Hauntings and High Jinx

Witch Haven Cozy Mystery - book 7

K.E. O'Connor

K.E. O'Connor Books

HAUNTINGS AND HIGH JINX

Copyright © 2022 by K.E. O'Connor

ISBN: 978-1-915378-34-7

Written by: K.E. O'Connor

Preface

The Witch Haven series has been created so you spend time with four amazing witches:

Books 1-3 tell Indigo's story: Spells and Spooks, Hexes and Haunts, Curses and Corpses

Books 4-6 tell Luna's story: Muffins and Moonlight, Cupcakes and Cauldrons, Pancakes and Potions

Book 7-9 tell Odessa's story: Hauntings and High Jinx, Hauntings and Havoc, Hauntings and Hoaxes

Book 10-12 tell Storm's story: The Case of the Screaming Skull, The Case of the Poisoned Pumpkin, The Case of the Cursed Candy

And there are two bonus origin stories to enjoy: **Fire Fang** and **Silvaria**

Chapter 1

"Those are his footprints. I'd recognize Michael's size thirteen feet anywhere. I accidentally gave him an extra toe on his right foot." I kneeled beside the deep imprint in the mud and placed my hand inside it.

My faithful scarecrow companion, Shamrock, loomed over me. The glow in his eyes helped to illuminate the darkness, but there was still no sign of Michael. We'd been looking for over an hour, and I was trying not to panic.

I stood and brushed dirt off my leggings. "What's gotten into him? This is the fifth time he's escaped."

Shamrock shrugged a huge shoulder as he scanned our surroundings.

I'd given Michael plenty of chances, but he wouldn't use his super strength for good. I hated when my scarecrows misbehaved. And if I got any more warnings from the Magic Council about my boys breaking out of their barns and scaring the locals, there'd be consequences.

"There must be a reason he keeps going walkabout, or rather, rampage about." I raised a light spell over my head, casting a pale glow to chase away the shadows in the forest. When I got back to the production barn, I'd run through each step I went through to bring my incredible scarecrows to life. I was certain I hadn't gotten anything wrong, but maybe I'd muddled the steps.

And a Grimsbane scarecrow couldn't afford to be muddled. I made the best scarecrows in the business, so my reputation was at stake. My workload felt never-ending, though, and I sometimes worked tired, which could cause problems like this.

Shamrock's large hand rested on my shoulder.

"Do you see something?" I whispered.

He moved in front of me and growled. My scarecrows didn't talk much, but I had a strong bond with Shamrock that enabled us to link thoughts and communicate telepathically. I trusted him to put my safety before anything else. And when he growled, I listened.

Shamrock stalked toward a patch of trees, and I took a moment to pull out a pouch of my powdered pumpkin and tipped the contents on my tongue. This was another talent of mine. Fresh pumpkins, magically enhanced scarecrows, and my secret powdered pumpkin. It went great with everything.

Buoyed by the energy giving properties of the powdered pumpkin, I continued tracking Michael's footprints. I squeaked as Shamrock lifted me off my feet and spun me around, using his back as a shield. A second later, something heavy thudded against him.

I sparked orange magic on my fingers as I squirmed out of his grip. A large rock lay by

Shamrock's feet, and when I examined his back, there was a dent in it.

"Michael, stop throwing things. We're trying to help." I raised my hand to allow the orange glow to light the trees. Several small pairs of eyes blinked at me for a second before vanishing among the foliage.

Shamrock growled again and punched away a huge branch that flew toward us.

"Come home and we can get you fixed," I said.

There was a rustle from nearby trees, and Shamrock took off running toward it.

I was right behind him, but had to dodge a large chestnut brown fox as it rocketed out of the shrubs. I almost lost my balance, but righted myself and kept running.

"Shamrock, don't hurt Michael. There's a chance we can help him." But it felt like a slim chance. Lately, I hadn't been on top of things. The farm was busy, the scarecrows were rambunctious, and my closest friends had recently gotten entangled in some puzzling mysteries that had distracted me. And then there was my ongoing search for Brodie.

Two heavy things colliding reached my ears, and I sped up. I glanced down to see the fox trotting beside me. "I suppose you think this is funny."

The fox glanced my way and kept running, his thick tail swishing from side to side.

"I would too if I saw a witch and her scarecrow sidekick chasing around the woods in the dead of night. You'd be wise to keep away from my boys, though. They're mean when they're angry." They could be mean most of the time, but that was how I made them. My scarecrows were the best bodyguards a magic user could wish for.

The fox slowed, but I kept running. I dove into the deep shadows of the forest without pausing. This wasn't the safest place to visit in the middle of the night, but I had my scarecrows as backup, when they weren't pounding each other to pieces. And there were dozens of them back at the farm. All I needed to do was whistle, and they'd come running.

They were the best protective army a witch could want. Although they came with a frustrating habit of chasing delivery people who came to my farm. But it was a small price to pay. And I loved my work. Even if it led me along a twisty, dangerous path at midnight to fix a small problem of my making.

I emerged into a clearing to see Michael just breaking free from Shamrock's headlock. He slammed his huge fist into Shamrock's chest and bolted away.

"Michael! This is your last warning. Come back to the barn with me now."

Michael didn't stop running.

I fired up my magic, regret simmering inside me. Michael was a failure, and it made me sad to extinguish one of my creations. With a heavy heart, I launched a powerful jet of bright orange magic at him. It slammed into Michael's back and sent him to the dirt.

I strode over, turning him with my foot, and pressed my hand against his chest where his heart should be. "I'm sorry, but you're out of control. Michael, it's time for you to sleep." I dragged out my life giving magic.

Michael struggled for a few seconds, twisting beneath my hand. But it was no use fighting. This was my magic, and I could give and take it easily.

A lump formed in my throat as the glow in his large eyes faded, and he returned to nothing more than a huge pile of straw, sticks, and baggy clothing.

Power tingled on my fingers before trickling up my arm and settling as a warm glow in my chest. It was a glow I'd always feel. It would remind me of Michael.

The fox appeared in the clearing and ambled over. It sniffed around what was left of Michael a few times, and then sat, curled its tail around its feet, and looked at me as if waiting for the next scene to begin.

I sat back on my heels and stared at the sky. "We've had two blood moons recently. They always make the magic in Witch Haven unstable."

The fox flicked its tail as if it wasn't sure it believed me.

A low warning growl rumbled behind me. There was a rush of air over my head as Shamrock launched at the fox.

I scrambled to my feet. "Shamrock, no! Let that fox go."

The fox was squirming in Shamrock's huge hands. It twisted around and sank its teeth into his arm.

Shamrock wouldn't feel the bite, but I'd be the one making repairs once we got home, so I needed to minimize the damage.

"No more fighting. We can all be friends."

The fox wriggled out of Shamrock's grasp, bounced against his chest, landed on me, and shot off.

I hit the dirt and sprawled on the ground as Shamrock bolted after the fox. As much as I loved my scarecrows, I sometimes wished they weren't so intent on killing everything they saw. But they'd always been like that. My scarecrows protected those they worked for. And they went to some impressive households. I'd even sent a troop of scarecrows to Windsor Castle to look after a member of the royal family.

I stared at the moon, taking a minute to get my breath back. I should do more investigation to see how badly these blood moons were affecting my boys. If things got any worse, I'd have to halt production. But with a six-month waiting list, and customers paying huge down payments to get their own custom-made killer scarecrow, the option to take a break wasn't there.

Rolling to my feet, I brushed off fox pawprints and took off after Shamrock.

When I thought about it, it sounded like I lived in a twisted fairytale. Twisted being the right word. Nothing was straightforward in Witch Haven, but I wouldn't have it any other way. I loved this tiny village. I had my friends around me and a thriving business. I had so many happy memories here. And a few tragic ones, too.

It was easy to follow the path Shamrock and the fox had taken. The smashed branches and trampled bushes showed me their route. Unfortunately, it was back toward the houses. People could be at risk if I didn't stop them.

I sped up and caught a glimpse of Shamrock. I whistled for him to come back. He ignored me. That was unusual. Shamrock was one of my more well-behaved scarecrows, and it wasn't like him to disobey a return command. That fox must have really annoyed him.

"Shamrock! If you don't behave, I'll take you to the stables, along with what's left of Michael. I know you hate the horses."

That made him slow. I never liked anything to go to waste, so the scarecrows who didn't turn out quite right were gathered up, and I took them to the local equine sanctuary. Hettie Crane was always grateful to have the extra straw, and the horses loved the pumpkin.

Reduce, reuse, recycle. That was a motto I lived by. And even if I was sad my failed scarecrows didn't get the long life I'd planned for them, the horses got a tasty feed.

I'd almost caught up with Shamrock and was about to give him a piece of my mind, when something with large black wings and a wicked sharp beak swooped from a branch, glinting talons aimed for my eyes. I fell to the ground and rolled, but not before the creature snared my hair in its talons.

"Hey, let go." My scalp burned as the feathered beast tried to take me with it.

The bird, which looked like a cross between a vulture and a Bald Eagle, squawked and kept beating its wings. Sharp feeling magic prickled off its talons as it struggled to restrain me.

"Quit yanking on my hair. I'm not a midnight snack." I reached up for the bird, getting a stab on the hand for my trouble. The forest was full of creatures like this, so it was only a matter of time before I encountered one. And it was just my luck that Shamrock was intent on destroying that innocent fox, rather than helping me.

I tried to get my fingers in my mouth to whistle for more scarecrows, but the bird critter was jerking me about so hard I could only make a pitiful hissy noise.

A warm whoosh of air blasted past me, and a second later, my feet hit the dirt. I crouched as I assessed the threat. "Oh! Sol. What are you doing here?"

Sol Vossen held the huge bird in a large, suntanned fist. He'd been working with me for almost five months, and I wasn't sure what I'd done before he joined the farm. He was hard working, steadfast, always turned up on time, never complained if I asked him to work overtime, and the scarecrows liked him.

"Odessa, are you hurt?" He strode over and caught hold of my elbow as he tossed the bird free. The bird cawed its unhappiness, but a glare from Sol sent it flapping away.

"I'm okay. More spooked than anything." My heart raced as Sol examined my head.

"That was a diamond griffin hybrid. It could have ripped your head clean off your shoulders. Are you sure you aren't injured?" His voice had a deep, reassuring rumble to it.

I patted my head, my fingers brushing his large, calloused palm. "I don't think so. It got its feet caught in my hair and didn't want to let go."

"It's their breeding season. It was probably looking for a meal for its young."

I chuckled. "I would have made some meal."

There was a glint of something I didn't recognize in Sol's eyes as his gaze flickered over me. But it was gone as soon as it arrived. "It's not a good idea to be in the forest on your own."

"I'm not alone. Shamrock's out here. We had a situation with Michael."

Concern crossed Sol's face. "He got out again?"

"He did."

"I thought we could bring him back, get him to focus." Sol lowered his hand, but remained close. I could smell the familiar scent of apple wood smoke and pumpkin he carried on him. The smell always made me relax and think of home.

"I've had to let him go. Michael was too difficult to handle." I smoothed down my hair. "I'm wondering if I'm losing my touch with the scarecrows."

"You could never do that. It's what you're known for."

It was rare I doubted myself, but standing here with a stinging scalp and a recently deceased scarecrow on my hands, it made a woman wonder.

"Odessa, you can't save them all. Some scarecrows are simply too intense."

"My magic makes them that way." I shook out my hands. Was I the problem? Was it time to do things differently?

Everyone needed to evaluate their lives and figure out when it was time to change things up. I was a third of the way through my life, so I was maybe due for an early midlife crisis. People wouldn't think it weird if I slid off the rails. After all, things hadn't gone how I'd planned them. There should be children in the farmhouse by now, and I should be happily married to Brodie.

Sol's gentle sigh knocked me from my early midlife crisis musings. "Is there anything I can help you with?"

"You can help me stop Shamrock. If he goes running through the neighbors' backyards again, someone will report him to the Magic Council. I can't lose him, too. Shamrock is special."

Sol stepped back and nodded. "Then let's go find Shamrock."

It took twenty minutes of tracking before we found him. He was hunkered down by a large outbuilding in the back of Raina and Alastair Chalice's large, neatly manicured back yard. Well, it had been manicured, but it looked like the fox and Shamrock had led a merry dance around the lawn a few times.

"Shamrock, get your straw-filled butt over here," I hiss-whispered. "And leave that fox alone. You'd better not have eaten him."

Shamrock looked my way, then glared at the base of the outbuilding.

"I'm not playing around." I raised a warning blast of magic.

He didn't move. Stubborn scarecrow. But then I made him that way, so I only had myself to blame.

"Shamrock! I've had enough for one night, and I'd have been in trouble if Sol hadn't been here to help." I glanced at Sol. "What were you doing in the woods so late?"

"Looking for moonflowers. I was making a tincture for my shoulder, and they're more powerful when the moon is full."

"Your shoulder is still troubling you?" He'd pulled it when dealing with three angry scarecrows who wouldn't behave.

Sol rolled the joint and gave me an easy smile. "It's getting better."

I went to touch his shoulder, but Shamrock suddenly loomed next to me, a sullen look on his face. He clutched my arm and moved me away from Sol.

"Stop. You know Sol is safe. And he just saved me from a diamond griffin. That should have been your job."

A humming noise filled my head as Shamrock formed a mind link with me.

"Sorry. Bad fox." Shamrock's voice was a jumble of growls and tweets mixed in with the words.

"No, just a curious fox."

"You hurt?"

"I'm fine, thanks to Sol." I nodded at Sol. I should give him more responsibility on the farm. He hadn't put a foot wrong since he'd started working for me. It was time I rewarded him.

I returned Sol's warm smile. I could find him a girlfriend. He hadn't mentioned anyone special, but he was an attractive man if you liked the large, cuddly teddy bear type. And who didn't like a beefy guy to squeeze you tight on a cold night?

"Shamrock, go find what's left of Michael and take him to the farm," I said. "Then get yourself in the barn and rest."

His gaze shot to the outbuilding, and his menacing growl filled my head.

"No! No more foxes. Foxes are our friends. They deserve to live just as much as we do."

Shamrock stamped his foot before marching back toward the forest.

Sol chuckled as he crossed his arms over his broad chest. "I've never seen anyone handle scarecrows the way you do. It never ceases to amaze me."

I wriggled my fingers, and magic sparkled on the ends of them. "As you said, it's what I do. Now, how about we—"

"Odessa Grimsbane! What are you doing in my yard?" Raina Chalice stood by the open back door of the house, dressed in a dark green set of pajamas.

"Sorry to disturb you, Raina. We were out for a late-night stroll, when I thought I saw someone in your yard. I wanted to make sure no one was stealing." It sounded a convincing lie to me, although I wasn't sure how I'd explain the messed up lawn if she noticed it.

Raina arched an eyebrow, her approving gaze moving over Sol. "I thought you two had snuck in here for a sneaky canoodle."

I burst out laughing. "Don't be silly. I'm not single." My fingers went to my empty wedding ring finger.

Sol sucked in a breath, and his gaze cut to me. "I should make sure Shamrock's behaving himself. Or I could stay. Walk you back."

"No. I'll be fine. Thanks for tonight. I'd have been in a mess if you weren't here to help." I patted his arm.

"Anytime. I'm always here for you." He nodded a good night to Raina and me before striding away.

I walked over to Raina. She was a well put together woman in her mid-fifties with short dark hair and intense green eyes. "I didn't mean to wake you."

Raina's gaze shifted from Sol to me. "You're fine. I hadn't gone to bed. I've been having trouble sleeping lately, so I was making a hot drink and thought I'd sit up and read."

"You're not sleeping? Are you worried about something?"

"Well, I have been having a few problems recently." Raina clenched her hands so tight I could see the white of her knuckles beneath her skin.

"Is there anything I can help with?"

She shook her head. "Only if you know how to deal with an unhappy ghost who doesn't want to move on."

I grinned at her. "Ghost hunting is a hobby of mine."

Raina's eyes widened. "Are you being serious?"

"Of course. Are you sure it's a haunting, though?" My stomach fluttered with hope. Could this be the ghost I'd been searching for?

"Yes. Absolutely." Raina bit her lip and glanced over her shoulder. "I'm getting desperate and don't know what to do. Have you got time to come in now?"

"Um... sure. I was going home, but I've got time."

"You're an angel. The ghost has been active all evening, and I don't know what to do to make him happy." Raina ushered me inside.

So, it was a male ghost. This sounded promising. "I'd be happy to help. Lead the way and introduce me to your ghost friend." And maybe, just maybe, I'd finally find my lost ghost and have my missing piece back.

Chapter 2

Raina led me into a low-ceilinged hallway. Dark wooden beams ran across the ceiling, giving the place an ominous look, despite the bright light she flicked on over our heads.

"I didn't know you were interested in ghosts," she said.

"It's been an interest of mine for a while. Ever since... well, ever since I decided to find a new hobby."

"I'm surprised you have time to go ghost hunting." She walked along the hall in front of me, flicking on more lights. "The farm must keep you busy all year round."

"It does. But I'm learning to delegate, and I hired an assistant for the first time. Sol has been sent to me from the angels."

"That's great to hear. And Sol must be good with his hands. Having a practical man around takes the weight off."

"He is. And it does. Although I have two hands of my own. And I know how to use them."

"Of course. Call me old-fashioned, but I prefer a guy to do the laboring, especially one that looks like Sol does in those fitted jeans."

"Uh... I guess. I'm glad I found him."

"And it's about time you got back out there," Raina said.

I narrowed my eyes. "Back out there?"

She turned, and her cheeks flushed. She pulled her pajama jacket tightly around her. "I mean, with everything that happened. With Brodie. He was a good man, but you're young and very pretty. You'd easily find another man. And... I wondered when I saw you with Sol—"

"No, it's not like that between us. I'm his boss. And I'm not moving on. I have no reason to. Brodie hasn't gone for good." I pressed my lips together. I'd said too much.

Her gaze turned curious. "Whatever you say. I just thought... Well, perhaps I shouldn't make assumptions."

She was right about that. My love life was no one else's business. "Tell me about this ghost."

"Of course. Let me show you around, and I'll pick out where the hauntings are the most intense. Although he gets around. I don't think there's a room he hasn't been in."

"You keep calling the ghost 'him'. It's definitely a male ghost?"

"Oh, yes. I'm certain of it." Raina opened a door and peeked around the side before shoving it open and flicking on the light. "This is the dining room. He comes in here most evenings when we eat. Sometimes, it just feels colder and he doesn't bother us, but he can get angry, and things get thrown. And I'm sure I've seen a man's face once or twice."

"Is there anything in particular that makes him angry?" I walked around the wood paneled dining room. There was a long table set in the center of the room and a grand fireplace at the other end that was laid with fresh logs.

"All kinds of things trigger him. Sometimes, it's the music playing in the background, or he gets agitated depending on the meal we have. He hates it whenever we serve fish."

"Anything else?" I paused to admire several large portrait paintings hung on the wall in gilded frames.

"There's no real pattern." Raina followed me closely, glancing around all the time. "He's unhappy, though, and I can't figure out why."

"When did you first notice this ghostly presence?" I tried to keep the excitement out of my voice. "Have you had the ghost for several years?"

She shook her head. "No. Just under a year."

I frowned. That was the wrong answer. "Sometimes, when a new ghost manifests, its presence is weak. Unless you were paying attention, you wouldn't have noticed it for months, sometimes years. This ghost could have been lingering and slowly growing stronger. Ghosts feed off our energy, after all."

"This house has always felt warm and inviting. Not like now." Raina rubbed her hands together. "Does it feel cold to you?"

"It is chilly in here." There was a spooky, intense vibe to the place, but I didn't mind. It gave me hope.

"You sense something, don't you?" Raina said.

I looked at the paintings on the wall again. They showed Raina looking regal as she stood beside an empty chair. There was also one of her and her daughter, Glory. There was also one with her husband, Alastair. "Let's look at another room. The ghost's energy could be stronger in there."

We explored several more rooms, ending our search in the hallway. Each room had a hint of spookiness about it, but I didn't see a ghost.

I turned to Raina. "I can sense a presence. But I need you to be clear on the timeline. Are you sure this didn't start about three and a half years ago?"

"Positive. And if it had been here all this time, I'd have gotten help a long time ago. Why do you think it started then?"

My stomach sank, but I wasn't giving up. This village was full of magic, so ghosts weren't unusual. Most ghosts kept to themselves and rubbed along with the living, causing no harm. I was certain that would be the case with my Brodie.

"I'm wondering if I know this ghost," I said.

"Oh! Does the energy feel familiar to you?"

"I'm not sure. I need more time to investigate." I knew when I found Brodie's ghost, everything would click into place, and I'd just know it was him.

So far, I'd hunted over fifty ghosts and hadn't recognized any of them. This one was feeling the same, but I had to be thorough. Brodie would never leave me. He'd just gotten lost. So it was up to me to bring him back to where he belonged, right by my side.

"Odessa, can you help me?" Raina said. "I don't know what I've done to offend this ghost, but I want him gone. He needs to be at peace."

"Give me a few minutes to see what else I can sense." I paced the hallway slowly, my eyes closed as I tapped into any otherworldly energy. I whispered Brodie's name several times, allowing any spirit in the house to take my energy and feed until it became strong.

Weak ghosts often got muddled. It was no surprise. After all, you don't become a ghost and simply know how to be all ghost. It was just like when a witch was born. She doesn't know how to cast a basic spell or what her particular ability will be. We grow into our powers.

After several minutes of pacing, I reluctantly accepted this wasn't Brodie. He wouldn't keep me hanging on or play with me.

I turned to Raina. "I think you have a haunting, but I don't sense any anger in the ghost. Perhaps he simply wants to keep you company. He could have made a home here and doesn't want to leave."

Her expression tightened. "If this is the ghost I think it is, he's overstayed his welcome."

"You know who the ghost is?"

"Not for certain, but it wouldn't surprise me if it was Eldridge. My first husband."

"Oh, of course. You remarried not so long ago."

"That's right. To Alastair. He's a wonderful man. We're very happy." Her gaze flicked around the room. "Although maybe not everyone is happy for us."

"Eldridge hasn't been dead for long, has he? Don't you think..." I bit my tongue before I said something I'd regret. My opinion was you married once and forever.

Raina lifted her chin a fraction and met my gaze, a glint in her eyes. "Eldridge had been dead six months before I remarried. That was long enough for me to be single. And he'd want me to be happy and move on. After he died, I wasn't ready to give up and become a widow dressed head-to-toe in black and mourn him forever."

My eyebrows lifted slowly. There was forever, and then there were six short months. It must have taken almost that long to plan her second wedding. "Of course not. And you deserve happiness. It just seems a little fast."

"Maybe to some. And I know the neighbors gossiped about me marrying Alastair so soon after Eldridge's death, but we already knew each other. Alastair has been a family friend for over thirty years, and he was Eldridge's best friend. Yes, it's strange to outsiders that we married, but we both loved Eldridge. He wouldn't have wanted me to be alone in this huge old place."

"I'm sure he wouldn't. Don't think I'm judging you." A tiny part of me was. I couldn't help it.

"You wouldn't be the first." The fight deflated from Raina, and her shoulders slumped. "I thought I was doing the right thing by marrying Alastair and moving on, but what if Eldridge wanted me to retreat from the world and mourn his loss for longer? I did love him, and I miss him terribly."

"Have you seen a clear image of the ghost? Maybe it's not him." I didn't want Raina stressed by this haunting or thinking the worst.

"Who else could it be?"

"Without seeing the ghost, I couldn't say. But it sounds like you loved each other. I'm sure you're right. Eldridge would have wanted you to be happy. Although I'd have struggled to move on so soon." I hadn't moved an inch since losing Brodie. And I had no plans to do so.

"I don't believe you only get one shot at true love. We change as we grow up. I think back to my feckless twenty-year-old self and the mistakes I made. I was a different person. My tastes changed, too. Alastair is different to Eldridge. Sweet, but assertive. He's taken over so much from me, and I appreciate that. And we all need someone in our lives to love us."

I nodded as she spoke, but didn't believe her. You only ever found true love once. It had struck me with Brodie and was taken as we were making plans for our forever future. I'd never forget Brodie. He'd always be my one and only, and no one would replace him.

"Would you mind if I looked around on my own? Perhaps the ghost is taking his time to show up because of my presence. I could walk about and see if any spiritual energy is out of place," I said.

"Of course. Look wherever you like. We have no secrets," Raina said. "Although three of the bedrooms could be occupied. My husband has already turned in for the night, and Glory is in the end room on the right. My brother-in-law is around here somewhere. You'll usually find him in the study or games room, if he's not passed out on his bed."

"I'll stay away from the bedrooms. But it would be good to get a feel for the place. Some ghosts pick particular rooms they have a strong connection with and stay there."

"I wish that was the case with this ghost, but he gets everywhere. I even sensed him in the shower one day. It gave me a fright."

"I'm sure we'll sort this out. And if it is your late husband, we'll convince him to leave."

"You can really talk to ghosts? I barely see them. I can only sense them." Raina wrapped her arms around her middle. "And I know we're supposed to welcome all magical beings in Witch Haven, but ghosts are eerie."

"They're not so bad. And yes, I can speak to them. Give me time, and we'll find out if this is Eldridge."

I spent the next half an hour looking around the downstairs. It was a huge place, with a dozen rooms. There was an expansive kitchen that felt warm and homely, and the dining room that I'd already seen. I explored a room that looked more like a museum exhibition and was full of vases and small statues I made sure not to touch in case I broke something. I also found a library, games room, a room with lots of comfy chairs, two studies, and a home cinema.

Not once did I sense anything to alarm me that this ghost was trouble. I also didn't get a sense Brodie was here. But I'd keep looking, and I'd find him. It was a matter of perseverance. He'd never abandon me. We'd promised to be together for the rest of our lives, and a small thing like death wouldn't keep us apart.

I returned to the library, with its floor-to-ceiling shelves jam packed with everything from the latest romance to psychological thrillers and classics.

After checking back in the hallway to make sure no one would hear me, I eased the door shut. "Brodie, are you here? It's Odessa." I waited a moment, tuning into the energy, hoping to pick up something that felt like Brodie. Nothing stirred.

"This must be confusing, but I'm here, and I'm waiting for you. I've been searching for you for such a long time. I know I'd be scared if I was in your situation, but there's nothing to be afraid of. I've found a solution to our problem. I know how to get you back."

A small picture of a countryside setting flipped off the wall and hit the thick, pale green carpet.

I tensed, my heart pounding. "Brodie, are you trying to communicate with me?"

I stood in silence in front of the picture, hoping to get another sign. As I waited, I studied the oil painting. Maybe there was a clue in that. Was this picture important to Brodie?

The scene wasn't of anywhere local. It could be one of a hundred places. And Brodie had never been a fan of hiking. He'd go for a walk now and again, but we didn't have a special place outside we visited. I couldn't connect this picture to him.

My frown deepened as I looked at the wall. The nail that had been holding the picture was bent. A sigh slid from my lips. Maybe the picture had simply fallen off the wall and this had nothing to do with a ghost. Brodie, Eldridge, or anyone else.

I did another circuit of the room. "There's no hurry. I understand if you've gotten stuck. We can work together to find you a way out. But you have to talk to me. There must be a way we can connect."

There was nothing but a faint tick of a clock to fill the silence. I refused to give up on my love. If this ghost wasn't Brodie, he'd be somewhere else. I would find him.

I walked back into the hallway and saw Raina coming out of the kitchen with a mug in her hand.

"How's it going?" She walked toward me.

"I may have encountered a ghost, but if it was Eldridge, he wasn't strong, and he didn't communicate with me."

"What happened?"

"A picture fell off the wall."

Raina's sigh sounded so sad it made me want to hug her. "What if Eldridge is unhappy with me remarrying?" She shook her head. "No. He always said he wanted me to find happiness and not be alone."

"You had that conversation before he died?"

"Yes. You sound surprised."

"I... yes, I am. It's morbid."

"I prefer to think of it as sensible. I assumed most couples talked about what they'd do if things changed between them or the other one died. You always need a plan. And Eldridge liked to have the bases covered. He said if you fail to plan, you plan to fail. He was a sensible man."

"What did he tell you to do in the event of his death?"

"Eldridge didn't want me lonely and pining for him." Raina walked along the hallway with me beside her, clutching her mug. "But with everything that's happened in the house, I wondered if I should have waited. But everyone deserves another shot at happiness, don't they?"

"Of course. But true love only strikes once. You won't find it again."

"I... no, I don't believe that. I started looking at Alastair differently after Eldridge passed. When I was married to Eldridge, I never paid much attention to other men. I was content. Once he was gone, and I spent more time with Alastair, I realized sometimes you get more than one chance at true love. It's refreshing to believe that, don't you think?"

I pressed my lips together and decided not to comment. I didn't agree. Brodie had always been my happy place, and I was adrift without him. I missed his warm smile and his laugh that used to curl my toes. I missed his big hands and the way he'd hold me late at night and make me feel safe. There could be no one else. I'd never feel that love again.

A loud thud over our heads made us jump.

"That could be our ghost," Raina whispered.

"Let's investigate," I said. "Maybe we can get to the bottom of this tonight, and you and your family can be left in peace."

Raina led the way along the hallway, and we crept upstairs.

Two more thuds came from different parts of the house, at opposite ends of the corridor.

"I'll check the noise this way." Raina pointed to the right. "Glory sleeps along here, and I don't want her scared if she meets a stranger."

"I'll go the other way." I reached into my pocket as I crept along the corridor and found my usual bag of powdered pumpkin encrusted treats. I was about to pop one in my mouth when my fingers brushed another packet, and I pulled it out. I grinned. This was an unexpected treat. Another small pouch of pure powdered pumpkin greeted me.

Now we were talking. I'd get an instant hit of energy from a tiny amount of this pure powder and have plenty of focus to root out this ghost.

Opening the pouch, I lifted it to my nose to have a sniff. It was sweet, tangy, and bright orange, showing it was triple strength. I'd only need a little to keep me going for the night.

A soft thud behind me caught my attention. I backed up a few steps, and as I turned, I came face-to-face with a pale ghost with large dark eyes, his mouth stretched wide in a silent scream. I squeaked and stumbled back. The entire pouch of powdered pumpkin shot into my mouth and up my nose, making me choke.

I clutched at air, realizing a second too late there was nothing to hold on to. As the powdered pumpkin flooded my system, my heart raced, and dark spots filled my vision.

"Oh, dear. I'm going to..." As the world blacked out, I glimpsed another face. Was that Brodie? He was here to save me.

Joy and terror mingled as I plunged backward down the stairs.

Chapter 3

Moaning reached my ears. Someone was in pain, and it sounded like they needed to be put out of their misery. It was only when I opened my eyes and clarity slid into place that I realized I was the one making the noise.

"Brodie?" I whispered. "Where are you?"

A middle-aged man with pale blond hair, pale eyebrows, and blue eyes appeared in my vision and peered down at me, concern clear on his face.

I shrank back. "You're not Brodie. Where is he? He was here." I went to move, but the man gently placed a restraining hand on my shoulder.

"No, I'm not Brodie. I'm Alastair Chalice. We've met several times at your farm. I'm Raina's husband."

I smacked my lips together and took a few seconds to get my senses in order. "Oh! Sure. What happened?" My gaze went around the room. I was on a couch, something soft under my head, and I was back in the library.

"You took a tumble down the stairs. I don't know how you didn't break your neck. Raina heard you cry out and then a crash. She checked you were alive and then came to find me." His hand hovered close to my face, as if uncertain whether to touch me.

"How's Odessa?" I heard Raina before I saw her as she hurried to the couch and looked down at me. "Was it the ghost? Did he push you?"

I struggled to sit up, and Raina helped me until I was propped against a pile of soft cushions. The back of my head throbbed, as did my right shoulder. "I... saw someone. I was at the top of the stairs and heard another noise. I turned and came face-to-face with a ghost. But I saw someone else, too. I thought..." I huffed out a breath. My head was a mess. What exactly had I seen? Had Brodie been here, or was that wishful thinking and too much powdered pumpkin messing with my head?

"You think there are two ghosts haunting this house?" Raina said.

I sucked in a breath to say Brodie's name, but stopped. I'd learned the hard way that, if I talked about my dead love, people got weird. They started avoiding me and making excuses not to be around me. My best friends, Storm, Indigo, and Luna, were patient, but even they got pitying looks in their eyes if I mentioned Brodie too many times.

"I don't know," I conceded. "I saw something, but it happened so fast."

"Piper, bring that water over here." Alastair turned to the door of the library.

Piper Brockwell appeared by my side, carrying a glass of water. She set it beside me. I knew Piper. She often came to the farm to select pumpkins for the family dinner.

"Thanks." I took a sip of water, my hand shaking so badly I spilled some on me. I had to pull myself together. I wanted to get back out there and see if I'd spotted Brodie. He'd saved me from that fall. He was the reason I hadn't broken my neck. Brodie had always been my hero.

"I used healing magic on you," Raina said. "It's not my specialty, but I hope it helped. I was so worried about you."

I felt wretched and shaky, but I was awake and talking. "Thanks. I'm certain you helped me. Shall we carry on the ghost hunt?"

"Absolutely not," Alastair said. "It's not safe. And those stairs are bad luck. That's where Eldridge died."

My eyebrows shot up. "He fell down those same stairs?"

Raina nodded. "He was tripped."

"By someone?"

"His familiar, Tuffin. It was a tragic accident." Raina patted my shoulder. "You rest up. We've done enough ghost hunting. I feel so guilty. I should never have asked you to look for the ghost so late at night. I didn't realize he'd be a danger to you."

"Eldridge had nothing to do with this," I said.

"He's a threat to the household," Alastair said as if he hadn't heard me. "He pushed you."

I shook my head and regretted it as the room appeared to spin. "No one pushed me. I simply got startled when I saw the ghost."

"Did it look like Eldridge?" Raina said.

"It's hard to say. This ghost didn't look completely human because his features were exaggerated. And it was dark."

"He hasn't turned into a ghost ghoul, has he?" Raina's face blanched, and she clutched Alastair's hand.

"No, I could still recognize him as human, and he wasn't aggressive." That was a fear I had for Brodie. If a ghost got stuck and couldn't move on, they changed. It didn't happen to all ghosts, but those with unfinished business, or those who'd had a violent or sudden death, struggled with their transition. They'd get lost on their journey. When that happened, they became unstable. Unstable and deadly.

And a ghost ghoul couldn't be brought back. The kindest thing to do was destroy or contain them in a ghost jar. My heart sank at the thought of ever doing that to Brodie. Even if he had gotten lost or stuck, he had memories of us to cling to. So long as a ghost had happy thoughts, they wouldn't change so quickly. And Brodie had always been the strong one in our relationship. He'd make sure he could come back to me.

I glanced down at my top and grimaced. I was covered in powdered pumpkin. I swiped a hand across my face and more came away.

"Would you like something to clean that off?" Raina said. "I wasn't sure what it was."

"Yes, thanks. I was holding some powdered pumpkin just before I fell."

"Piper, get a towel and a warm washcloth for Odessa. Unless you feel up to using the washroom?"

"You stay where you are," Alastair said. "You have a lump on the back of your head. You need to rest."

"I might just rest up for a few more minutes. I'm so sorry to inconvenience you." I nodded a thanks to Piper just before she hurried away.

"It's no trouble. And I should make amends to you," Raina said. "You wouldn't be lying on the couch covered in bruises if it wasn't for our ghost problem."

"Eldridge isn't a problem," I said. "He's misunderstood."

"Whatever he is, we must encourage him to leave," Alastair said. "It's getting difficult to live here. I've suggested we move, but Raina won't hear of it."

She squeezed his arm. "Of course not. This is our home."

I took another sip of water, slowly feeling more like myself. "Alastair, have you ever seen the ghost?"

"No, but I've sensed him. And things are always being moved. To begin with, I thought Glory was playing with me, but it's always things I use in the shower. I can't imagine Glory would have any need for them. I'm certain it was the ghost."

"What do you sense when you experience this ghost?" I said.

"I hear noises or see things out of the corner of my eye, but they're gone when I turn my head. There are cold spots as well."

"Do you ever sense how the ghost is feeling toward you?"

"No, but I'm not as attuned to ghosts as Raina, or you, by the sounds of it. When it first started, I thought it was just an old house creaking, or I was getting forgetful and putting things in the wrong place. But then Raina started pointing things out, and I realized these experiences were unnatural."

"And once you start looking for them, they're everywhere," Raina said.

"Can you remember exactly when you first sensed this ghost?" I said.

"Six months ago," Alastair said.

"You're sure?" Brodie died three years, two months, and sixteen days ago. This haunting wasn't linked to him. But he'd been at the top of the stairs. I had seen him. And Brodie always saved me when I got in trouble.

"I'm positive. Eldridge might have been here for a short time before I noticed him, but he died almost a year ago, and the haunting started not long after that," Alastair said. "Raina sensed something was wrong almost straight away."

"It's not Eldridge," I muttered under my breath. Brodie could have been weakened after his violent death. Ghosts could remain confused for months. There was a chance this was him. Please, let it be him.

"What was that?" Alastair said. "You mentioned another ghost. If we're experiencing a multiple haunting, we'll have to move."

"I'm not certain about two ghosts, but it was dark, and I am tired. I could have imagined it." I hadn't, and I would find my missing ghost.

Piper returned with the washcloth and a towel, and I took a couple of minutes to tidy myself up. My insides felt jittery because of all the powdered pumpkin I'd ingested. It would take a couple of days to work out of my system. I was always careful with how much I consumed. It was like supercharged caffeine with an added dash of adrenaline.

"I wondered if the garden renovations triggered Eldridge," Alastair said. "That began six months ago. It was after that the haunting grew noticeable."

"It's possible. Change unsettles spirits," I said, trying not to sound glum. The more I learned about this ghost, the more I realized it wasn't Brodie. And why would he haunt this house? We'd known Eldridge and Raina when they were together, but they were over twenty years older than us, so we hadn't mixed in the same circles.

A soft sigh slid out of me. I'd gotten things muddled. It wouldn't be the first time, but I so wanted to find Brodie.

There was a knock at the front door, and Piper left to open it. She returned a moment later, and my eyes widened when I saw Indigo Ash and Storm Winter stride into the room.

"What are you doing here?" I said.

"I called them," Raina said. "We thought you might need a hand to get home. We can't send you out in the dead of night on your own with a head injury."

Indigo kneeled beside me and placed a hand on my forehead. Storm remained standing, her arms crossed over her chest as she examined the room with her usual sharp glare.

"What have you been getting yourself into this time?" Indigo arched an eyebrow.

"Nothing bad. I was helping Raina. Things didn't go quite as planned."

"No kidding." Storm flipped her dark hair over one shoulder. "You almost got yourself killed."

"You're being dramatic," I said. "I had a small tumble."

"You fell down a flight of stairs," Storm said. "Where is your scarecrow bodyguard?"

"Busy. And that's why I was out. I was dealing with a scarecrow issue."

"I thought you were taking a walk with Sol?" Raina said.

"Oh! Yes, that too. I can multitask." I blushed at getting caught out on a lie.

Indigo wiped a finger across my cheek. It came away coated in some powdered pumpkin I missed. "You've had quite an evening."

"It has been an adventure," I said. "It didn't end the way I hoped."

"Let's get you home," Indigo said. "Or do you want to see the doctor? How are you feeling?"

"No, I'm already better." My head and shoulder still hurt, but everything felt like it worked. And I didn't want a fuss. I was embarrassed about this mess, and I'd wasted all that powdered pumpkin by throwing half of it on myself.

"I can stay with you tonight if you like," Storm said, "just to make sure you don't relapse in your sleep. But I need to leave early. I've got a lot on."

"I don't need babysitting," I said.

"You might have a concussion," Indigo said. "We're not leaving you on your own." She helped me off the couch, and I wavered on my feet.

"Maybe someone sticking around overnight would be good." I looked at Raina and Alastair. "Thanks for taking care of me."

"You're more than welcome," Raina said.

I looked around the room. "I don't think I can help with your ghost situation. If it is Eldridge, he didn't want to communicate, and when a ghost digs in his heels and refuses to let you know what's wrong, there's not much you can do."

Raina's gaze dropped. Then she nodded. "I understand."

Raina and Alastair walked us all to the door. I was taking my time and grateful for the arm Indigo gave me to lean on. We stepped outside and said our goodbyes before we made our way slowly onto the street.

"So, spill," Indigo said. "What are you playing at?"

"It's nothing dodgy." I was trying not to limp. My leg must have taken a whack as I fell.

"You're still ghost hunting," Storm said. "I thought you'd given that up."

"You thought wrong. Raina needed help. I was hardly going to turn her down."

"But you just did," Storm said. "Why were you so keen to help and then changed your mind?"

"I've just fallen down some stairs. I need to look after myself, not chase an unhappy ghost."

Neither of them spoke for a moment as we continued our slow journey along the street.

"You're still looking for Brodie, aren't you?" Indigo said quietly.

I bit my bottom lip. "Why would I do that? You all told me I was ridiculous for trying to find him."

"No one ever called you ridiculous," Indigo said. "Brodie's been gone a long time, though. He's moved on, just as he should."

I tried to tug my arm away, but Indigo kept a tight hold on me. "Brodie wouldn't do that. He'd never leave me."

"He would if he didn't have a choice," Storm said. "Sometimes, ghosts move on instantaneously. They're not aware of what's going on, and their path is clear. It was Brodie's time."

I wasn't in the mood for this conversation. My skin still felt sticky from the powdered pumpkin, my head throbbed, and every step I took made my leg complain. "I was just trying to help someone. That's not a bad thing."

"It is if you have ulterior motives," Storm said. "Looking for a dead guy is unhealthy."

"Forgetting Brodie existed is the only unhealthy thing in this scenario."

"No one is suggesting you forget Brodie. We know how much you loved each other," Indigo said. "But no one will think badly of you for moving on. If you want to find someone else—"

"I don't. Why does everyone keep telling me that? I've only ever wanted Brodie."

"That's impossible to make happen, since the guy is dead," Storm said.

I clenched my hands and dug my fingers into my palms, determined not to yell. I was a peace loving witch, but when my friends questioned me about Brodie, I saw red. It was none of their business. If I wanted Brodie back, then I'd get him back. I still had a few pieces to fit into place, but I would find him.

They didn't understand. Storm rarely dated, and when she did, she had a three date rule, cutting a guy off before she formed an attachment. And Indigo, she was happy now but had spent a long time hiding from any relationship. They weren't experts in finding true love and had no right to question what I was doing to get my happiness back.

"Where does your leg hurt?" Indigo said, breaking through the tense silence.

"I said nothing about my leg being painful."

"You're limping. Stop being a hero. I can use healing magic on you."

"And that way we can all get to bed before dawn," Storm muttered.

I pointed at the top of my right thigh, and Indigo pressed a hand against it. After a few minutes, the pain eased, and I could walk without a limp. I let go of Indigo's arm.

She tugged me back to her side. "Stop being like that. We're helping."

"And I appreciate you coming to get me, but I don't want help with anything else," I said.

"You're getting it," Storm said. "We're your friends, and that gives us the right to interfere in your life whenever we choose."

I gritted my teeth. Storm was so stubborn. "You can try to interfere. But I'm telling you this—" I yelped as something cold wrapped around my neck and hauled me off my feet. I lay on my back and stared at the pale face I'd seen in Raina and Alastair's house.

The ghost pressed his face so close to mine, I could feel an icy chill on my skin. "Help me. I was murdered."

Chapter 4

"Eldridge. Is that you?" I stared at the slightly ghoulish features of the ghost who had his nose jammed against mine.

A second later, a blast of magic slammed into him, and his form disintegrated, scattering in the cool night air.

"Wait! Don't hurt him." I scrambled to my feet and gestured for Storm and Indigo to lower their hands. They were sparking magic, and it was aimed at Eldridge.

"He was trying to kill you," Storm said.

"It's the ghost from the house. He just told me he was murdered."

"That gives him the right to knock you on your butt?" Indigo said.

"No, but he's scared and confused," I said. "Give him a second chance."

"To successfully kill you?" Storm said with a shrug. "It's your funeral. Although I won't be attending, other than to spend a few minutes etching *Odessa Grimsbane was too trusting for her own good* on your headstone."

"Oh, hush. It won't come to that. Eldridge isn't mean." I looked around as the fragmented remains of Eldridge reassembled. "Look at the poor ghost. He needs our help, not our judgment."

Storm lowered her hands, still not looking happy.

"Are you sure you know what you're doing?" Indigo said. "You've whacked your head and overdosed on powdered pumpkin. You might not be thinking clearly."

"My thoughts are crystal clear."

"Confused ghosts turn difficult quickly. Remember what happened in Luna's apartment when she was being haunted," Indigo said.

"That was different. Anyway, where is Luna?" I kept an eye on Eldridge as his form slowly became solid. Ghosts always had a wispy outline, but some could pass for living, breathing entities if you weren't paying attention.

"One guess," Storm said. "What with her werewolf boyfriend demanding her time and the ever-expanding animal sanctuary, Luna has no time for us. She's ditched us for a smoking hot werewolf and a bunch of unloved furballs."

"That's not true," Indigo said. "But her wedding plans are her focus. And her parents are still interfering, no matter how many times she tells them to back off."

"Luna keeps trying to get me to go to dress fittings," Storm said. "I told her I'd grab something from the store nearer the time. Why does she have to go to all that expense of tailor made dresses?"

"Because it's a special day," Indigo said. "And as her bridesmaids, we have to support her, not mess with her plans and not show up for dress fittings." Her gaze shifted to Eldridge, who was looking almost normal. "So, what's the deal with this ghost?"

I turned to Eldridge. "You're Raina's first husband, is that right?"

His form wobbled for several seconds. "Yes. Eldridge Talbot. And you have to help me." He made a grab for me, but I dodged out of his way.

"Ease up on being so handsy," Storm growled, "or you'll get knocked back. The next time that happens, you won't be getting up so easy."

"Everyone take a breath. We've all had a hectic night." I smiled encouragingly at Eldridge. "Start at the beginning. You're the ghost who's been haunting the house?"

He nodded. "It's still my house. I have every right to live there, or haunt it, as much as I like."

"Not if you're messing with the living residents, you don't," Storm said.

"You said you were murdered," I said. "Who killed you?"

Eldridge blinked out of sight for a second, and when he returned, his features were distorted and his teeth too big for his mouth. This ghost was turning ghoul at a rapid rate. "I don't know. But it wasn't an accident. I didn't fall down those stairs."

"When I spoke to Raina and Alastair, they said your familiar tripped you. Do you remember that happening?"

He hid his face in his hands. "That's not true. Of course, she was there. Tuffin went everywhere with me, but she'd never hurt me."

"Cats can be sneaky," Storm said.

"So can killer mutant hellhounds, but you keep Fire Fang around," Indigo said.

"He's only a foster. I just haven't found him the right home." Storm had been saying that ever since she took in Fire Fang. Those two would never split up.

"Was Tuffin on the stairs the night you fell?" I said.

"She was. At least, I think she was. It was a confusing time. And it happened so suddenly." Eldridge looked over his shoulder.

"I didn't see any familiars in the house," I said. "What happened to Tuffin after your death?"

A sob flew from Eldridge's lips. "She was imprisoned, so she couldn't cause any more trouble. Raina had her frozen with magic and mounted. She's trapped in a glass cabinet in the house. It was her punishment for what happened to me. But she didn't do it. Tuffin is innocent."

"That's terrible. Even if she was involved in your death, no familiar deserves that," I said. "Raina could have sent her for rehabilitation or given her to another family."

Storm was scowling and shaking her head. "I can't say I follow all the laws set down by the Magic Council, but your wife has broken one too many by enforcing justice on your familiar. That's torture. Is Tuffin aware of what's going on?"

"She is. They all blamed my furry angel for my death," Eldridge said. "Please, you have to help me. My death wasn't an accident, but Tuffin didn't trip me. Someone wanted me dead, and Tuffin was used as a scapegoat."

"A scape cat," Indigo said with a grin.

"I'm really sorry about what happened to you."
I looked at Storm and Indigo. "If we work on
this together, we can figure out what happened to
Eldridge."

"When did you die?" Storm said.

"Almost a year ago," Eldridge said.

"Which means there's no evidence trail to follow."
Storm shook her head. "Cold cases are the worst. I
should know."

I gave her arm a squeeze. We all knew how
hard Storm worked to find her missing sister, Eden.
"You're good at this sort of thing. And your PI work
will come in handy to solve Eldridge's murder."

"If it even was a murder." Storm didn't look
convinced.

"I was killed." Eldridge spun around us in an icy
blast.

She held up her hands. "I've got a full workload,
and I just received two leads about Eden's
whereabouts. I don't know when I'll be available to
help. It could be weeks. And from the looks of this
guy, he doesn't have weeks before he turns." She
mimicked an evil ghoul by scrunching her face and
waving her arms around.

"What about you, Indigo?" I said.

"Sorry, but I've got the renovation project
ongoing, and my house is deeply unhappy about
having its bits and pieces torn down and repainted.
The magic is misbehaving, so I need to be on hand
to make sure it doesn't attack the builders. I've
already had two guys walk off the job."

"Don't give up on me. I was following you in the
house when Raina showed you around," Eldridge

said. "Odessa, you like ghost hunting. I can be your next project. I'll behave myself."

"That's not a good idea. I'm busy, too." I didn't look at Storm or Indigo. They'd only be all judgey faced if they knew how many ghost hunts I'd been on in my efforts to find Brodie.

"You said you wanted to give this ghost a second chance." Storm pursed her lips. "Or is this not the ghost you were looking for?"

I narrowed my eyes, but ignored her question. "We're all too busy to help, Eldridge."

"I've been in that house for almost a year, trying to figure out what happened. I think I'm getting somewhere, then I meet a dead end." He raised his shaking hands. "And I'm changing. I don't want to be a ghost ghoul."

"Are you absolutely certain you were murdered?" I said. "You said you've been feeling confused."

"I am confused, but I know for certain my last living emotion was fear. I didn't feel safe before I died, but I don't remember the last few minutes of my life."

"Ghosts never do," Indigo said. "Who wants to remember that?"

"You sound paranoid," Storm said to Eldridge. "Maybe that's all this is, and you've connected the dots wrong."

"I haven't." His teeth flashed for a second, but he drew back, a mortified look on his face. "Sorry! I struggle with my anger, and it's getting worse."

"It will if you don't move on," I said.

"How can I move on, when someone killed me?"

We all shrugged in sympathy and looked at our feet.

"Could this have to do with your familiar, Tuffin?" I said. "You're stuck because you know what happened to her and want to put things right."

Eldridge's forehead wrinkled, and he rubbed his chin. "I don't know about that. Although I'm miserable about what they've done to her."

"You could be getting your emotions muddled," I said. "You're unable to move on because you need to make sure Tuffin is safe. How about we help your familiar? Once she's free, you might feel you can go."

Eldridge blinked several times, and two concentration lines formed between his eyebrows as he considered my offer. "I do want to help Tuffin. It's wrong what they've done to her."

"You won't hear any disagreements about that," Storm said.

"And we can all help with that, can't we?" I said.

Storm and Indigo nodded.

"All we have to do is sneak into the house. You show us where Tuffin is stored, and we rescue her." I rubbed my hands together as I warmed to the idea. This would solve Eldridge's haunting. "We'll get Tuffin out, reverse the magic that froze her, and find her a new home. We have a friend who runs an animal sanctuary close by, so she can look after Tuffin until we fix a permanent solution. How does that sound?"

"I would like Tuffin free." Eldridge nodded slowly. "Raina always said she loved Tuffin but turned on her quickly enough when things were difficult. It makes me wonder what else Raina's been lying about."

"You think your wife shoved you down the stairs?" Storm said.

"One step at a time," I said. "Let's set things right with Tuffin then deal with any other loose ends." With luck, this was the only problem haunting this ghost. Eldridge would realize his death was an accident caused by a misbehaving familiar and there was no murder to solve.

We turned and retraced our steps back to his house. Eldridge floated along beside us, his form shimmering in and out of focus as tension radiated off him.

"Try to relax," I said. "You'll upset the magical energy in the house if you go in all ghost anger blazing. We need to be stealthy. They can't know it was us who took Tuffin."

"Stealthy and careful. There's deflection magic around the case Tuffin's in," Eldridge said.

"What does it deflect?" Storm said.

"Attention. They want to hide her in plain sight. I know they can all see Tuffin, but whenever they have visitors, they never comment on the mummified looking cat on display. It's creepy. Why keep her to look at if she caused my death? It doesn't make any sense." Eldridge heaved out a sigh. He'd be dragging his feet if he wasn't floating. The weight of the world was squashing this unfortunate ghost.

"What's the best way to get in without being noticed?" I said. We'd reached the house and stood outside looking at the dark windows.

"There's a small door around the back," Eldridge said. "The lock sticks, and Raina always forgets to check it or turn the key. You can get in that way."

We headed around the back of the house, and Eldridge took the lead to show us the door. It was partially hidden behind a huge swathe of ivy that had grown over the top. If you weren't looking for it, the door would be easy to miss.

"Where does this take us?" Indigo whispered.

"Into a pantry and then through to the kitchen. The room where Tuffin is on display is the second door on your right along the corridor," Eldridge said.

"I went in that room," I said. "I didn't see any cat."

"Because they don't want you to see her. My family is up to something, and I'm not happy about it."

I tried the handle of the door, but it stuck. "Maybe Raina has had it repaired since your death."

"Just use your shoulder on it," Eldridge said. "Give it a shove, and it'll open."

"Or wake the entire household," Storm muttered. "How many are we dealing with if things go sideways?"

"It's Raina, Alastair, Glory, their daughter, and Eldridge's brother," I said.

"Don't worry about him," Eldridge said. "Lars will be passed out drunk somewhere. It's what he does every night."

I tried the door again and leaned on it with my shoulder. It gave an inch, but moved no more. I shoved more weight behind it, and it sprang open. I staggered into a large, cool, well-stocked pantry.

For a few seconds, I didn't move and listened to see if anyone had heard us and was investigating the noise. But there was no movement in the house.

I gestured the others in. "Storm, Indigo, you wait in the hallway. Listen for anyone coming down the stairs."

"Indigo can wait there. I'll check out the rooms to make sure no one is awake. I'll put them to sleep if they are." Storm stalked away before I could stop her.

"Just don't kill anyone," I whispered.

She raised a hand in acknowledgement. Storm's weather magic came with a side of bluntness. When she shot out a spell, she always meant it.

Eldridge gestured us to a closed door. "It's this one. Tuffin's in here."

I nodded at Indigo as she positioned herself beside the door, and I eased it open.

All the lights were off, and nothing stirred. Eldridge floated along beside me as I tiptoed across the room.

"It's this case." He jabbed a finger at a large glass cabinet.

I stopped in front of the case and lit a small orange ball of light. I examined the case from top to bottom. "Raina's magic is good. There's no sign of Tuffin."

"Can you feel the protection magic?" Eldridge said. "They know they've done wrong by trapping Tuffin, so they've layered magic around the case."

Carefully, I lifted my hands and pressed until I felt resistance from the magic barrier. "When I break through, the magic could alert the family, so we won't have much time. And I still can't see Tuffin."

"You see that squat Roman urn on the second shelf?"

I nodded. "That's Tuffin?"

"Yes. It took me weeks of staring in the cabinet before I realized something was wrong. I sensed she was close, but I couldn't locate her. Then I saw the magic covering her waver, and it all made sense."

By habit, I reached into my pocket and pulled out a piece of candy encrusted with powdered pumpkin. I stuck it in my mouth and sucked it as I investigated the magic. There was power behind this spell, but I was stronger. And with my system flooded with a pouch of powdered pumpkin, there were few spells I couldn't break.

"Check with Storm and Indigo to make sure the coast is still clear," I said. "And warn them I'm about to break through the magic. We need to be ready to run."

Eldridge skimmed out of the room, leaving me surrounded by eerie tribal art masks and ominous statues that loomed out of the corners of the room. I focused on the magic, pressing against it to test for weaknesses.

My spooky new friend swiftly returned. "They're ready to go."

"Did Storm find anyone who could cause us trouble?"

"Only my useless brother. As I predicted, he's as drunk as a skunk. Even if alarms were blaring and lights flashing on and off, it wouldn't wake him."

"He likes a few drinks?"

"Lars says it's his way of unwinding. I hoped when he got more responsibility, he might grow up. It seems the reverse has happened."

My eyebrows flashed up, and I grinned at Eldridge as my hands slid through the barrier and touched the glass. "I'm through."

As the magic faded around the glass case, Tuffin appeared in front of me. From the way she'd been posed, it looked like she'd been running for her life when the magic hit. Her ears were flat against her fuzzy black head, her nose wrinkled, and her teeth bared. Her beautiful amber eyes were just visible, as if she'd been squinting against a bright light.

I grabbed the base she was mounted on and yanked it through the barrier. I was almost out when my hand got stuck and I was hauled toward the case, smooshing my nose on the glass.

Eldridge flew to the door. "Someone's moving upstairs. They must know we're here."

I twisted and turned my arm, trying to get free of the magic. "Distract them. Do some ghostly moans and groans and throw things about. They can't catch us in here."

Eldridge sped back to me. "Why aren't you running?"

"The magic is stronger than I realized. Go! Make sure no one comes down those stairs."

"Are you sure you can do this on your own? I could get your friends," Eldridge said.

"Yes! Now, scoot. Go be a bad ghost and scare the pants off your wife and her new husband."

"Got it. I can do scary." He zoomed to the ceiling and shot through it.

A few seconds later, Indigo poked her head around the door. "I can hear groaning upstairs. What's Eldridge up to?"

"Distracting the family. Get over here. I got stuck inside the magic barrier. The display case was booby trapped."

Indigo dashed over. "Hey, you found the cat. She doesn't look too happy, though."

"Would you be if you got stuck looking like this?" I squirmed against the magic. "Hurry! See if you can lower the barrier. I thought I'd got it, but it's strong, and my arm is freezing." White ice crept up my fingertips and covered my hand. The same thing was happening to Tuffin.

Indigo shoved her hands against the magic barrier. Pulses of powerful dark purple magic washed around the room, coating the display case. She lowered her hands after a couple of minutes. "Whatever it is, it's not budging."

"Where's Storm? We need her primal weather magic to cause maximum destruction."

Indigo arched an eyebrow. "So much for a discreet in and out."

We jumped as someone screamed and a door slammed over our heads.

"I'll grab Storm," Indigo said. "Maybe between us we can get you out. Don't go anywhere." She hurried away.

The cold was biting into my forearm and making my teeth chatter. This magic felt unhealthy. I couldn't let it reach my heart, or I'd be in trouble.

I squeaked as ice raced across my skin. Time had run out, as had my desire for subtlety. I grabbed a handful of powdered pumpkin encrusted treats with my free hand, shoved them in my mouth and chewed. I slammed my hand against the magic barrier and shattered it, along with the glass case.

My ears popped, and I staggered back, only just keeping hold of Tuffin. The ice covering my arm faded, leaving me with a tingle from my fingertips to my shoulder.

Indigo and Storm appeared in the doorway a second later.

"Move!" Storm said. "There's someone coming down the stairs."

"We can't go back to the kitchen," I said. "We'll get seen."

"We go through here." Indigo pulled open a window. "We jump into the yard and make a run for it."

Indigo hopped out first. I handed her Tuffin and followed her out. Storm was the last one out. She shoved the window closed, and we sprinted away. We'd reached the edge of the lawn when lights flashed on behind us, and I heard a door opening.

We ducked behind a bush and waited to see what would happen.

"Someone was in the house." That was Alastair, and he sounded furious.

"It was the ghost, darling."

I peeked around the edge of the bush to see Raina holding onto Alastair's arm.

"If that was Eldridge, I don't appreciate it. What's his problem? The man was supposed to be my best friend," Alastair said.

"Until you married his wife," I muttered.

"Eldridge must have been agitated about something," Raina said.

"He can get agitated, but why bang the doors open and shut at night? Glory will be terrified."

"She wears a blackout sleep mask that plays music all night. Hopefully, she won't have heard a thing."

"I like the sound of that mask thingy," Indigo whispered. "I might get one. Olympus sometimes snores."

"But I heard voices. There were female voices in the house," Alastair said. "It couldn't have been Eldridge. And I'm certain I saw someone running from the house just now. I should take a look."

"No! You could get hurt. We'll call the Magic Council, and they'll see off any intruders. Are you sure it wasn't just Eldridge?" Raina said.

"I'm certain of it."

We stayed crouched behind the bush until Raina and Alastair went inside and shut the door. I remained hidden, watching as the house was lit up as they explored inside.

"They'll soon find out we pinched their kitty," Storm said. "And you wrecked that display case when you blasted it with your magic. I thought this was a covert op."

"I had no choice. Whatever spell they put on Tuffin was freezing me."

Eldridge joined us, his dark eyes lit with delight as he spotted Tuffin under my arm. "You got her. Thank you. I never thought you'd break through the magic. Raina is an ice witch, and it always makes her power chilly."

"I almost didn't get through," I said. "You could have warned us how much protection they'd put around Tuffin. My arm almost got frozen off."

"You wouldn't have helped if you knew. You didn't get hurt, did you?" Eldridge patted Tuffin's head.

The cat remained frozen in place.

"I'll survive. But we have to get out of here. Raina and Alastair will call the Magic Council once they figure out they've been broken into."

"They won't. What they did to Tuffin was illegal," Storm said. "They'll get in trouble if they report the theft of a magically frozen familiar. So they should."

"Even so, let's not wait around." I adjusted my hold on the frozen familiar as we hurried away, and we were soon heading to my farmhouse.

"I hate to break and enter and then leave," Indigo said, "but Olympus will be wondering where I am. I said I had an Odessa emergency when I got the call from Raina."

My nose wrinkled. I never had emergencies, just minor mishaps. "Check with him to see if Raina and Alastair report the break-in."

"You're suggesting I use my relationship with a member of the Magic Council for unscrupulous means?" She grinned at me.

"Not unscrupulous. We were doing a good deed and just had to bend a couple of tiny laws to achieve it."

Indigo chuckled. "I'll see what I can find out. Catch up with you both soon." She raised a hand in farewell and walked off.

"You're still staying the night?" I asked Storm.

"Yep. But I'll be gone by dawn. I'll check you survived the night before I leave."

That was Storm's way of telling me she loved me. "There are breakfast muffins on the counter in the kitchen. Help yourself to whatever you like. You know where everything is."

"Thanks. I always do."

I turned to Eldridge, who was hovering by my side. "You're welcome to come back to my farmhouse. The magic on Tuffin will take a while to deactivate. You can stay with me until you figure out what to do next."

"That's kind of you. I would like to wait with Tuffin and make sure she's feeling okay when she snaps out of this. She can be grouchy when she doesn't get her own way."

"Tuffin will be fine in the morning. And then you'll be ready to cross over."

He nodded, although his expression suggested that wouldn't happen.

We walked to my farmhouse slowly, the frozen familiar still tucked under my arm and Eldridge hovering so close I kept getting chills down my spine. I hadn't found Brodie during my ghost hunt, but I'd done a good deed. And as convinced as Eldridge was he'd been murdered, I was sure he was simply confused.

In the morning, everything would be set to rights.

Chapter 5

The next morning, I woke with a frozen back, a boiling chest, and something soft and warm covering the best part of my head and preventing me from breathing properly.

I reached up and patted my head. Something sharp slashed across the back of my hand. "Ouch! What in the world..."

A familiar growl rumbled in front of me.

"Shamrock! I've told you before about sneaking into my bedroom. Get off the bed. I'm boiling to death under these covers."

There was more growling, but a weight lifted off my mattress and a welcome cool breeze wafted over me. I still couldn't get the fluffy thing off my face, though, but I had a good idea what it was.

"Eldridge, are you in here, too?" I said.

A loud yawn came from behind me, and the icy chills faded. "Sorry, I dozed off. I was tired after our adventure last night, and I wanted to stay close to Tuffin."

"Tuffin is on my head?" I decided not to risk feeling around again in case I got scratched.

"She is. Tuffin must have woken after we went to sleep. She loved to sleep on my head when I was in bed. It was her favorite place."

"It's not mine. Can you get her to move?" I said.

"Tuffin, come here." Eldridge made a kissy sound. "We'll find you fresh fish if you're a good girl."

The warm, furry bundle didn't move.

"You did a great job with her, Odessa. Tuffin looks as good as new," Eldridge said.

"I wouldn't mind seeing that or even being able to breathe without inhaling cat fur."

The warm bundle of fluffiness shifted a bit.

"That's it. You're such a good girl. Leave Odessa alone," Eldridge said.

There was a grumbling noise from the cat.

I loved cute fluffies but didn't appreciate having one sleeping on my head. "Any time this morning would be great, Princess Tuffin."

"Give her time. She's very independent," Eldridge said.

There was another warning growl from Shamrock.

"Tuffin, I'm happy you're back with us, but you should move your furry butt as quickly as you can. My scarecrow isn't keen on you. Shamrock sees you as a threat. And when my boys sense a threat, their instinct is to destroy," I said.

There was a faint hiss, and the warm bundle leaped off my face, digging her claws in as she pushed off. Typical cat.

Tuffin sat at the end of the bed, blinking her large amber eyes at me. Eldridge hovered beside her, and

Shamrock remained crouched on the other side of the bed, looking like he wanted to kill someone.

I sat up, pulling cat furs out of my mouth. Talk about a ménage à trois. Or was that a ménage a quatre? I'd never shared a bed with three people. Well, a ghost, a scarecrow, and an indignant looking black cat. It wasn't something I planned on making a habit.

After a big yawn and a stretch, I slid to the edge of the bed. I was exhausted, but there was no rest for the scarecrow queen of Witch Haven.

Once we'd gotten to the farmhouse last night, I'd spent an hour reversing the magic that had frozen Tuffin. There'd been layers of spells trapping that poor familiar. It must have been horrible for Tuffin. She'd been aware of what was going on, but had been unable to move or communicate. My opinion of Raina had changed as I'd unpicked that magic. I needed to be careful around that witch. She could be trouble.

"How are you doing, Tuffin?" I slid my feet into a pair of orange slippers.

"I'm cold. And I'm unhappy." Tuffin's voice was a combination of a deep grumble and a hiss.

"How would a nice breakfast cheer you up? I'm always starving after I've performed lots of magic. And last night was a doozy."

"Do you have fresh salmon?"

I bit my lip and tilted my head. "Maybe in the freezer. I'm not big into fish, though."

"That's all Tuffin eats," Eldridge said. "That and prime rib. She likes steak, too. But only sirloin. And then it has to be medium rare and pan fried in butter."

Shamrock snorted what I could only describe as a noise of disbelief.

I waved at him. "You're growling again. Be nice to our guests."

He looked away, as if embarrassed.

"We'll figure things out. This is new for all of us." I went to pet Tuffin, but she slashed out at me with her claws.

"Tuffin! Be on your best behavior. We're Odessa's guests." Eldridge shot me an apologetic look.

"No worries. We're all still stressed after our big adventure. And Tuffin has had the biggest adventure of all. You're free now, though. That must make you a tiny bit happy," I said.

"Salmon would make me less miserable. And I'm not talking the cheap tinned stuff." Tuffin flipped her fluffy tail around her paws.

This gloomy welcome to the morning needed an injection of joy. "Eldridge, you must be thrilled to have Tuffin back."

"Oh, yes! I couldn't be happier."

"And Tuffin..."

She huffed out a tiny snort. "I'm not frozen. This is slightly less dreadful."

"Excellent. You can spend time together today and then say your goodbyes. And you have nothing to worry about leaving her behind, Eldridge. I'll make sure Tuffin finds the perfect new home."

Eldridge's expression morphed into a terrifying caricature of a human face, with an overly long jaw and narrowed eyes. "I'm not sure. I'm still not ready."

"This was your problem, though. You weren't murdered. You were just worried about Tuffin. Now, you don't have to be. She's free and won't come to any harm. And if you want, Tuffin, you can help decide where you'd like to live."

"How kind of you," Tuffin said. "Allowing me to make my own decisions."

This was a tough fur ball to crack. All I was getting was sass. "Aren't you happy to get out of that display case?"

Her cute, silky nose wrinkled as her gaze shifted around my bedroom. "This is tolerable."

"Tuffin! Odessa risked a lot to set you free. You must be nice to her," Eldridge said.

"This is me being nice. Where's that fish?"

I climbed out of bed and grabbed my dressing gown, ignoring the few seconds when Eldridge changed into a full on ghost ghoul as I busied myself looking in the mirror. My head no longer hurt, and although my thigh had a wicked bruise on it, my fall down the stairs had done no permanent damage.

I headed into the kitchen, trailed by Eldridge, Shamrock, and Tuffin. There was a note on the table from Storm saying goodbye, and an empty coffee mug in the sink.

"Shamrock, go outside and make sure there are no problems in the yard," I said.

He nodded, then bounded out the door.

"I was looking around your barns last night while you were sleeping," Eldridge said. "Your scarecrows are impressive. Several of them tried to grab me."

"They can be overprotective. I'm working on that." I turned to him, my mouth pursed. "You didn't go into the far barn, did you?"

"You mean your workshop? The one with the scarecrows that look eerily human?"

Hmmm... a nosy ghost. This could complicate things. "That's the one. It has several huge keep out notices on it. I don't put them there for decoration."

"I figured that, since I was a ghost, I couldn't get hurt if the scarecrows were unstable. They can see me, but they can't hurt me. I hope. They can't hurt me, can they?"

"It's best to stay out of there, just in case." I busied myself with making coffee and toasting a pumpkin bagel. The contents of that barn were part of my big plan to get Brodie back, and I couldn't afford any interference.

"Why are you making scarecrows that look human?" Eldridge said.

"Why not?" I stabbed my knife into the jar of marmalade and swirled in some powdered pumpkin.

"Doesn't that defeat the point of them being scarecrows? They're supposed to stand out and act as a deterrent before anyone gets too close and causes problems."

I pulled out a mug and thumped it down. "Yes, some people use them for that purpose."

"But you want to create a different kind of scarecrow?"

"That's the plan." I refused to look at Eldridge in case he could tell I wasn't being truthful.

"I saw several of them that looked unfinished, as if you'd abandoned them. One guy's head was missing, and another had a stake through the heart. Why was he staked?"

"It's a delicate process to make the perfect scarecrow. They don't always turn out how I want them to." I speared the butter with the same knife, making a mess with the marmalade. "But I recycle or reuse any parts I can. This is a sustainable farm. Nothing goes to waste."

"And the stake?"

"A precaution." I added a second bagel to the toaster. A busy night of magic use meant a rumbling belly in the morning.

"Huh! So, the humanlike scarecrows—"

"Can I get you anything?" I didn't let anyone in the end barn for a good reason. Nothing would get in the way of what I was doing. And, just like Eldridge, if anyone saw my experiments, questions would get asked.

"Um... I'm a ghost. We don't eat," Eldridge said. "Although that coffee smells amazing. I'll have to live through you and watch you eat. Food is something I miss. Raina knew how to cook."

An engine rumbling close to the farmhouse had me looking out the window. Sol was hard at work, transporting a loaded trailer of hay to the barns. I could always rely on him to get on with his work.

I finished my coffee and bagels, had a quick shower, and got dressed. I made sure Eldridge remained downstairs. I didn't want this nosy ghost around while I showered. Not that I had anything to be ashamed of, but every woman deserved privacy.

"I've got work to finish up on some custom scarecrow orders," I said to Eldridge as I walked through the kitchen. "You and Tuffin can come with me if you like. Then we can figure out what we need to do to make sure you move on."

"I'm not going right away." He went to pet Tuffin, but she skipped out of his reach.

"You don't have to cross over this second, but are you sure you don't feel ready to go now Tuffin is free? There's nothing to keep you here."

"I'm sure." Eldridge shook his head as he floated beside me, out of the farmhouse and down the steps of the wooden porch. "Although I am grateful for what you did for Tuffin."

"You're still thinking you were killed?" I raised a hand to Sol, who was heading off on the tractor, and he returned it with a big arm sweep of a wave.

"I do. And until I know what happened to me, I'm stuck here."

"Then we'll have to work on getting you unstuck." I grabbed supplies from the biggest of my six barns and headed to my production barn. This was where I worked most days, bringing to life my scarecrows to sell to people all around the world.

Tuffin mooched through the barn door. She hopped onto a workstation and glared at me.

"Is something wrong, Princess Tuffin?" I grinned at her.

"You forgot my fish."

"Sorry! I'm not used to having a cat around. Shamrock, where are you?"

"And you can keep that flea ridden straw bag away from me," she hissed out.

"Hey! Be nice. None of my scarecrows have fleas."

Shamrock blasted through the door and stopped in front of me. His glowing eyes flicked to Tuffin, and he growled.

"Can you help me with Tuffin?" I said. "There's salmon in the deep freeze in the storage barn. I think it's under the spare tubs of pumpkin maple ice cream. Can you get it out for her?"

"What am I supposed to do? Cook it myself?" Tuffin's eyes narrowed.

"Shamrock is domesticated. He does an amazing barbecue. Although he tends to catch fire if I don't watch him."

Shamrock grabbed at Tuffin, but she dodged out of his way. "Keep your scratchy hands off me, fleabag."

"There's no need to carry Tuffin. All four of her furry paws work just fine. Shamrock, go to the kitchen, heat the oven, and cook the fish for twenty minutes." I stood in between them to prevent the brewing fight from escalating.

"I suppose the scarecrow can't get those simple orders wrong," Tuffin said. "I'll stay here and supervise until it's ready."

Shamrock issued another growl before vanishing out the door.

With the drama over, I set out my wand, powdered pumpkin, bale of straw, and a heap of clothing. When my scarecrows came to life, they didn't want to be naked. Well, I didn't want them naked. I made them with fully functioning anatomical bits.

I warmed my hands by rubbing them together and picked up my wand. Magic was easy without a wand, but it helped direct the spells when I created life.

My hand went automatically to my powdered pumpkin to get a boost. After chewing on some powder, I laid out a basic human shape for the scarecrow. He needed a solid trunk, arms, and legs. I added the pumpkin head at the end. Get the body right, sort out the brain, and add the final touches of magic to make the scarecrow a complete unit.

"This is boring," Tuffin said. "All I'm seeing is a pile of straw and some grubby clothes."

"My scarecrow art takes time. Have patience." My gaze was focused on the individual items as I imagined them alive. I breathed the first batch of magic over the scarecrow and directed it with my wand. After a few minutes, it settled into place and pulsed through the body.

I turned to Eldridge. "That'll take a few minutes to catch and get things moving. Tell me about your life."

"Um... what do you want to know?"

I took a moment to compose the scarecrow's arms and legs. "When I spoke to Raina, she said you had a happy marriage. Is that true?"

"Yes. There were never any problems between us."

"You must have had a few arguments." I crouched by a heap of pumpkins and selected several, testing the weight of each before I found the right one.

"Every relationship goes through its trials. I'm sure you and your young man bicker." Eldridge pointed out of the barn at Sol.

"I'm Sol's boss. We work together. That's all."

Eldridge nodded. "Well, we had a few arguments, but the marriage was peaceful. We were content with each other."

"Raina married again quickly enough," Tuffin said.

"I thought that was strange, too," I said.

"It's not strange. Alastair was a family friend, and they've known each other for years. It wasn't as if the relationship started from scratch," Eldridge said.

I guided a rogue strand of magic back into my scarecrow as it tried to escape. "Were they attracted to each other before you died?"

"No! Nothing like that. Raina was a loyal wife. I had no doubts about her fidelity."

I glanced at him. "What about your fidelity?"

Tuffin snort laughed and almost fell off the workstation. "Good one."

Eldridge's face flickered out of shape for a second, and an inhuman snarl crossed his face. "That's unkind, Tuffin."

"You had no choice but to be faithful. No one else would want you." Tuffin whipped her tail from side to side.

"You're not all that nice for a familiar," I said.

Tuffin pointed a front paw at her chest. "Cat. Frozen for a year. Starving. Allowances."

"Okay, Princess Sassy Frass. Moving on, we can rule out cheating as a reason for Raina wanting you out of the way."

"We can," Eldridge said.

"I'll give you a good motive. Raina needed an upgrade and all the cash," Tuffin said.

"Do you think Raina was bored with Eldridge?" I said to Tuffin.

"Sure. Eldridge isn't exactly the life and soul of the party. One of his hobbies was collecting bow ties."

"That's not fair. I always looked after you. Besides, bow ties make an outfit," Eldridge said.

"I know you bought me the cheapest salmon when I wasn't paying attention."

"Salmon is salmon," Eldridge said.

Tuffin simply closed her eyes and looked away, as if too disgusted to respond.

"If that's true, we have a motive for Raina," I said. "She wanted a new relationship, and you were standing in her way. She wasn't prepared to break her vows, but once you were dead, she could move on with Alastair."

"Raina wouldn't do that." Eldridge's face blanched, and his jaw stretched wide.

"Look at what she did to me," Tuffin said. "Raina has secrets."

Eldridge's expression wavered. "I can't believe she's capable of murder. If Raina was unhappy, she could have asked for a divorce. I'd have let her go if she was miserable."

"What about Raina getting her hands on the money? What did you mean by that?" I said to Tuffin.

"It's obvious, isn't it? Eldridge had all the cash. Now he's gone, Raina can play Lady Muck in the big house and buy all the pearls. She's in charge."

"It didn't seem that way to me," I said. "Alastair seemed like a take charge kind of guy."

"Raina didn't want extra money. I always gave her a generous allowance," Eldridge said.

"Not generous enough for her liking," Tuffin said. "When people have money, they always want more. Humans are greedy."

"Unlike cats and their salmon," I said.

"That's basic survival. It's a different thing," Tuffin said.

"Raina never wanted for anything in our marriage. She was free to work and earn her own money, but I preferred it when she stayed at home." Eldridge drifted about, not looking happy about the prospect his wife bumped him off so she had unlimited access to the family treasure chest.

"She didn't get bored with being a kept woman?" I said.

"Raina wasn't kept. She had full control over what she did. But the house is huge, and it's a full-time job taking care of it. And she also brought up our daughter. Raina was happy. She never complained about money. And I was always giving her gifts to show my appreciation. She only had to mention something once, and I made sure she got it."

Tuffin didn't look impressed.

"What about Alastair?" I said. "He said you were old friends. Did you ever have any problems?"

"He was a great friend. Almost like a brother. There were no problems between us."

"Alastair is the younger model," Tuffin said.

"Stop that nonsense. He's only a few years younger than Raina," Eldridge said.

"Raina wanted an upgrade," Tuffin said.

I tilted my head as I compared the two men. Physically, they looked similar in build, but Alastair had an alpha edge over Eldridge. Perhaps Raina had wanted a change.

"We can't forget Lars. He's a drunk and an idiot." Tuffin's nose wrinkled. "I don't think he's ever worked a day in his life."

"He has! But Lars has issues. He tries his best," Eldridge said.

"If his best is loafing about like an incompetent sloth drinking your cellar dry. He's got that down to a fine art."

"Lars is your younger brother?" I said.

Eldridge drifted around the barn some more. "By five years. As the older brother, I assumed responsibility for the family business and the estate once my father died. It's the way things have always been."

"Did you mind doing that?"

"No, I was happy to take on the role. I knew what was expected of me."

"And it doesn't bother you that Lars gets to lounge around and take no responsibility? That could cause tension in some families."

"No, and he'll find his way, eventually. Lars is enjoying himself while he's free and single." Eldridge smiled and shook his head. "Sowing his wild oats while he can."

"The only oats coming out of Lars are marinated and worthless. Did you know, he's drinking your collection of rare wines? The buffoon is always stumbling to the cellar to grab another bottle. He should have been the one to fall down the stairs," Tuffin said.

Eldridge glowered at the familiar. "Tuffin..."

She flicked an ear. "And then, if you don't have enough suspects already, we have the brat."

"Glory is not a brat. She's an intelligent young woman." Eldridge scowled at Tuffin. "You like her."

"I never said that. She always wants more, no matter what you give her. Glory doesn't work either," Tuffin said to me. "She's almost as useless as Lars. Although she sometimes gave me treats, so I let her off of being a lay-about. But Glory isn't so great. She didn't object when the family froze me and stuffed me in a display case. If she was a halfway decent person, she'd have gotten me out."

"I understand Raina's motive, but I'm not clear why Lars would want you dead," I said, "or Glory."

"Some detective you are," Tuffin said.

"I'm not a detective. I run a pumpkin farm and make scarecrows." I raised my eyebrows at Eldridge, but he simply shrugged and shook his head.

"Is that scarecrow bringing my fish out here?" Tuffin said.

"I don't know. Why don't you check?" Although Tuffin's snarky comments were throwing up a stream of suspects, I could do with some peace so I could focus on my work.

"No, I'm staying."

"Maybe it's better if you find someone else to deal with this mystery." I grabbed my wand and glared at my pile of unfinished scarecrows. I had enough going on without dealing with a possible murder that may not be a murder at all.

"I'm sure you'll be a great detective," Eldridge said. "Please, don't give up on me."

"Tuffin is right. I don't know the first thing about solving a murder. I should speak to someone at the Magic Council. I know a couple of people there. Maybe they'll reopen the investigation and find evidence of foul play."

"I've been dead almost a year. No one will be interested. My fall down the stairs was written off as an accident." Eldridge dipped his head.

"Corruption is rife in the Magic Council," Tuffin dramatically whispered.

"There's no point in getting them involved," Eldridge said. "You solve this case for me. I can sense you're a good person."

"It was just a thought. Besides, if I ask them to reopen your case without fresh evidence, it won't get me anywhere."

"Don't give up on me, Odessa," Eldridge said. "Something terrible happened to me. And I'm changing. I'm not always in control. I try hard to stay calm and keep my thoughts together, but sometimes everything scatters. I feel this rage building inside me, and I direct it at whoever's closest."

Tuffin shuddered and did a whole body shake. "Spare me. I won't become the familiar to a ghost ghoul."

"Stop being so spiky," Eldridge said. "And be nicer to Odessa. She'll find you a new home and make sure my murderer is brought to justice, won't you?"

"Well, it seems there are plenty of motives in your immediate family. Raina could have gotten bored in the marriage, Alastair might have decided to make a move on your wife and needed to get rid of you, or maybe Lars didn't like being your understudy, so he killed you. And your daughter—"

"No, Glory's innocent."

"More like super annoying," Tuffin muttered.

I rested my hip against the workbench. "We need to find out their alibis for the night of your death."

"We have a genius on our paws," Tuffin said. "This'll be solved in no time."

"Tuffin..." Eldridge wagged a finger at his familiar.

She hopped off the workbench. "I know. Be nice. But you have to remember, I'm a cat. We're bred to be difficult."

I really didn't have time to poke around in a cold case, but I couldn't ignore the pitiful look on Eldridge's face. It just about broke my heart in two to see him so morose. And having a ghost buddy might work in my favor. I needed an inside source to finish my project.

"I'll help you," I said.

Eldridge beamed at me. "I knew you would. Thank you so much."

"I'll help but on one condition."

Chapter 6

Eldridge continued to smile. "Name it. Whatever you want, I can do it."

"I need you to find someone for me," I said.

"Oh. Sure. I didn't expect you to ask me that. Who's missing?"

"His name is Brodie Barclay."

"That sounds familiar." Eldridge scratched his cheek. "Is it the Brodie who lived here? The two of you were involved, weren't you?"

I assembled the next scarecrow, then placed my wand down. Whenever I talked about Brodie, my magic scattered, and my pulse raced too fast. "That's right."

"I knew you dated him. He died, didn't he?"

I took a second to let the tears clogging my throat clear. "Yes, and yes. We met when we were teenagers and started dating. We were together for ten years. He was my first love. He is my only love."

"Young love is the best," Eldridge said. "I met Raina when we were young. It's nice to have so many shared memories with one person."

I nodded. "We were great together, and we had so many plans for our future, but then... I lost him."

"It was an accident?" Eldridge said. "I remember there being a fire, or was it an explosion? Am I remembering right?"

"You are. Brodie managed the gemstone ore works in Wonderland Pines. There'd been rumors the trolls were about to make a move on the site. Brodie dismissed the whispers and said they'd never do that." My throat stopped working, so I shut my mouth.

"Ah. Yes. But the trolls hit the ore?"

"They did. Brodie was working late one night, he was one of a handful of crew left, and the trolls broke in. They thought the place was empty. Brodie tried to stop them, but they'd rigged explosives to cover their tracks. He got caught in an explosion." I focused on breathing as sadness hit me like a jagged ice shard.

"I'm so sorry," Eldridge said.

"Brodie's death was sudden and unexpected." I concentrated on the task at hand. If I dwelt too much on Brodie's accident, I'd retreat to my bed, and no one would see me for a week. "And as you've experienced, when you die unexpectedly, it makes the transition confusing."

"I have struggled to move on, but that was because I was murdered."

"Possibly murdered," I said.

"Definitely murdered," Tuffin said.

I frowned at her. "Brodie is missing, and I never found his ghost. That's who I need you to find."

"You want me to find your dead boyfriend's ghost after all these years?" Eldridge shook his head. "It's been too long."

"Not that long. Just over three years. And he died quickly and violently. Brodie's still here. He's just gotten lost."

"There's lost, and then there's—"

I stopped Tuffin's snark with a raised hand. "No! He's here. We always planned to spend the rest of our lives together. Brodie won't have forgotten that. He's just having trouble coming back to me."

Tuffin gave me a long, hard look. "When you get this missing ghost back, what do you plan to do with him? How do you spend the rest of your life with a ghost?"

"Easily." My special human-scarecrow project would solve everything.

"Is it even safe to look for him?" Eldridge said. "I feel myself changing, and I've only been adrift for a year. I can't imagine what state a ghost would be in after three years of confusion." His hand lifted to his mouth. "Oh, that was thoughtless. I... I'm sure Brodie is fine. You know him best."

I held back the sadness that wanted to rip out of me in a flood of messy tears and runny nose. "He is fine. Maybe we'll have work to do when he gets back to me, but I'm prepared for that. I have a plan. But I can't do anything until I've located Brodie. I know he's around here somewhere. I've been looking for years."

"That's why you were so keen on helping Raina with her ghost problem," Eldridge said. "You thought Brodie was haunting my home?"

"I take every haunting seriously. I never know when I'll meet him. I won't give up searching until I do." I forced a bright smile. "And now I have you.

You can be my contact in the ghost world. Will you ask around and see if anyone has heard about Brodie or knows where he is?"

Eldridge shrugged. "I can try. But I'm sure I'd have heard about him. I'm sociable. I've been all over the village, meeting the resident ghosts."

"But you haven't been asking specifically about Brodie, so why would they tell you about him?"

"That's true, but I'd have heard about a stuck ghost, especially given the way he died. People talked about that explosion for weeks."

My hands flexed, but I took a calming breath. It had almost destroyed me to hear people gossiping about the mine being raided. "Maybe Brodie's stuck somewhere else. Did you haunt any places other than your home?"

"Sure. I can go anywhere I like."

"Then I'll make a deal with you. You help me find Brodie and bring him here, and I'll investigate what happened to you. I can ask around and see if there were any holes in the investigation into your death."

Eldridge hovered about for a few seconds. "Very well. I'll check out everywhere I can and see if anyone's heard of Brodie. But don't get your hopes up. There are ghosts around here, but I've met them all, and Brodie wasn't among them."

"You can't have met them all, because you haven't found Brodie." I looked back at the door. "He's out there. I know it."

Eldridge hovered close and patted my arm. "I'm sure you're right."

"I'm not," Tuffin muttered.

"We're helping Odessa," Eldridge said.

"You can do what you like," Tuffin said. "I'm not chasing a fantasy."

"Ignore her. She's hungry. I'll do my best to help you," Eldridge said. "And Tuffin will help, even though she pretends she doesn't want to."

"I'm pretending nothing."

A sparkle of joy flickered in my heart. This might work. "Thanks, Eldridge. And Tuffin. I'll also do my best for you. I'll get to the bottom of what happened to you."

"Come on, Tuffin," Eldridge said. "Let's go ghost hunting."

"I've got fish to eat. Odessa promised me breakfast, and it's almost time for my elevenses already. I should get two meals for being forced to wait so long," Tuffin said.

I looked at my half-finished scarecrow. I was in no mood to create new life, and the magic wasn't settling. "Let's go to the kitchen. I'll get a top up of coffee, and we'll see if your salmon is ready."

"Two bowls. I want two bowls of salmon." Tuffin darted out of the barn.

"Ignore her grump. She's secretly happy I'm back. I'll let you know when I have any news about Brodie." Eldridge touched my arm, then floated away.

I headed back to the farmhouse with Tuffin trotting in front of me. I needed a plan. First, some refreshments, then I had to work on the outstanding orders for my scarecrows. I'd also need to dry some pumpkins since I was running low on my powdered pumpkin, and I wanted to squeeze in some baking. Oh, yes, and I had to solve a murder.

I'd just stepped outside with my mug of coffee, leaving Tuffin to eat her warm salmon off a plate in the kitchen, when my gaze landed on Sol. A very bare chested Sol.

My eyes drifted over his broad shoulders and down to his stomach. I hadn't realized how warm the day had gotten, and sweat glistened off his skin. He was a large guy, kind of like a big teddy bear, with a little belly and a smattering of dark hair across his chest.

I looked away, my cheeks warm. As my gaze scanned the pumpkin patch, I was amazed to see all the pumpkins had been collected. I stepped off the porch. "Sol, did you do all this yourself?"

He lifted his head and raised a hand before striding over to me.

I kept my gaze averted. I wouldn't look at his chest. I'd always had a thing for big, cuddly guys. I loved to have something to squeeze.

"Morning. I got a few of the scarecrows involved, but we got an early start. The pumpkins are in the barn, ready for you to make your selection. I know you had a large custom order come in last week, so I figured you'd need extra."

"Thanks. That was good of you to remember."

"I never forget when you need something. And I don't want you to run out of pumpkins and disappoint your customers." He rubbed the back of his neck with a broad, tanned hand.

My gaze remained on the field. I wasn't looking at his chest. "The pumpkin patch already looks tilled. You aren't planting again, are you?"

"No, I'm following your rotation pattern. We'll do an annual wildflower patch here to give the soil a break so it can replenish the nutrients. I planned to till the next field over this afternoon and get it ready for planting. Unless you want me to do something else."

"No, that's perfect." I turned and faced him. "You know the farm better than I do. It's exactly the plan I had in mind, I just hadn't had time to talk to you about it."

Sol flushed under my praise and ducked his head. "I always enjoy working your land. It's great to see life flourish."

"I love that, too. I get such a thrill when I see the first green shoots of life. It makes the hard work worth it."

Sol tugged his T-shirt out of the back of his pants and wiped it across his brow.

I tried really hard not to stare, but failed. How could such a handsome guy not have a string of girlfriends? Maybe he did. I knew little about his private life. Sol wasn't married, but that was all I knew.

"I was thinking of taking a break, if you'd like to join me," he said.

My gaze lifted to meet his eyes. "I should get back to the scarecrows. I got off to a slow start this morning."

"I've set something up for us."

My head tilted, surprised by the comment. "Something like what?"

"Come take a look." He reached out a hand and settled it lightly on my elbow.

I pretended not to feel the heat of his hand on my arm as he guided me to the nearest barn. My eyes widened when I saw a small picnic table. There was a flask on it and a cooler box. "What have you been doing in here?"

"I wanted to treat you to something nice. You're always working so hard on things that make other people happy. I figured you'd like a break. I've got freshly made lemonade and iced buns with a strawberry filling. They're fresh from the bakery. I didn't make them myself. My thumbs are green, not flour-covered."

I stared at the picnic table and then at Sol, my heart thudding uncomfortably fast. "You did this for me?"

"I'd hardly do it for the scarecrows." His laugh was self-conscious. "I thought you might like to relax. After all, last night was hectic."

Last night felt like a long time ago. Since then, I'd agreed to become lead investigator in a possible murder case, moved in a sassy cat and a ghost, and gotten a new way to find Brodie.

When I didn't reply, his smile slipped. "It was just an idea. We could do it another time."

I stepped back. "It's thoughtful of you, but I'm so busy. I've got my scarecrows to finish, and powdered pumpkin to make, and some baking to do. And then there's the ghost..."

"The ghost?"

"I, um... Yes. I've agreed to help a ghost with a problem. I'll tell you about it another time." I was still backing away to the door, my panicked gaze flicking from the food to Sol. It was sweet of him, but I couldn't do this. It didn't feel right. "And I have to take Michael's remains to the stables. Hettie is expecting me." That was a lie, but I needed to find a way out.

His mouth turned down a fraction, then he nodded. "I understand."

"It was a great idea. You stay. Have a break and enjoy yourself. You've worked so hard, and it's not even midday. You eat my cake if you like. Sorry. I have to go." I turned and blundered out of the barn, tripping over my own feet.

My heart was lodged in my throat, and my palms were damp as I dashed away. I was glad I had this ghost mystery to focus on. Sol was a sweet man and so thoughtful, but in my heart, I knew you only found real love once. I'd had my happiness, and nothing would compare to that.

I glanced over my shoulder to see Sol standing with his shoulders slumped and his hands gripping his T-shirt. His gaze was fixed on the picnic table. It looked like he was talking to himself.

I shook my head. No, I couldn't contemplate a new love. It was wrong.

Chapter 7

"Indigo sends her apologies." Storm strode through the front door of my farmhouse, Fire Fang on her heels.

"What's she doing this evening?" At the last minute, I'd invited the girls for dinner to see if they could help with the Eldridge problem.

"It's the house again. It trapped a builder inside a bedroom for three hours. Indigo is still calming the place down."

"She should stick with a rustic style. It's my favorite look." I pulled out a chair for Storm.

She settled in it and grabbed a handful of appetizer nuts I'd put on the table. "Sure, it suits this place, but Indigo wants an upgrade. She's got Olympus there trying to help, but he's making things worse by doing his uptight Magic Council overlord act. He got a tin of paint dumped on his head."

"Poor Olympus. I'm guessing Luna is busy with Cole?"

"Yep. It's just the two of us. And Fire Fang."

I risked petting Fire Fang's head. He was an incredible cross breed hellhound who stood higher than my waist. He had a tendency to growl and snarl at everyone, even when he was being friendly.

"Well, I'm glad you could make it," I said.

"My social calendar is always wide open." Storm grinned at me. "I didn't disturb you when I left this morning?"

"Nope. I heard nothing."

"I checked on you. You had plenty of company, so I figured you'd be fine."

"I was. Although the bed guests weren't welcome. Anyway, I need your expertise the most." I checked the pot roast and then sat at the table and poured some drinks. "The ghost who tackled me to the ground is still convinced he was killed. Even after I unfroze his familiar, it wasn't enough to get him to move on. Eldridge wants me to figure out who murdered him."

"Most people wouldn't touch that case. The evidence is gone. If there were witnesses, their memories won't be reliable, and if someone killed Eldridge, the chances are they didn't hang around."

"I promised I'd help him. The guy is a mess. And he's changing."

"Yeah, I saw flashes of ghost ghoul when he jumped you. The kindest thing to do is put him out of his misery. Why drag things out? You'll only be disappointed when you can't find out who killed him."

"No. I'm seeing this through. It's important."

Storm chewed on a handful of roasted nuts. "What's it to you if this ghost makes it or not? Have you got a vested interest I don't know about?"

I hopped up and checked the pot roast again. "I don't like seeing anyone unhappy. And if someone killed Eldridge, then they have to pay."

"You sure that's it?"

"Certain. How many roast potatoes do you want?"

"As many as you've got spare. Whatever I can't finish, Fire Fang will inhale." Storm tipped back in her seat. "If this dinner is a bribe to get me to help you, you're out of luck. I'm heading out first thing tomorrow to investigate another lead on Eden."

I set down the tray of potatoes and sat back in my seat. "Is it good news?" Eden had been missing for years. She was Storm's younger sister and the reason Storm set up a private investigation agency, so she could track every lead that came up. She took on private cases too, but her driving force was always to find Eden.

"I'm not sure. This guy's been in touch a couple of times." Storm fiddled with the zipper on her leather jacket. "He sounded legit, but so many people do, then they turn out to be whack jobs. I questioned him on the phone, and he wants to meet. He reckons he saw Eden a couple of months ago." She rearranged the salt-and-pepper shakers on the table several times. "Someone knows something. I plan to find out if this guy is legit. If he isn't, he can make friends with Fire Fang. It'll teach him a lesson that lying is always bad."

I gave her hand a quick squeeze. Storm wasn't big on emotional displays, but she was hurting. "I'll get the food dished up, and then we can talk about Eldridge's murder." I plated up the chicken pot roast, roast potatoes, and pumpkin balsamic glazed carrots with a side order of roast pumpkin.

Fire Fang got his own bowl of dinner, and I left him munching in the corner of the kitchen while I settled in my seat.

"What does your ghost remember about the night he died?"

"Not much. I'm hoping talking things through will clarify his memory, but nothing has jogged it so far. He is certain he didn't just fall down the stairs, though."

"And you're determined to do this? Help a ghost who's been drifting around for ages, wondering about his murder."

"Yes. We made a deal."

"Sucker." Storm shook her head as she munched on a potato.

"You could be more supportive."

"I am. And even though I can't help you, I've got a contact who can. He's my go-to guy for finding out all the dirt and information. I don't know how he does it, but if there are any black marks against this family, he'll dig them up."

"Thanks. I'll take all the help I can get. I'm thinking it must be one of the family. They were all in the house when Eldridge died. I want to talk to each of them to discover their alibis. But any information I can get in the meantime would be great."

"He calls himself John Smith." Storm smirked. "I'll let him know you're interested in speaking to him. He'll be in touch. Be careful, though. John is rough around the edges. Give him an inch and he'll dig up the foundations, sell the land under your feet, and have you married to a foreign prince before you've changed your underwear."

"I'm sure he's a sweetie. I'll make him a basket of pumpkin muffins. That'll make him happy."

"Not much makes John happy, but you can try. I'll send him a message tonight. He'll need all the information about Eldridge, when he died, and anything you know about the family."

"Got it. Thanks. The sooner Eldridge can move on, the better."

"Before he turns killer ghost ghoul and suffocates you in your sleep. You're not letting him stay in the house, are you?" Storm said.

"Yes! And he's no trouble. Eldridge is under control."

Storm stuffed a piece of pumpkin in her mouth. "For now. But watch him. When they turn, they go fast."

Storm had a tough exterior, but she always looked out for her friends. "I will."

"And take Fire Fang with you when you meet John."

"Can't John just email me the information?"

"He always hands over information face-to-face. He likes to check out his clients."

"Oh, well, we can meet. But there's no need to borrow Fire Fang. I have my boys. I'll take a couple of them as backup."

"That'll work." A gleam of wickedness entered Storm's eyes. "What about taking Sol with you?"

I speared a roast potato into my mouth, then pointed at my face to show I couldn't answer. It was rude to speak with your mouth full.

Storm arched an eyebrow. "When are you going to give that guy a break?"

"Do you think I'm working him too hard?"

"This has nothing to do with how hard he works on the farm. I saw Sol heading to the bar on my way here. He didn't look happy. Did you turn him down again?"

"There was nothing to turn down. Sol works for me. That's all."

"We all know that's not all. The guy's been crushing on you ever since he started here."

"That's inappropriate. I didn't hire him to have man candy around the farm. His references were excellent."

"You admit he's great to look at?"

I remembered seeing Sol with his top off. "I can't say I've noticed. Do you want more potatoes?"

"I'm good for potatoes. What have you got against Sol? I don't like many people, but he's a good guy. And he's reliable. You haven't complained about him once since he started. And you interviewed over thirty people before deciding on him as your assistant."

"That's because none of the others were suitable. Sol is qualified. He even worked on a pumpkin farm. He was the ideal candidate."

"For Mr. July in a man candy calendar." Storm pursed her lips. "No one is perfect, but he comes close."

"If you're so interested in him—"

"No, this isn't about me. You've been on your own for years. Find a nice guy."

"So I can be completed by him?"

"Sarcasm doesn't suit you."

"That's your forte."

"Exactly right."

I chewed on a large piece of pumpkin. Storm didn't understand. She'd never been in love. If she had her own Brodie, she wouldn't question me about dating anyone else. I couldn't replace him. It was pointless trying. Sol was a good man, and he'd make someone a great husband, but that someone wasn't me.

"You know what your problem is?" Storm said.

"I have a feeling you're about to tell me."

"You look at your relationship with Brodie through pumpkin powdered tinted spectacles."

"I have no clue what that even means."

She set down her knife and fork. "It means you filter your experiences through that orange fairy dust you always have on hand. Brodie wasn't Mr. Perfect."

"You didn't like him?"

"He wasn't awful, but he was too flashy. And he wanted to modernize the farm. You argued about it."

"We had a disagreement. And all couples argue. Eldridge argued with Raina when they were married, but that doesn't automatically mean she killed him."

"Maybe it does," Storm said. "You have to stop idealizing the past. Brodie made you happy most of the time, but you also had plenty to complain about.

You've chosen to forget the bad times because he's dead."

My throat felt tight, and my appetite faded. The food in my stomach sat like a lead weight. "And you only think that because you filter the world through cynicism and meanness. Why can't you leave my relationship status alone? I don't prod yours and ask why you never let a guy stay around for more than five minutes."

"You make me sound easy."

"Well, if the shoe fits."

Fire Fang growled as Storm shoved her seat back. "I'm done. Come on, Fire Fang. We know when we're not welcome."

I opened my mouth to apologize and call her back, but nothing came out. The front door slammed. I stared at the remains of my dinner but was no longer hungry. I hated arguing with Storm, but she could be so blunt. And she was dead wrong about Brodie.

But I shouldn't have lost my temper and suggested she slept around. She didn't.

I reached into my pocket to grab a small pouch of powdered pumpkin. I took it out and set it on the table. I didn't have a problem with this stuff. It was all natural. Storm was just being grumpy, as usual.

With dinner ruined and a pumpkin and peach cobbler still in the oven with another twenty minutes before it was ready, I went outside. The air was warm and balmy with just a gentle breeze blowing my hair around as I headed to the end barn and unlocked it.

I stepped inside and took several long, deep breaths. When Brodie was back, Storm would realize her mistake. She was misremembering our relationship. Sure, we'd had different ideas, but there was nothing wrong with that. We'd always talked things through.

Before Brodie died, he'd even written a business plan for the farm. He'd always wanted me to expand and get more land. I had to admit, I was hesitant about taking on more work, but he'd assured me we could make it a success. He'd even said he'd get me help to manage everything. It had never happened.

My hands drifted over the tools on the workbench, where my latest experiment was underway. My gaze ran over the humanlike features of the scarecrow. It had taken three weeks to get to this point, and I'd had to work on the scarecrow every day to keep the magic topped up. But I would get it right. I was simply missing a spell or two that would create a permanent living vessel for Brodie's ghost.

Bringing a ghost back to life in a vessel was difficult and technically illegal. Some ghosts rudely jumped into a living person and used their body as a shell, but that wouldn't work for Brodie. He needed a permanent vessel to live in.

I rested my hands on the scarecrow's stomach and pulsed gentle magic through it to see how the latest combination of spells was holding. The scarecrow jerked around, and one arm shot up.

My magic was as scattered as my thoughts, and it was no use trying anything productive on Brodie's vessel tonight. Besides, I needed his ghost to make this work. Until Brodie was found, I'd keep perfecting the magic.

"Am I allowed in?" Eldridge poked his head around the side of the barn door.

I waved him in. "You've already seen this. I can hardly hide it from you."

"Why would you want to hide it?" He floated in, Tuffin skulking along behind him.

"Oh, no reason. I just don't want my designs stolen. There are unscrupulous scarecrow traders out there. I've had a few passing off their work as mine. I'll have you know, my scarecrows come with authentication tags. You'll always be able to tell an Odessa Grimsbane scarecrow from everything else."

Eldridge floated around the workbench where Brodie's scarecrow vessel rested. "You make amazingly terrifying scarecrows. I've been hanging out here today waiting for you, and I got to meet some of them. Those things have issues."

"Not really. I mean, a few struggle with their primal urges. When you get to know them, they calm down. Usually."

"I saw your friend leave," Eldridge said. "She was muttering to herself. I hid from her giant wolf dog. That thing looked straight at me and snarled."

"Storm isn't happy with me. I'll have to sort things out with her. But she gave me a contact so we can work on finding out what happened to you."

He zoomed over to me. "You're really going to help?"

"I said I would." Since I couldn't solve my own issues, I'd do something useful and make sure Eldridge found peace.

"What are we waiting for? What do you need me to do?" Eldridge swirled around.

"Hang tight. Storm's contact will start by investigating your family. I need information from him before we do anything else."

"Oh. You're still thinking it was a family member?"

"Unless a random person broke in and shoved you down the stairs for no reason, that's the direction I'm headed."

Eldridge's forehead furrowed, but he didn't protest. "I suppose we must cover all bases. You tap your sources, and together, we'll crack my case wide open."

Maybe we would, or maybe I'd be wasting my time. But with the chance to locate Brodie and move on with my life, I was willing to take that chance.

Chapter 8

"You two, stay outside the inn. I'll whistle if I need you." I guided Shamrock and Marmaduke to the alleyway that ran alongside the inn in Witch Haven. Cornelia Norwood had banned my scarecrows from going inside. She said they were a disruptive influence and put off customers. I couldn't see it myself.

I smoothed down my tunic dress, scrubbing away a small piece of dried pumpkin on the hem. I'd spent the day working on my scarecrows and was looking forward to a break. But what I was most looking forward to was finding out what Storm's investigator friend had found out.

John Smith had contacted me first thing this morning, taken down the information he needed, and said he'd be in touch. Sure enough, I was eating dinner when he sent a message saying he had the information and to meet at the inn at nine o'clock.

He said he'd wear a black hat with a red feather on it so I'd be able to identify him. When I'd asked if he wanted to know what I looked like, he said he already knew. I wasn't sure if I should worry about that. How easy was it to find out information about me? If I knew the answer to that question, I'd probably have sleepless nights.

I settled in my scarecrows and headed inside. It was mid-week, so the inn wasn't busy, but there were ten people in there, most of them on their own, and two couples. I recognized several people and waved at them as I looked for John.

When I finally spotted him, he was tucked at the back of the inn, his head down and his long legs stretched out in front of him. The red feather gave him away. There was an untouched pint of ale on the small round table next to him and an orange-colored drink in a tall glass.

I headed to the table. "John Smith?"

He lifted his head to reveal a broad face with a flat nose that looked like it had been broken once or twice. He had large green eyes and a grim set mouth. Several days' worth of stubble covered his face. "That would be me. I got you your favorite drink."

"How do you know what I like?" I remained standing. I didn't sense any threat from him, but John had a dark undercurrent. If I said the wrong thing, I'd get in trouble.

"Nothing is private these days. And I can find out everything for the right price."

I settled in my chair and lifted the drink. It looked like the pumpkin rum cocktail I usually ordered. "Cordelia told you I drank this, didn't she?"

"Like I said, I know how to do my job."

"Well, thanks. And cheers to solving this murder quickly." I raised my glass.

He gestured for me to keep my voice down. "We're casual friends catching up. Don't draw any attention by saying the M word."

"No. Of course not." I looked around, but no one was paying us attention. "Did you get the information on Eldridge's family?"

John lifted a file he'd wedged behind him on his seat and placed it on the table. He rested his hand on top of it. "I have the basics. This'll get you started while I do more digging. Why are you interested in this family?"

"Didn't Storm explain when she got in touch?"

"She was unusually abrupt when we spoke. Even for Storm. Did you annoy her?"

"Nope." I reached for the folder, but he pulled it back.

"Answer the question. Did you know the dead guy?"

"Not really. I knew of him when he was alive, though. Eldridge moved in different social circles to me. And he was older than me, so we didn't spend time together."

"And so..."

"Well, he reached out to me."

"Reached out?"

"He's convinced he was killed. I see ghosts, and I found him haunting his former home. He's sad and confused."

"Which is tragic but doesn't explain why you're helping a guy you had no association with."

"I'm a nice person."

"You are."

I beamed at him. "Thanks."

"But being nice doesn't get you anywhere. Nice gets taken advantage of. Is that what this ghost is doing? He's got something on you."

"Eldridge has nothing on me. I have no secrets."

"Yeah, that's not true."

I stiffened in my seat. "If you're going to be rude, I'm leaving."

"Leave. I've already been paid."

"Wait! Storm paid you to do this?"

"I don't run a not-for-profit, sweetheart. Storm brings a lot of business my way, so she got a discount for this job. And she said there'd be cake. Did you bring the cake?"

"Um... yes, I have muffins. I make them from my leftover pumpkins."

He made a come closer gesture with his hand. "Hand them over."

I passed him the bag I'd brought with me. "There are three kinds. Pumpkin and lemon with a cream frosting middle, cranberry jelly and pumpkin, and dark chocolate and—"

"Let me guess, pumpkin?" He took out a muffin and ripped off a chunk with his teeth. "Not bad."

"I'll pay Storm back. I didn't know you charged for your services."

"You learn something new every day." John kept his finger on the file. "Do you want this or not?"

"Will you be nicer to me?"

"Unlikely. So... what's the deal with the dead guy?"

I wanted the information. I needed to know what the family had to gain from Eldridge's death, and I wanted his help to find Brodie, so that meant a little more opening up. "I'm fixing Eldridge's problem, and he's helping with mine. We made a deal."

John nodded and slid the file my way.

My eyebrows shot up. "You don't want to know more?"

"I wanted to see what you were prepared to share. Some people poke around in others' business to cause trouble. You don't."

"If it turns out Eldridge was murdered, I'll be causing trouble for his killer."

"Which is not something I'm interested in. When someone does something wrong, they pay for it. Although you don't strike me as the hunt them down and destroy them type." He took another muffin and ate it in three bites.

"Have you ever paid for doing wrong?"

John flashed his teeth at me. "What makes you think I'd break the law?"

I dropped my gaze to the file. "I'm not answering that question."

He chuckled and drank his ale. "That family you're investigating is complicated. If I was snooping in their business, I'd reckon someone wanted Eldridge dead to get his money."

"That's what Tuffin said." I opened the file to discover pages of information on Raina, Glory, Lars, and Alastair.

"The familiar." It wasn't a question. "I looked into her, too."

"Yes. Tuffin has a bad opinion about everyone in the family."

"Check the financial arrangements. They're a traditional family. Even though Eldridge has a daughter, his estate passes through the male line. And his closest living male relative is his brother."

"The drunken brother has control over the house and all the money?" I nodded to myself. That explained what Eldridge meant by Lars growing up.

"He does. And the guy's a lush. He's been barred from most places that serve alcohol. I wouldn't want my money or business dealings in such incompetent hands."

"Maybe Eldridge was going to change the succession line and pass the estate to someone else. That would give Lars an excellent motive."

"It would. And Lars also has a criminal record. He's been a bad boy."

"What was he charged with?" I flicked to his page of information.

"Mainly idiot behavior that happens when a guy can't hold his booze. Fighting and disorderly conduct."

"I imagine no one in the family was happy about Lars being put in charge." I flicked through more of the paperwork. It would take me a while to sort through this.

"You're thinking the brother is the prime suspect?" John said.

"It makes sense. He gets everything, but he had to kill his brother to achieve that."

John nodded, although his mouth was turned down. "It's never that simple, though. Have you met the guy?"

"No. I've heard about him, so I know Lars enjoys a drink. Everyone says he spends most of his time passed out drunk."

"And there's your problem. Would a drunken layabout have the spark to commit a murder? Would he have even considered it through his haze of alcohol and hangovers?"

"Lars could have gotten drunk to give him the courage to kill Eldridge."

John grunted and stretched out his legs. "Being drunk sounds like his default. If his focus is on getting wasted every day and doing no work, should Lars be your number one suspect?"

"I suppose, if he inherited the estate and Eldridge's business, it would be a lot of work."

"And a drunk like Lars will always go for the easy option. You'll see when you read his information that he never holds down a job for more than a couple of months. He even worked for Eldridge for a while, but it ended badly. Eldridge gave him a monthly allowance, so he was free to do what he wanted."

"Was it a generous allowance?"

"Depends on how rich you are. Ten grand a month isn't to be sniffed at."

I thumbed through the file. "If he's not my number one suspect, should I be worried about him? If someone killed Eldridge for the money, will they go after Lars next?"

"You're the one playing detective, but it's not a ridiculous idea."

"Should I warn him?"

John raised his hands. "It's not my business. But if there's one less drunk littering up the place, I won't be unhappy."

"Lars doesn't deserve to die."

"There are some people this world won't miss," John said.

I closed the file. "Where do you place yourself on that scale?"

John downed the rest of his drink. "If we do more business together, you'll get to find out. Enjoy." He stood and strode away.

I sipped some of my drink. Maybe Lars was too obvious as a suspect, or maybe he was the next victim.

After finishing my drink, I stood to leave. I nodded goodbye to Cordelia, who was behind the bar, and pulled open the door, almost walking into Sol as I stepped outside.

"Odessa! I rarely see you out on a week night." A flush crossed his cheeks as he smiled at me.

"I was just meeting someone. I'm heading back to the farm."

"May I walk you home? It's getting late."

"Thanks. Although I already have backup." I whistled for Shamrock and Marmaduke. They ambled out of the alleyway, both nodding and grinning at Sol.

"I was taking a walk out your way, anyway, so it's no trouble," Sol said. "And it's a nice night for a walk."

"Sure. We can walk together. I'd like that." I turned to Shamrock and Marmaduke. "You two can take off for the night."

Shamrock jabbed a finger at Sol and then passed it across his throat as his eyes glowed.

Sol chuckled. "Odessa is safe with me. I won't let anything bad happen to her."

Satisfied with that answer, my boys strode away.

We walked side-by-side for a few seconds, neither of us seeming keen to get the conversation rolling, even though there was a lot I needed to say to Sol.

I gripped the file I held. "I'm glad I've seen you. I owe you an apology."

"For what?"

"You did a nice thing for me, and I didn't appreciate it. You were being friendly with the offer of drinks and cake, and I behaved badly. I didn't mean to, but it was unexpected."

"That was my fault. I presumed too much. I didn't want you to feel uncomfortable."

"I... it wasn't that. I was shocked. You surprised me."

"You work so hard on the farm and never take breaks. And you're often working in the barn until gone midnight."

"I enjoy what I do. Although, yes, sometimes it feels like hard work when the magic won't take and the scarecrows don't behave, but I look after myself."

"You look after the scarecrows better than you do yourself. When was the last time you had a vacation?" Sol said.

"Brodie took me away for a long weekend to Silver Falls not so long ago. We swam under waterfalls and drank wine from the local vineyard. It's so beautiful there. Have you been?"

"I have. That's the place with the wild adventure course, isn't it?"

"Unfortunately, yes. Brodie also booked us on the course. I was terrified. I was screaming for my life while hanging from a thin piece of rope. He thought it was so funny."

"It doesn't sound like you enjoyed yourself much."

"Maybe it wasn't the most relaxing of vacations. And I told him I didn't want to do it, but Brodie insisted, and I didn't want to let him down. It was fun when I got past the dangerous bits. But I don't like heights. My knees were shaking for the rest of the day after we'd done the course."

Sol hummed under his breath, but made no comment.

"It was a great vacation, overall. Brodie was always doing that. Taking me away on spontaneous trips."

"That vacation must have been over three years ago."

I pursed my lips. "That's right."

"It must have been tricky with the farm to run. You can't drop everything when you're in the middle of a harvest or dealing with animation magic for a new batch of scarecrows."

I tugged on my bottom lip. Brodie had never checked how things were going on the farm. He'd toss our bags in the truck and insist we go. And he was always right. I'd come back happy and refreshed most of the time.

"It would have been easier if you'd been working for me," I said. "You could have looked after things while we were away."

Sol didn't say anything to that comment either, so I hurried on. "In fact, I've been wondering if you'd like more responsibility. Brodie planned to expand the business, but I never had time to think about it. And after he was gone... Well, it would never have worked out with me being on my own. But now I have you, it's time for a change. What do you say?"

"It's an interesting proposal. What do you have in mind?"

"I'm not sure. But the place has been transformed since you came here. Would you like more responsibility?"

"I wouldn't say no. I enjoy working here, and I enjoy having you as my employer."

"I'm not too bossy for you?"

"That would be impossible." Sol chuckled. "And you make the best muffins. The farm is already perfect as it is, but if you want to expand, I'd be happy to help. I worked on a mixed soft wood farm that made broomsticks for a couple of years while they expanded, and I learned a lot. I set up most of the logistics."

"That sounds great. We'll work out your new tasks together. And of course, there'll be a pay raise."

"I enjoy working here so much, I wouldn't mind if you didn't pay me."

I chuckled this time. "You have to be able to pay your bills. Besides, you deserve more money. You do an amazing job. And my scarecrows love you."

"I wouldn't say they love me. Although Shamrock has stopped stalking me."

We continued to the farm, chatting about new duties Sol might like to be involved in. He had a wonderful range of experience, from hands-on farm laboring to dealing with the accounting. I had an asset on my hands, and I'd been under-using him for too long.

"What have you got in the file?" he said as we reached the porch steps.

"It's to do with the ghost I'm helping. He thinks he was murdered, and I'm looking for evidence to support that."

"A murder. That sounds dangerous."

"It's safe enough. I'm just asking questions and hoping to reassure the ghost he has nothing to worry about."

"Where did you meet this ghost?"

"It's Eldridge Talbot. I met him at his house. He died a year ago, but he's still here. I met him after we had to deal with Michael and Shamrock the other night."

Sol nodded, a thoughtful expression on his face. "I like crime dramas. They use suspect boards to get the information straight. Have you got one of those?"

"A suspect board?"

"They look easy to set up. You need pictures of everyone you think could be involved, and then you figure out their alibis and motives. It helps you see if anyone is lying or if there are holes in their stories."

"I was planning to talk to them all to see where they were when Eldridge fell down the stairs. I hadn't thought about setting all the suspects side-by-side, though. It might make things easier when I'm comparing motives and opportunities."

"I can give you a hand. Set something up. It might help to work with visuals."

"Thanks. That would be helpful."

"Give me a minute. I've got some cork boards in a storage barn. I'll bring one inside."

I headed into the farmhouse and laid out the information John had given me. He'd included pictures of each suspect, so I had everything I needed when Sol came in with a large cork board and a box of pins.

"I'll put Raina up first. Eldridge was Raina's first husband. He told me they had a happy marriage, but maybe she got bored or fell for Alastair, her second husband, and got rid of Eldridge so she could remarry."

"Okay. Who's next?" Sol said.

I picked up Alastair's photograph. "The new husband has to be included. He's a nice guy, but he needed Eldridge out of the way so he could marry Raina. Although Eldridge said they were good friends and had no problems."

"I recognize this woman." Sol tapped a picture of Glory. "I've seen her around the village."

"That's Eldridge and Raina's daughter, Glory." I pinned her on the board. "According to Tuffin, she's not got any work ethic and was always demanding more from her dad. Maybe Eldridge turned her down when she asked for something too big and she got angry."

"Who's Tuffin?"

"Oh! Eldridge's cat familiar. You might have seen her around. Eldridge and Tuffin are staying here while I look into things."

"Is she small, with black fur, and kind of grumpy?"

"That's Tuffin."

Sol nodded. "I know Glory. I wouldn't say she has a temper. She's always friendly when I speak to her."

I slid him a look. "Is she your type?"

Sol rubbed the back of his neck. "That's not what I meant. I just can't see her hurting anyone. She's a nice lady."

"I'll take your word for it." I grabbed the final picture and pinned it up. "This is Lars, Eldridge's younger brother. According to all sources, he likes a drink, he can't hold down a job, and once Eldridge died, the entire estate and the money passed to him. Lars became an extremely wealthy man once his brother died."

"I've seen him around the village, too. Mainly in the inn. Those reports about him are accurate. Lars usually gets steaming drunk and has to be carried out. Cordelia is always threatening to bar him, but he spends a lot, so she lets him sit in the beer garden when it's quiet."

"According to Eldridge and Tuffin, Lars has no drive. Which could be a problem. It's a huge responsibility to keep an estate of that size going."

"Maybe Lars plans on spending the money and running things into the ground. Or selling the assets. He'll get rid of any businesses and sell the house and land then keep the money."

"And leave the family destitute?"

"Is he a family man? I don't know Lars well," Sol said. "Maybe he's cold-hearted enough to take it all."

"I'm not sure about that. We don't mingle in the same circles, so I know little about him." I mused over the pictures. "If it wasn't Lars, he could be vulnerable."

"You think the killer plans to strike again?"

I stood back from the suspect board. "If the motive is money, then maybe. And if Lars isn't a killer, one of the other family members must be. And they'd have to kill Eldridge and Lars before they could get the money. We can't let that happen." When I looked at Sol, he had a soft smile on his face. "You're enjoying this?"

"I'm not sure anyone would enjoy poking around in a murder case, but I'm enjoying spending time with you."

"I'm surprised you haven't questioned me about why I'm doing this. Everyone else has."

"You always want to help others. It's one of the many things I like about you."

My cheeks flushed, and I focused on the board. "Anyone would do the same."

Sol's mobile buzzed in his pocket, and he pulled it out. "Do you mind?"

"No, go ahead."

He checked the message. "I'm sorry, but I need to go. I'm running late."

"I didn't mean to hold you up. It's nothing important, is it?"

"No, just a catch up with an old friend. Let me know if you need any more help with your suspect board. I'm no detective, but I'm happy to listen to your ideas. We could puzzle this out together."

I walked to the door with him. "Thanks, Sol. I appreciate the help. I'm not cut out to solve crimes."

We said our goodbyes, and he strode away, turning and waving when he got to the end of the drive. I waved back, then smiled as I looked over the suspect board. This was really helpful. I was finally getting clarity into this mystery. I'd review the information John had given me, and after that, it was time to question each suspect.

"Eldridge, are you around?" I turned slowly, peering into corners to see if he'd been lurking while we'd looked at the suspects.

He materialized a few seconds later, and Tuffin strolled into the kitchen as if I'd also summoned her.

I gestured to the board. "What do you think?"

Eldridge studied the pictures for several seconds. "It's logical, but it doesn't make me happy that my family members could be involved in this."

"One of them has to be." I rested my hands on my hips. "So, let's get this moving. Out of all these people, who would most want to shove you down the stairs?"

Chapter 9

I yawned as I made myself a decaf coffee and sucked on my sixth powdered pumpkin candy. It might have been my seventh or eighth candy, but who was counting?

I'd hit a roadblock. After reviewing the suspects with Eldridge for several hours, I couldn't convince him any of them had killed him.

A low growl had me spinning around, and I gripped the countertop as Eldridge morphed from a pleasant looking middle-aged man into a seriously scary ghost ghoul. His teeth elongated, and his eyes grew too large for his head. He growled again, and his cold gaze settled on me.

"Eldridge, take a deep breath and remember who you are." I kept my tone soft and level so as not to alarm him. "You're having a brief ghoul episode. You're safe with me and Tuffin. We're looking after you. Remember who you are. Remember why you're here."

He snapped and snarled a few more times, but slowly his features became more human, although his eyes still looked too large. "Sorry. I had a moment. All these thoughts keep swirling around my head, and I get angry. How dare anyone kill me? I'm a nice guy."

"Let's take a break." I eased away from the counter and made sure I had an escape route, just in case Eldridge turned again. "We've been looking at this for hours, and we're no closer to finding out who killed you."

"Not any of them." His voice was still growly.

"You said you had a good marriage to Raina, you loved your brother and respected each other, and you never had problems with Glory. And you were best buds with Alastair. Everyone loved you."

"They did."

"And you're absolutely sure you were killed?"

"Yes! I felt hands on me before I fell. I was walking along the corridor toward the stairs, when I was shoved. Although..."

"Yes? You're remembering something?" I carried my mug to the table and settled in a seat, stifling a yawn behind my hand.

"I was feeling confused. I don't remember why I was out of bed," Eldridge said.

"Maybe you heard a noise?"

"I'm a sound sleeper. It takes a lot to wake me."

"Did your phone go off? I sometimes wake if I forget to switch mine to silent mode."

"No. I leave my phone downstairs so it doesn't disturb me. Or rather, I did, when I needed a phone. No one calls you when you're dead."

"Maybe you had a call of nature," I said. "That happens when you hit middle age. It's something to do with the prostate. You have to get up more often."

"Not me." He shook his head.

"There was a noise." Tuffin was flat on her stomach on the kitchen table.

"You heard it?" I said.

"I did. My hearing is far superior to Eldridge's, and I hadn't been drinking single malt all night."

"That's what got you out of bed." I tapped my finger on the table. "You went to investigate a disturbance."

"I didn't say it was a disturbance, just a bumping sound," Tuffin said. "There were no burglars creeping about the place. I'd have smelled them. My sense of smell is even better than my hearing."

Eldridge tilted his head from side to side. "Maybe I did hear something."

"It woke us both," Tuffin said. "You staggered out of bed mumbling about something, so I followed you."

"Why was Eldridge staggering?" I said.

"The single malt," Tuffin said.

"That's not true. I never get drunk these days. I can't handle the hangovers. My hard drinking days have long been over," Eldridge said.

"But you had been drinking that night?" I said.

"One or two. Lars insisted I have a nightcap with him, and he always pours large measures."

"You were three sheets to the wind," Tuffin said. "You could barely stay upright. And you almost stood on my tail."

"I'd had a few, but I could walk in a straight line."

"Not from where I was standing," Tuffin said.

I leaned back in my seat. "If you were unsteady on your feet—"

"Which I wasn't," Eldridge said.

"You'd had quite a lot to drink. It slows your reaction times," I said. "I'm thinking someone saw an opportunity to get rid of you. They made the noise in the hope you'd come out and give them the chance to kill you."

"But why?" Eldridge said.

"All your money is behind this. Serious wealth makes people do terrible things. Even kill people they care about."

He shook his head. "Not my family. We respect values and traditions. We were taught from an early age to value what we have and follow the family rules. Everyone understands that."

"They may understand, but that doesn't mean they like it if it leaves them in the cold," Tuffin said.

"That's true. I need to question each member of your family," I said, "find out who is hiding secrets from us."

"You can do it tomorrow," Eldridge said. "It's the one-year anniversary of my death, and they're having a gathering in the rose garden on the estate. Everyone you need to talk to will be there."

"Then we have the perfect solution. I'll show up pretending I know nothing about the event. I'll bring a muffin basket and some fresh pumpkins as an apology for being caught in the yard the other night. And I'll tell them I'll help with their ghost problem. It'll give me a reason to keep dropping by."

"Don't accuse anyone of being my killer, though," Eldridge said.

"I'll be tactful, but we need to sort this out." I rose from my seat, happy we had a plan. "By the end of tomorrow, your problems will be solved."

After our unsuccessful trawl through the suspects last night, Eldridge had left to get details of his memorial service. I'd caught up on some much-needed sleep and then spent most of the next day working on my scarecrows. I had three ready to ship out.

I headed into the kitchen and filled a basket with pumpkin and mango sugar encrusted muffins. I also chose two of my best specialist variety pumpkins to add. They weighed down the basket but were so beautiful and tasted amazing.

My dark navy dress was a conservative length. It wasn't my favorite bright color, but it was appropriate for the occasion.

I looked around for Eldridge and Tuffin, but there was no sign of them. Maybe he'd gone on ahead to watch the family set up the memorial.

After locking up, I headed out of the farmhouse. Although the sun was shining, it was cool with a sharp wind. I'd only taken a few steps away from the house before Shamrock appeared. He yanked the basket out of my hand.

"Hey, I need that. I'm taking it to the memorial service at Eldridge's home."

He hooked it over his arm and gestured along the road.

"You're coming with me?"

Shamrock nodded.

"Very well. But stay in the background. I can't afford any trouble at this event."

Shamrock mimed zipping his mouth shut, then grinned at me.

There was no point in arguing with him, and it would be nice to have someone carry the heavy hamper. Besides, I didn't mind Shamrock tagging along. He was one of my more well-behaved scarecrows, so I could almost guarantee he wouldn't cause trouble.

He set a brisk pace, and I hurried along beside him until we reached the house.

I tried the door at the front and knocked several times, but no one answered. "Shamrock, make yourself scarce. Go hide behind those trees in the back yard. I'll whistle for you when it's time to go."

He handed over the hamper and strode away.

I walked around the side of the house and into the backyard. I spotted the family gathered around a recently turned flower bed. They were dressed in black and looked suitably somber.

Rather than heading over, I stayed back as the gardener came out and placed a rosebush in a hole in the middle of the flower bed.

Raina stepped away from the group and turned to face everyone. "It's been a year since we lost Eldridge. I thought it was right we gave him a permanent memorial in a place he loved. Eldridge always enjoyed the garden, although some of what he attempted to grow didn't turn out right."

"I remember him planting all those grasses. They spread like wildfire and had to be dug out because they were crowding out everything else," Alastair said.

"Eldridge was always trying new things." Raina nodded, her smile indulgent. "And he didn't mind if they went wrong. He said every failure was a learning experience. And that particular experience taught him never to plant ornamental grasses ever again."

Her gaze lifted to me, and surprise crossed her face before she nodded an acknowledgement. "We will dedicate this flowerbed to Eldridge. I intend to have his favorite flowers planted here so every time any of us look out the window, we'll remember Eldridge."

No one spoke as the gardener bedded in the rosebush and filled the hole with soil.

"If anyone would like to add additional plants to the flowerbed, let me know, and it'll be arranged," Raina said.

A shiver ran down my spine, and a second later, Eldridge appeared. "I wondered where you were. I figured you wouldn't want to miss this."

"I've been drifting around the house. Tuffin is sulking back at the farmhouse. She didn't want to come because, you know, the whole glass case thing." He watched the group for a minute. "It's a nice thing to do, but I'd have preferred a statue. It should have been placed so I was staring in the window at them."

"They might have found that creepy. Did you enjoy gardening?"

"I gave it a go, but I was no good at it. This is okay, though. It shows they care and makes me think it even more unlikely any of them killed me."

"Or it could be a front," I said. "Heads up, Raina is coming our way."

"Odessa, I'm surprised to see you here. We're having a private family event to remember Eldridge." Raina stopped in front of me. She wore a black silk dress with a string of diamonds around her neck.

"Sorry for intruding. I wanted to see how you were getting on with the haunting, and I brought you these." I held out the hamper.

Raina peered inside. "Thank you. That's thoughtful. Give the basket to Piper." She looked over her shoulder. "We're having a few of Eldridge's close friends over shortly. You're welcome to stay."

"Thanks, but I don't want to get in the way."

"It's fine you're here. How's your head? Any aftereffects from the fall?"

"I'm all better. And I wanted to see if you'd had any more problems with Eldridge."

"He was hyperactive after your visit, and a display case got smashed."

"Eldridge did that?" I hoped I looked more innocent than I felt.

"Who else would it be?"

"I don't know. Was anything taken?"

Raina cocked her head. "Why do you ask?"

"Oh! No reason. I figured a display case might contain valuables. If it wasn't Eldridge, maybe someone broke in to steal the family heirlooms."

She let out a sigh. "Of course. No, nothing was taken. I'm certain it was Eldridge. Although Alastair thought he saw someone running from the house, but he was mistaken. It was just our unhappy ghost."

Raina was lying to me. But then she could hardly confess what she'd done to Tuffin.

"Has Eldridge been a problem since that evening?" I asked.

"Actually, no. Everything is quiet. Maybe he wanted to go out with a bang. He could have left us alone."

"Really? I was planning to offer my help if you still needed it." Eldridge had been spending too much time with me. I needed him back in the house, haunting the family. Otherwise, there'd be no reason for me to keep coming by.

"Your first visit must have done the trick. I haven't heard a peep since the display cabinet was broken. You must have a knack for getting rid of ghosts. I must admit, I'm relieved."

"I did nothing special. Maybe Eldridge hasn't gone." I didn't want to scare Raina, but I had to keep a foot in the door. "Ghosts are tricky. They go quiet for days, but they're conserving energy as they build up to something big."

"Oh, do you think it could be that? I'd really hoped he'd gone." Raina bit her bottom lip. "I mean, I'm sad he's no longer around, but life is easier when you're not living in a haunted house."

"Why don't I look into it some more? I've been doing some research and come up with a few ideas about how to get Eldridge to move on."

"What are you thinking?"

"He could have unfinished business that needs sorting out before he's ready to leave."

"I can't think of anything left incomplete after his death. Eldridge was an organized man. And he left me well provided for, so it can't be me he's worrying about."

"Maybe not, but I'm happy to keep looking into things. Even if it's just to confirm Eldridge has gone."

"I'd welcome that. I'd like to know he's happy and doesn't feel he has to stay for any reason." Raina leaned closer. "I was worried he might be changing. You know, turning into a ghoul."

"It often happens to confused ghosts. And we definitely don't want to deal with Eldridge if he changes."

"No, that would be dreadful. Yes, please help us. I need to know this is over."

I was surprised how easily Raina agreed to me being involved. If she'd killed Eldridge, she'd want to keep things quiet in case I uncovered something unsavory.

"I know this must be difficult," I said, "but may I ask you a couple of questions about the night Eldridge died?"

"Of course. If you think it'll help."

"Any details could be useful. Why was Eldridge out of bed that night?"

"I don't know. I only woke when he fell down the stairs."

"You were both in bed just before he fell?"

She nodded. "We stuck to a routine. We always had a tea before bed. I'd turn in first because I like to read. That night, Eldridge stayed up with Lars, and they had a drink. He was tipsy when he came to bed and was joking around. I told him to stop being silly and have a glass of water to avoid a hangover. He got ready for bed, and then it was lights out. There was nothing unusual happening that night."

"Do you know what Eldridge and Lars were talking about?"

"No, but it was most likely one of Lars's ridiculous ideas. He's always coming up with big ideas for new businesses but never follows them through."

"Lars is ambitious?" That didn't sound like the guy I'd been learning about.

"No, Lars is a daydreamer." Raina pursed her lips. "And I am worried about the future of the estate now it's in his hands. Lars is in charge now, and managing everything is challenging. You need to be organized. I keep gently prodding Lars to encourage him to become focused, but he's not interested."

"Is he interested in spending the money now it's under his control?"

She sucked in a breath. "Not really. He spends some, but he's not excessive. He likes his vacations and expensive cars, but there are several of those in the garage already."

"He's not got extravagant tastes?"

"No more than the rest of us. I need to sit him down and talk to him again." Raina adjusted the neckline of her dress. "Eldridge could get through to him. Maybe if Alastair has a talk to him, man-to-man, Lars will see he needs to be more involved in the estate."

"Is he running things at the moment?"

"No, he's a figurehead. I deal with the day-to-day things, along with Alastair. Do you think Eldridge is staying around because he's worried Lars might make a mess of things?"

"It could be that. I'll see what I can find out. If Alastair can help Lars get things moving, it might give Eldridge closure."

"Then I'll make sure it happens. If you'll excuse me, I should get back to the family." Raina turned away.

"Before you go, was Alastair around the night of Eldridge's fall?"

She turned back. "He was. He'd often stay at least once a week. It saved him from having to make the trip home. Now, I should really..." Raina gestured to the group.

"Of course. I won't hold you up. I'll make contact with Eldridge and get to the bottom of this."

Eldridge had been hovering nearby the whole time, listening intently to Raina's answers.

"Thank you. Let me know if you need more information. And do stay around if you can. We're having drinks inside in half an hour. And look at the rosebush we planted. Eldridge loved yellow roses. He'd often bring me a bouquet."

"Thanks. I will stay a little longer." As Raina walked away to join the family, I turned discreetly to Eldridge. "What do you think?"

"Nothing Raina said surprised me. And she concealed nothing."

"Could Raina and Alastair be in on this together? She knew you'd had a lot to drink, so she got Alastair to make a noise and get you out of bed. Then he shoved you."

"I hate that theory."

I held in a sigh. "You don't like any theories when it comes to your family. I need to speak to Alastair next. Come with me so you can hear what he has to say."

I headed to the flowerbed, where the gardener was tapping down the soil. The family had moved away, so I stood and admired the glossy green leaves.

The gardener stood. He was a young guy with shaggy dark hair and scruff on his chin. He nodded at me and walked away with a spade in his hand.

Piper walked over a few seconds later with a tray of drinks and a selection of tiny sweet, iced pastries. "Would you like one?"

"Thanks. I'll swap you a drink and some nibbles for this hamper. I brought over muffins and two fresh pumpkins I thought might be useful."

Piper nodded as she hooked the basket over her arm. "Great. I was thinking of making a pumpkin risotto one night this week. And your pumpkins are the best. They're so full of flavor." She glanced over her shoulder.

I dived into the tiny cakes and had eaten three before I could stop myself. "These are incredible. Are they your recipe?"

"No, it's from an old family cookbook. They're a family favorite. Eldridge loved them."

"Could I get the recipe?" I grabbed another iced pink cake and popped it into my mouth.

"Of course. You can borrow the book. I'll get it for you before you leave."

"Thanks." I turned to the flower bed as I licked icing off my finger. "It's nice the family has done this to remember Eldridge."

Piper smiled as she studied the rosebush. "Yes. And that will flourish under Ben's care."

"He's the gardener?"

"Assistant gardener. He's not been here long, but I knew this would be the perfect job for him. And it means I don't have to deal with cutting the flowers for the house. It always affects my allergies. Ben's handy to have around." Piper looked over her shoulder again.

"Is everything okay? The ghost isn't bothering you, is he?" Some magic users were sensitive to ghosts, and it looked like Piper was one of them.

"No, I haven't heard him for a while." She inclined her head to the right. "But I'm worried about that huge scarecrow skulking in the bushes. He looked in the kitchen window and gave me a fright. Is he one of yours?"

Chapter 10

After a swift goodbye and an apology to Piper, I dashed to the bushes, checking no one was watching as I slid behind them to confront my misbehaving scarecrow. "Shamrock, you were supposed to be discreet. You're scaring Piper. She thinks you're going to attack her."

Shamrock's eyes glowed red. He caught hold of my arm and stared at me.

"It's not time to go yet. I've still got suspects to talk to."

He tugged my arm, almost yanking me off my feet.

"Behave yourself. What's the matter with you?" A buzzing filled my head, but I couldn't get any sense from Shamrock as he continued to pull my arm. "Go home. Sol will need help to put away the equipment."

Instead of following my orders, Shamrock grabbed me around the waist and hid me behind a tree, covering me with his huge straw scented body.

"What are you doing?" I said. "Let me go."

He shook his head and jerked his chin in the direction of the house.

I poked my head around the tree. Someone wearing a wide-brimmed black hat was approaching the family. "That's a member of the Magic Council. I'd recognize that silly hat anywhere. Maybe they're here about the damaged display case."

Shamrock growled and clutched me tighter. My scarecrows didn't like the Magic Council.

I looked up at him. "You were protecting me from this visitor?"

He nodded.

"That's lovely of you, but we have nothing to hide. I run a respectable business, and everyone loves my scarecrows." Although I didn't want the Magic Council discovering my sideline in creating humanlike scarecrows. That was nobody's business but mine.

From this distance, I couldn't make out who the person was, but she was female, with jet black hair hanging down her back in a straight curtain. She spoke to Piper for a moment, and Piper pointed to the bushes where I was hiding.

"Uh-oh. We've been rumbled. Shamrock, you need to get out of here. We can't give the Magic Council any reason to have a problem with us."

His grip grew so tight, I squeaked.

"Go on. I'll be fine. You know I'll whistle if I get in serious trouble."

He heaved out several sighs to show his unhappiness before he let me go.

"Get back home. I'll be right along with you." I waited until Shamrock was out of sight before walking through the bushes, attempting to make it look normal that I'd been poking around the hedgerow. As I emerged, the woman from the Magic Council was striding toward me.

She raised a hand. "What are you doing?"

As soon as she got closer, I recognized Selma Black. I didn't know her well, but she'd been in Olympus's office a few times when I'd dropped by with Indigo. "I thought I saw a fox."

"They're vermin." Selma was in her late thirties, with pale skin and a permanent downturn to her lips.

"They're adorable. People should be kinder to animals. After all, we're just animals when you take away the fancy phones, clothing, and lack of fur."

Her small nose crinkled. "You may be."

I ignored her slight. "Is there a problem with the family?"

"I'm not here to see them. I'm here for you." Selma set her feet apart as if she felt the need to brace for trouble. "You're a difficult witch to find. I had to use a location spell to see where you were hiding out."

This didn't sound good. "I'm not hiding. What do you need to see me about?"

"We have a problem of the scarecrow variety."

"Are you sure it's my scarecrows? They're always well-behaved. Although the newer models need more intensive training. They're just like cars; the fancier the model, the more bits can go wrong."

Selma opened her large purse and pulled out a thick file. "You admit you're having problems?"

"No, that was just an example. My scarecrows are works of art. They're—"

"I've been put in charge of dealing with this problem. It's my top priority."

I studied the file in her hand, my stomach dipping. "Go on. I'm sure it's something I can fix."

"Over the last three months, we've had a number of complaints about you. As a result, I've been monitoring the farm and your activities."

"You've had me under surveillance? Is that legal?" I'd been spending lots of time working on my human scarecrows. What if Selma had poked around and seen what I was doing?

"It's legal. We have every right to assess threats in the village and make a judgment on how to handle them."

"You're mistaken. Everyone loves my scarecrows. And I have orders coming out of my ears from all over the world. If people didn't like them, they wouldn't buy from me."

Her nose did that crinkle thing again. "I've been investigating your over-inflated claims about how impressive your scarecrows are as well. False advertising is against the law."

"Over-inflated?" My fingers flexed. "My scarecrows are perfection. I always tell customers, if they have any concerns, they come straight to me. I can fix the problem or give them a replacement. And if they remain unhappy, they can return the scarecrow, and I'll give them a full refund. It's a guarantee I always offer."

"And yet I have complaints from a number of villagers about your scarecrows breaking into their houses, damaging property, and being menacing.

Six villagers have also reported being intimidated by your scarecrows."

"They're misunderstanding the situation. My scarecrows look intimidating, but that's their purpose. If I made them sweet and cuddly, they wouldn't be able to do their jobs properly. Let me speak to these villagers and explain the situation. Are they new residents? If they've recently moved in, they won't understand the scarecrows."

Selma clutched the file to her chest, as if expecting me to yank it from her hand. "These complaints were made in confidence."

"I know almost everyone in Witch Haven. They won't mind if you tell me their names so I can have a friendly chat with them."

"And take your menacing scarecrows with you to make sure they keep their mouths shut or even withdraw their complaint?" Selma flipped the file back into her purse.

"I wouldn't do that. Some people need educating when it comes to my scarecrows, though. I'd hate for there to be any misunderstandings."

"They don't need your kind of education." Selma adjusted the waistband of her black pants. "When I visited the farm this afternoon, I spoke to your assistant."

"Sol can't have a problem with the scarecrows. They love him."

"He didn't." Her thin, dark eyebrows arched. "I asked him to show me around."

This nosy posey was pushing her luck and my friendliness envelope. "And did he?"

"No, he said this was your business. You've got him well-trained."

"Sol is a loyal employee. He wouldn't let anyone poke around without my say so. Creating magically enhanced scarecrows is a sensitive business. What if you'd stumbled into the middle of a project and ruined it? You'd have cost me money."

"I never stumble when I investigate dangerous magic practices. But I do plan to get a warrant and explore every inch of your farmhouse and barns. Unless..."

"Yes? I can show you my records and permits if that would ease your concerns. Everything is aboveboard."

"I've already checked your paperwork is up to date. But if you give me permission to look around now, it'll be considered favorably when I review the complaints."

I frowned. There was no chance I'd let the Magic Council snoop into my business.

A sly smile slid across Selma's face. "Since you claim there's nothing untoward going on with your business, I'm sure you won't have any objections."

I bristled under her smug tone. "Actually, I do. Despite you saying my scarecrows are a problem and people don't like them, I have a backlog of orders. I can't afford any delays."

"If you're so busy, why are you here? If you've got time to look for foxes, you can spare me an afternoon so I can bring over a team to comb through your assets."

"That's different. I'm here for Eldridge Talbot's memorial event."

"You're a friend of the family?"

"In a way. I'm helping Raina. She was happy for me to be here."

"When I spoke to her, she said she was surprised to see you. You didn't get an invitation, I take it?"

"I didn't, but I wanted the family to know I was thinking of them on this sad day."

Selma shook her head. "You need to get your story straight. One minute, you're dropping by to offer condolences, and the next, you're looking for vermin in the flowerbeds."

"My story is as straight as your hair."

Selma folded her arms over her chest. "Are you going to let me look around the farm?"

I copied her posture, crossing my arms and jutting out my pelvis. If she wanted to play alpha with me, I'd happily out alpha her. "No. There's nothing you need to look at. My business is respectable, and my scarecrows are under control. It would be a waste of time."

"Then you leave me no choice."

The gleam in her eyes made me sweat. "What do you mean?"

"I'm suspending your license to trade."

My mouth dropped open. "You can't do that."

"It's within my rights. We can shut down any business that poses a threat to customers."

"The business isn't a threat."

Selma tapped the file. "These complaints say otherwise. Destruction of property, menacing behavior, and intimidation. This has to end."

"I can fix that, although it's an exaggeration. Some of the scarecrows get bored. I'll give them more to do to keep them occupied. That's all this is."

"That's not good enough. If you're housing unstable scarecrows on your land, they need to be destroyed."

"I'm not destroying my scarecrows. If you lay one finger on them, I'll—" I pressed my lips together, holding back my threat.

Selma arched an eyebrow. "Yes? Were you about to say you'd set your dangerous scarecrows on me? You'll send a bunch of them in the middle of the night to intimidate me? Is that how you make your money? You use a thug scarecrow army to keep people quiet."

"No! My scarecrows aren't thugs."

"I expect I'd have dozens more complaints if you weren't using intimidation tactics to keep people silent."

"I have no need to do that." I needed to shut this problem down. "Why don't you come to the farmhouse and we can talk some more?"

"No, you had your opportunity. I came here offering an olive branch, and you snapped it in half. Now, this is official. I'm filing the paperwork so we can search your property."

"If you do get that warrant, I hope it comes with a huge apology when you find nothing." I held my hands behind my back, my fingers digging into my palms.

"I'm only doing my job. If you and your scarecrows are a threat, then you'll be shut down for good. You won't be able to trade, and if you try to get a new license, I'll make sure it's refused."

I glowered at her. Selma was loving this power trip.

"I'll be in touch within seventy-two hours. And if you've hidden anything from me, I'll know. Don't make any new scarecrows and confine the ones you have." She turned and marched away.

Anger blazed through me. I grabbed a pouch of powdered pumpkin from my purse and shook it into my mouth, chewing on the gooey, sweet powder as it transformed on my tongue.

I wasn't giving up on my scarecrows. Selma could make all the threats she liked, but I had to keep working to ensure that, when I found Brodie's ghost, I had the perfect vessel for him. Nothing would stop me from getting him back.

I glared at Selma as she stopped to talk to Raina for a moment. Selma shot a disdainful look over her shoulder as if she sensed me watching and then walked away.

A sigh slid from my lips as the anger faded. I didn't need this complication. I had Eldridge's murder to solve and Brodie to find. And thanks to Selma's intrusion, I'd lost my chance to question everyone at the memorial event.

As I rounded the side of the house, people were arriving and going inside. It would be impossible to talk to the family about Eldridge's death now they had guests to look after. My chat with Alastair about his alibi would have to wait.

Piper waved at me and jogged out to give me the recipe book. At least one good thing had come out of this visit, and I'd be making plenty of delicious mini cakes to cheer myself up.

I stamped back to the farmhouse, still fuming at Selma's treatment. I slowed by the locked barn and rested my hand on the door. I had to do something about my experiments. Selma wouldn't understand what I was doing.

Sol rounded the corner and pulled up short. He was dressed in a smart white shirt and a pair of dark blue jeans. "Odessa! I didn't know you were here."

My gaze flickered over him before returning to his face. He scrubbed up well. "I just got back from visiting the Chalice family. They were having a memorial event for Eldridge."

He ran a hand down his neatly ironed shirt. "We had a visit from the Magic Council while you were gone."

"I know. Selma Black found me. Thanks for not letting her poke around while I wasn't here."

"She kept asking questions, and I got the impression she was trying to trip me up. She was looking for a problem, and asked me what you were like to work for, and if you'd ever done anything I found threatening."

"It would be impossible for me to threaten you. I'm half your size."

Sol grinned. "You can be intimidating when you need to be. And you can always placate the scarecrows, no matter how teeny you are."

"I do my best to play the mean boss when I have to. What else did Selma ask about?"

"She kept talking about the scarecrows and what you did to them. She thinks you're using dark magic."

"I'd never do that. The scarecrows go to families and businesses. If I was using anything illegal, everyone would know about it."

"That's what I told her, but Selma wasn't convinced. She kept on and on and even tried to look in a barn after I told her she couldn't go inside."

"I need to add security guard to your expanded list of tasks on the farm," I said.

He shook his head. "No need. I'll always look out for you."

"And I appreciate that. I don't think we've seen the last of Selma, though. I told her she couldn't look around, so she's getting a warrant to do a search. Fortunately, the Magic Council is slow when issuing paperwork, so we've got a couple of days to make sure everything is as it should be."

"That won't be a problem. It's not like we're hiding anything dodgy. This is a legit place. I wouldn't work with you if it wasn't."

"Of course. I'll deal with Selma when she turns up." My gaze slid to the locked barn before returning to Sol. "You look nice. Are you going somewhere?"

He looked away and nodded. "I hope you don't mind. I'm leaving half an hour early because I have a date."

I stepped back, and my hand went to my chest. "A date. Well, that's good. I've been meaning to ask if you wanted me to set you up with my single friends. I mean, Storm is single, but she's kind of scary. I'm not sure she's your type. But I noticed you don't have a regular girlfriend. Or at least, no one I know about. Not that it's my business who you date. I'm just your boss. I'm just..." I clasped my hands together and took a deep breath. "Have a nice time. Enjoy yourself."

"Thanks. I didn't plan it. My brother set me up and only told me at the last minute. I don't want to go, but I won't stand the lady up."

"Absolutely. That would be horrible. No one should be stood up." I was slightly less bothered now I knew Sol hadn't met someone he liked. A blind date wasn't a real date. It was two strangers shoved together to have an awkward exchange.

Sol was about to step away, but hesitated. "If you need me here, I can stay. I got my tasks done for the day, but we haven't finalized details about my new role. We could grab a coffee and talk about it."

I was tempted to take him up on that offer. "What about your date?"

"I'll get my brother to contact her. He wouldn't even give me her number, so I couldn't cancel. I'll tell him I have a work thing. He'll understand."

"There's no need to cancel. We've got plenty of time to sort your job."

He kept his steady gaze on me. "You want me to go on this date?"

I bit my lip. "I don't want you to be lonely."

"I'm not lonely when I'm here." Sol looked away. "And what about Eldridge's murder? How did you get on talking to the family? We could look at the suspect board and see if it helps. That's more important."

"It is, but so is having a private life." I shouldn't be jealous about Sol seeing someone. He was a free agent. And he was a good-looking guy, so of course, it was natural someone would scoop him up and make an honest man out of him. I should be happy for him, but the twist of knots in my stomach made me think I was going to be sick.

"Are you positive?"

"Go and enjoy your date. We can catch up about Eldridge's murder tomorrow." What Sol did in his private life was none of my business. He could date who he wanted, when he wanted, and he could take them on amazing romantic candlelit dinners. I'd be happy for him.

"You're absolutely sure you don't want me to stay? You don't think Selma will come back?"

"No. We've gotten rid of that problem for now."

He opened his mouth as if to say something more, but then simply nodded. "Have a nice evening. I'll see you tomorrow."

"Yes. Have fun. Fall in love and sweep this woman off her feet." I winced at how high-pitched I sounded.

His shoulders rounded and he sighed. "Sure. Have a nice night."

I turned away and trudged into the kitchen. I switched on the oven and pulled out my muffin trays. I spent a few minutes flicking through the recipe book I'd borrowed. Raina had made notes on several of the recipes, altering ingredients and trying new flavors. I picked a recipe for triple chocolate pumpkin muffins with white icing and sprinkles.

All I wanted was to get my happiness back. Why was that so hard to achieve?

Chapter 11

The next morning, I woke to something icy stroking my left cheek. I blinked open my eyes and came face-to-face with Eldridge.

He breathed his icy breath on me, his eyebrows shooting up. "Thank the Wicca prophets. I thought you were dead."

"I kept telling you she wasn't dead. She's too warm to be dead." Tuffin was curled on my lap.

I smacked my lips together and blinked my gritty eyes. It took a few seconds to realize I'd fallen asleep in the easy chair in the kitchen by a cold fireplace. "I'm alive. Although I don't feel so good." My hand landed on one of the half-dozen empty silicone muffin cases scattered around me.

After baking my triple chocolate pumpkin muffins last night, I'd curled up in the chair with a blanket around me and eaten every single one. It hadn't improved my mood.

I'd been looking for comfort, but six giant sweet muffins for dinner left me feeling yucky and gave me a food hangover.

"Who was that scary lady visiting my house yesterday?" Eldridge said, still giving my cheek an occasional prod, as if he didn't believe I was going to make it. "I was inside when I saw her talking to you and Raina."

I shuffled up in the seat, being careful not to disturb Tuffin, and ran my hands through my hair. "Selma Black."

"What did she want? Is it something to do with my murder? Is my case being reopened?"

"No, her visit had to do with my scarecrows. She hunted me down to inform me there was a problem."

"I would have stuck around to hear what she had to say, but I wanted to see what my family was doing," Eldridge said. "I thought I might find out something useful."

"Did you?"

"No." His bottom lip jutted out. "They spent little time talking about me. They said a few words when new people turned up, but they didn't seem sad I was gone. Most of the conversation was about other things. Lots of vacation talk."

"Does that make you think the service was just for show?" I eased Tuffin off my lap and collected the muffin cases.

"Do you think they were all faking being sad that I was dead?"

"Maybe not all of them, but I'm still convinced one of your family members killed you. Your killer had to put on a good show, so no one got suspicious of them. If the first anniversary of your death passed with nothing being done, it could raise questions. People in this village love to gossip."

"I... maybe." Eldridge drifted around, not looking happy.

"Who suggested the memorial flowerbed?"

"Raina. She brought it up with Alastair over dinner one night. They both agreed it was a nice idea. Do you think Raina pushed me?"

"I think she did," Tuffin said. "I always thought she was the smart one in the relationship."

"I'm with Tuffin on this. Raina could have come up with the memorial plan to cover her tracks. She wanted everyone to think she was a respectable widow and hadn't forgotten you, despite her speedy remarriage." I placed the muffin cases in the sink and switched on the coffee pot.

"Raina was a good wife. And when the family was outside, she seemed sad about me being dead."

"Seemed being the important word in that sentence. Raina is evil. I'm living proof of that," Tuffin said.

"And maybe Eldridge is the dead proof," I said.

Tuffin's gaze cut to me. "Where's the fresh salmon for breakfast?"

My stomach turned over unhappily. "I don't think I can stand the kitchen smelling of fish this morning. I'll find you something else."

"Bacon cubes would be acceptable."

"Can't you catch your own breakfast?" I said. "The scarecrows are always chasing mice out of the barns."

"I don't catch my breakfast. What do you think I am, a common cat?" Tuffin's eyes narrowed to tiny slits. "Eldridge may be a forgettable lump, but he used to cook my meals from fresh every day. That's not going to change."

I rubbed my forehead. "It might have to. Let me find a scarecrow to hunt you something from the freezer."

"More frozen rubbish," Tuffin grumbled.

"It's that or go hungry. Or you could turn vegetarian. What are your thoughts on pumpkin?"

Tuffin hissed and turned her back to me.

"She's grumpy because you moved her off your lap when she was comfortable," Eldridge said. "When you get to know her, she's a real lap cat. I can tell she's warming to you."

"That's Tuffin getting warm?" I brewed the coffee.

"Be gentle on her. Remember, she was frozen for a year."

I nodded slowly as I inhaled the delicious aroma of roasted beans. "I haven't forgotten. It's why I haven't tipped her out of here for being such a sassy puss."

"My ears are working fine," Tuffin said, her back still to me. "Where is the scarecrow with my breakfast?"

I glanced out the window to see three scarecrows loitering. I whistled them over, and they gambled my way. Shamrock was among them.

I caught hold of his hand so we could two-way communicate. "Shouldn't you all be busy? Hasn't Sol given you your tasks for the day?"

A familiar buzzing filled my ears as we made our connection.

"Not here," Shamrock said.

I checked the time. It had just gone eight o'clock, and Sol was always here before that, even though his official workday didn't start until eight-thirty. "Are you sure?"

"Sure. No work. We're chilling."

"Go to the barn with the freezers and find something suitable for Tuffin to eat, please. Anything meaty or fishy will do."

Shamrock looked at Tuffin and growled.

"No, Tuffin is a friend," I said.

"Tuffin a mean jerk."

"Why do you say that?"

"Shredded pant leg."

I looked at Tuffin. "Have you been messing with my scarecrows?"

She wrinkled her nose. "You don't have any scratching posts."

"I live in a farmhouse made mainly of wood. Can't you scratch on some of that?" I leaned out the window and inspected Shamrock's shredded leg. "Tuffin! That's not nice."

"He chased me for half an hour, but he was too slow to catch me. Even so, I had to get my revenge when he was snoozing." Tuffin sounded far too happy about destroying Shamrock's calf.

Shamrock lunged through the window, but I placed a restraining hand on his broad shoulder and pushed him back. "No! Tuffin won't do it again, will you?"

"I make no promises. Eldridge bought me a multi-tiered scratching play station when he was alive."

"Which you never used," Eldridge said. "You sat in the box it came in for three months and then started scratching on the couch corner. Raina was so angry when she caught you."

Tuffin simply twitched her nose in response.

"Let's have breakfast and figure out what we're doing with the day." I looked at the other scarecrows. "You can start the planting in the lower field. Shamrock, find food for Tuffin, then you join them. Understood? No fighting with each other."

He nodded but was quietly growling. "Cat's still big jerk."

"And you're a useless bag of straw." Tuffin strutted out the door.

"Huh! I only just noticed Tuffin can hear Shamrock. Not all magic users have an ability with my scarecrows. Maybe if they get over their differences, they can be friends," I said.

Shamrock growled again and shook his head before racing after Tuffin.

"He won't hurt her, will he?" Concern crossed Eldridge's face.

"Looking at Shamrock's leg, he's met his match." I headed back to the coffee pot, poured myself a strong mug, and settled at the table. "I didn't get far with my investigation into your death yesterday. Raina revealed nothing new, and I was planning to talk to Alastair, but I got distracted by Selma."

"You're looking in the wrong place. My marriage to Raina was fine. There were moments of dullness, but it was stable. I'm sure it wasn't her."

"How about Alastair? Have you bumped him up the list of killers?"

"No, and I've been thinking about this long and hard since you laid out the suspects."

"There were no signs of an affair between Alastair and Raina while you were alive?" I sipped my coffee, grateful for the warmth as it slid down my throat.

"No. He was a good guy and respectful."

"They could be in on this together. They were both in the house when you fell."

"I was pushed."

"By some mystery person you don't know, since you won't believe anyone you're connected to did this."

Eldridge floated around so I couldn't see his face. "I watch them, sometimes."

"When you say watch them, what do you mean?" I asked.

"When Raina and Alastair are getting ready for bed."

"Eldridge! I hope that's all you do. They deserve their privacy."

He glanced over his shoulder at me. "And I always give it to them. When things get frisky, I shoot through the wall. I don't want to see my wife and best friend getting hot and heavy."

"Okay." I stretched out the word, uncertain I believed him. "Why have you been watching them?"

"To see if they let anything slip."

"Pillow talk. And... anything suspicious come out? Have they discussed your death?"

"Hardly at all. Alastair sometimes asks to move my things into storage, but that's it."

I felt sorry for Eldridge. Life really had moved on without him. "If it wasn't Raina and Alastair, that leaves us with Lars and Glory as suspects."

"No, it wasn't either of them."

I tipped back my head. We were getting nowhere with figuring out what happened to Eldridge.

A cold draft blasted across me, and I looked up to see Eldridge standing too close, his features mildly ghoulish. "Don't give up on me. I'm sorry. I'll try harder."

"I'm not giving up on you. But I'm stuck. Tell me more about Alastair. What does he do for work?"

"He runs a business selling refurbished broomsticks. He also has a line of custom-made broomsticks. They're popular. He makes them himself."

"Does the business make a lot of money?" I said.

"I believe so, although broomsticks bore me. He had no money worries that I know of."

"So, Alastair didn't marry Raina for the money?"

"He'd be wasting his time if he did. Lars is in charge of the estate. Raina has savings, but I really think they married for love."

"We should still look into Alastair's business. If he was having struggles, he might have gotten desperate and married Raina to get access to your assets or her savings." I finished my coffee and stood. I looked out the window again, but there was still no sign of Sol. The place would be fine if I left, but the scarecrows could get rambunctious if they were alone for long.

"What are you going to do?" Eldridge floated along beside me.

I lifted a hand as I got to the stairs leading to my bedroom. "You stay down here. I'm going for a shower and a change of clothes. Then I want to speak to Alastair. We need to get cracking on this investigation so you can move on."

"Very well. But I don't think it'll help."

"We have to find a lead somewhere." I dashed upstairs, sorted myself out, and rushed back down, my hair still damp. I hadn't bothered with makeup and was wearing an oversized orange dress with pink flowers dotted all over it. It wasn't a flattering outfit, but I loved these colors.

As I went into the kitchen, Tuffin was eating something out of a bowl. Good, that might make her happy for five minutes.

"Eldridge, you're with me." I dashed out of the farmhouse and down the porch steps. "Where does Alastair run his business?"

"He has an office in the grounds of the house."

"Then that's where we need to go."

"How will you get him to talk about his money worries? If he even has any."

I sped along, raking my fingers through my hair as it air dried. "I need a broomstick."

"You do? I've never seen you fly."

"I did when I was a child. And I want to try out my skills. It's a perfect reason for me to see Alastair."

We arrived at the house twenty minutes later. I was out of breath, having dashed along, but I was determined to make progress today. Yesterday had been a disaster, so I needed to make up for it.

"The office is around the back, by the willow trees and the lake," Eldridge said. "Follow the gravel path."

I looked around as I walked, but apart from seeing someone working in the garden in the distance, there was nobody about. I headed to a large single-story wooden building painted in a sage green. The door was open. I poked my head in and saw Alastair sitting at a desk.

"Knock, knock. I hope you don't mind me disturbing you," I said.

He looked up and smiled. "Of course not. What brings you back here? Any news on Eldridge?"

I made sure not to look at Eldridge, who had drifted into the office and was slowly moving around. "No. Actually, I'm here to look at your broomsticks. I've been hearing amazing things about them."

"Excellent. You've not bought from me before, have you?" Alastair pushed back from his seat and stood. He was dressed in a casual blue shirt and jeans.

"No. And my skills are rusty, but I want to get back into the tradition of riding."

"The fine art of riding a broomstick is much maligned in favor of cars and bikes. They have their place, but sometimes a witch needs to feel the wind in her hair. I ride several. I made them myself. Where did you hear about my work?"

"People love to talk in the village, and someone suggested I come to see you."

"Take a seat and have a look through my design books. I can make just about anything you want. I've got all the tools right here."

I flicked through the colored brochure he'd placed in front of me. "These are amazing. You're talented."

"Talent that comes from years of study and hard work," Alastair said. "That one you're looking at is a Master Whip 5000. She's a speed demon. Like riding a rollercoaster."

"I'm not looking for anything that sophisticated. Just a basic model, in case it's not for me." I flicked through a few more pages. "Did you ever design anything for Raina or Eldridge?"

"I have given Raina a broomstick, but she only rides to keep me happy. She always looks magnificent though, sitting astride a broomstick and whizzing through the air. Eldridge had a few goes, but he didn't like it."

"Riding a broomstick made me queasy," Eldridge said. "And Alastair always shows off. He made me feel inadequate."

"We used to mess around with the broomsticks after we'd had a few drinks," Alastair said. "But Eldridge preferred something with four wheels and a beast of an engine. Poor guy. We won't ever get to fly together again."

I set the brochure to one side. "I was talking to Raina about Eldridge and what she heard just before his accident."

"She mentioned that to me. I think she feels guilty that she wasn't able to stop his fall. She knew he'd been drinking and wasn't stable on his feet."

"I don't think anyone could have stopped it," I said. "What about you? Did you hear anything that night? You were staying in the house, weren't you?"

"That's right. No, I heard nothing. But that's not unexpected. I was in a room at the far end of the corridor. The family rooms are closer to the stairs."

"And how did Eldridge seem to you that night?"

"His usual self. He was always a friendly guy. It's rare you meet a person and that friendship carries on over the decades. We all change as we age, but Eldridge always had that easygoing way about him."

There was no way for me to check if Alastair was telling the truth about where he was, since he was in bed alone, so I changed tact. "Did Eldridge show an interest in your broomstick business?"

"I can't say he did. I mean, I talked things over with him now and again, but broomsticks weren't his thing."

"Broomsticks make me nervous," Eldridge said. "I worry about getting a splinter in my behind."

I held back a smile at that comment. "What you're doing here looks great. Have you ever thought about expanding? Although I suppose you'd need a lot of investment to do that. Did you ever suggest to Eldridge that you should go into business together?"

"I wouldn't have asked Eldridge to do that. You need a passion for broomsticks to be successful with them. Riding magic is sensitive." Alastair clasped his hands together. "I tell you what, I have a couple of models out back. If you're interested, why don't you take one for a spin?"

"Oh, I couldn't do that." I hadn't ridden a broomstick since I was a teenager. I was likely to face plant in the dirt if I hopped on one.

"I insist. Once you get the feel of a broomstick again, you'll fall in love with it. You can try a couple of models to see which one is best for you."

I glanced over at Eldridge. He was grinning and shaking his head. He'd be no help at getting me out of this situation. "I guess it couldn't hurt. But only a quick ride."

"You go outside, and I'll grab the broomsticks. I just need to check in with someone before we start. I'm interviewing for a new estate manager, and my latest candidate is finishing the budgeting test. I won't be a minute." Alastair dashed away before I could think of an excuse to get out of riding a broomstick.

"I didn't pick up anything odd from that conversation. I don't think Alastair is hiding anything," I said to Eldridge, keeping my voice low so no one would hear me talking to thin air.

"Same here. And he was right about me not being interested in his business." Eldridge drifted along beside me as we headed outside. "I never understood the fascination with broomsticks. I find them uncomfortable."

"Me, too." I forced a smile as Alastair appeared and handed me a pale brown broomstick with a side saddle.

"Give that one a whirl. It's a model three series, so it doesn't come with mod cons, but it's a great basic broomstick to get you from A to B."

I shuffled into the saddle and clasped my hands around the stick. This was like riding a bike. You never forgot the technique.

The broomstick rose under me, and I squeaked. Then it shot off. I had no control over it. I shrieked again as I rocketed from side to side.

"She's got a kick in her, hasn't she?" Alastair yelled as I zoomed past.

"I can't get it to stop. Where's the brake?"

"Hold on and go for another circuit. You'll soon get the hang of things."

I wasn't getting the hang of things. The world whizzed by, and the broomstick shook as it plummeted and weaved. My eyes widened, and I drew in a breath to scream as I headed straight toward a gigantic oak tree.

From out of nowhere, Sol appeared, caught hold of me, and pulled me off the broomstick.

Chapter 12

The broomstick whizzed away, leaving me in Sol's arms.

I stared at him, too stunned to speak for several seconds. "What... what are you doing here?"

"Saving you. Are you okay?"

"I'm fine. I'm just out of practice when it comes to riding broomsticks. Um... Thanks for the rescue."

He set me on my feet but kept hold of me. "I've never seen any broomsticks at the farm. What made you suddenly want to buy one?"

"Odessa, are you okay?" Alastair rushed over with a toolbox in his hand. "I'm so sorry. There must be a fault on the broomstick. I've never seen it behave like that."

I eased away from Sol's arms, even though it felt great to be wrapped in them. "I'm sure your broomstick is fine. It's my lack of practice that's the problem."

"You're already proving yourself. I have a feeling you'll be an asset to this place." Alastair patted Sol on the arm. "Odessa, if you're sure you're okay, I'll collect my errant broomstick and check the magic isn't faulty. I've got every tool I need to fix her, and then you can try again."

"No, thanks. But you go. I'm fine." I was studying Sol's face. He was no longer looking at me.

Once Alastair walked away, I cocked my head at Sol. "You didn't answer my question about what you're doing here. And why does Alastair think you're an asset?"

Sol kept his gaze on the ground and pushed his hands into his pants pockets. "I came here for a job interview."

"Oh! You want to leave the farm? Why? I've just offered you more responsibility. I know we haven't figured out the details, but isn't that what you want?"

"There's so much I want, but I can't get it from you."

My stomach plummeted. This wasn't about his workload. "You can tailor the job however you like. And there's plenty of work to keep you busy on the farm. If there's a job you don't like doing, we can work something out."

"You know that's not what I mean."

"Got it." Alastair strode back toward us, clutching the broomstick.

I stared at Sol for a few more seconds before turning to Alastair. "Great. I'm glad it didn't get damaged."

"My broomsticks are hardy. I'll give this one a service and make sure it doesn't happen again," Alastair said. He looked from me to Sol. "Ah. I see this might be awkward, Sol being here for an interview and all."

"It's not awkward," I said. "I'm just surprised. This is the first I'm learning that Sol wants to leave the farm."

"I don't. I'm exploring my options," Sol said.

"And I'm in desperate need of an experienced estate manager," Alastair said. "I hate poaching from your team, Odessa, but Sol has excellent references and experience."

"He hasn't asked me for a reference," I said. "Maybe you'll change your mind when I give you one."

Alastair chuckled and rubbed the back of his neck. "Maybe so. And I'm still interviewing. I'm seeing two more people this morning, so nothing is decided."

I glared at Sol. "That's good. You need to find the best person for the job." And since Sol was walking away from me, it looked like I'd picked the wrong person for my farm.

"I'm terrible at estate management," Alastair said. "Raina does a lot of it, but I want us to ease up on the workload and enjoy what we have. We need a reliable manager to keep things under control."

I was trying hard not to sulk about Sol keeping this from me. After all, he could go where he liked and take any job he wanted. I had no say over what he did. But as his employer, he could have kept me informed.

"This was something Eldridge was much better at doing," Alastair said. "He enjoyed all aspects of running the estate, but I'm not great with the grounds management. We've got a lad who does the gardening and a few maintenance bits, but I need someone who understands all aspects of estate management."

I looked around for Eldridge to see what he thought about this, but he'd drifted off.

My gaze went to Sol. I wouldn't be childish. Sol deserved better. "Even though I'm risking losing a great employee, you won't find a better estate manager. Sol's helped transform my farm. I was always losing things and having problems keeping up with orders, but Sol makes sure I have enough supplies. I can't remember the last time I've run out of anything. And he always knows the right time to harvest the pumpkins."

"That's an excellent reference." Alastair took a step back. "Well... I should get on with some work. Thanks for coming for the interview, Sol. I'll be in touch soon. And Odessa, let me know if you want to go ahead with a broomstick purchase. You're welcome to come back and have another go. We could try a more sedate model."

"Thanks. I'll think about it." I watched Alastair walk away and took several deep breaths. I didn't know what to say to Sol. I wasn't just annoyed he hadn't told me what he was doing, I was also hurt. I didn't want him to leave the farm. He was a perfect fit. Where would I find another Sol?

He touched my elbow, and I flinched and stepped away. "Odessa, I want to talk to you about this. I shouldn't have kept it from you. The interview was a last-minute thing."

I shook my head. I was in the wrong mindset to discuss Sol's future. "You do what you like. In your contract, I asked for a month's notice, but you can go straight away. There's no point in staying if you don't want to work for me."

"Hang on, I only just interviewed for this job. I might not get it."

"You'll get it. Alastair seemed impressed with you." I had to keep deep breathing and thinking happy thoughts, or I'd say something I'd regret. "And I will give you a reference if you ask for one. I'll only say good things."

"I'd appreciate that. But I haven't made a decision yet."

I looked at him, and my heart sank. I was about to lose Sol. What I could offer at the farm wasn't enough, but I couldn't give him anything else.

"How was your date last night?" Yes, I was going there, even though I was in a terrible mood.

"Err... it was fine. She was nice."

"You're seeing her again?"

"Do you care?"

"I... no."

Sol sighed. "I'm not seeing her again. There's only one woman I'm interested in."

Panic slammed into me like a goblin's hammer. "I need to get back to the farm. And if you're leaving, I'll have to put out a vacancy for a new assistant." I walked away without saying goodbye.

A few seconds later, Sol strode after me and matched my pace. "Don't leave. We should discuss this."

"It's been discussed. You'll soon have an amazing new job, and I'll be down a member of staff. Well, I only have you, so I'll be working on my own again. Maybe I should figure out a way to do that permanently. At least I won't let myself down." I'd slid into petulant mode, despite my efforts to stay in the mature woman lane.

"Odessa, you're a smart, creative lady. You can always figure things out on your own. But I know you've enjoyed working with me. I've loved working with you."

"Perhaps I shouldn't have enjoyed it. I rely on you, and you're letting me down." I was marching along, pumping my arms to get some distance from Sol. Unfortunately, his long legs made it easy for him to keep up with my frantic stride.

"I'm sorry you think that. I enjoy my work at the farm, and I was pleased when you suggested I take on more responsibility."

"But it wasn't enough to make you stay?"

Sol said nothing for a few seconds. "I stay because I want to be around you. I like the work, but I like you more."

I shook my head. I wasn't prepared to listen to this. "That's all I can offer you."

"I don't think it is."

My face was too hot, and I was breathing deeply. I also had a stitch in my side, but I kept walking. "You should take the estate management job if you're offered it. And you will get it. Alastair isn't stupid. He knows what an asset you'll be."

"I will take it if you don't want me around. But you need to tell me that."

I slid him a glare. Sol wasn't even out of breath, and I was power walking like an Olympic athlete. "I just offered you more responsibility."

"Because you want me around?"

That wasn't fair. Everything had been going smoothly, and now it was crashing down around me.

"I don't want to leave you," Sol said, "but sometimes, it's painful to be around you when I know you're hung up on someone else. Someone you can never have."

"Sol, I've always been clear about this. I'm not available. I'm married."

"No, you're not." He caught hold of my elbow and stopped walking.

"I am! You know about Brodie."

"I know your version of Brodie. But I know from other people that you never married him."

"We were as good as married. I feel married." I pulled my arm out of his grip. "I gave my heart to Brodie, and he gets to keep it."

Sadness simmered in Sol's eyes. "And what about you? Is it healthy to fixate on a ghost? Brodie can't give you the love you deserve."

I shook my head and backed away. "He can. You don't understand."

"I understand more than you think. You want him back."

"What's wrong with that? We were perfect together."

"Even though he took you on vacation and made you do things you didn't want to do, when he knew you hated doing them?"

"I shouldn't have told you that. And it was a one-off. That wasn't typical. And no one is perfect. Not even you."

"Brodie was also pushing you to expand the farm, but he expected you to do it all yourself. Is that a fair partnership?"

I fanned my hot face. "That's not true, either. You're twisting my words. Brodie is a good man."

"Maybe he was, but Brodie wasn't perfect for you. Brodie is also gone."

"It's none of your business. We were happy. I can't consider being with anyone else. It would be wrong."

Sol reached out and took hold of my hand. "You should. Because I care for you. When I started working at the farm, it took about five minutes before your quirky ways and sweet laugh got to me. I began to make up reasons to stay late so I could be around you and get to know you more. Nothing I've learned about you has put me off. The opposite."

"Sol, I can't do this." My heart was racing so fast I felt dizzy.

"Odessa, I love being around you. I love your ambition and your creativeness with the scarecrows, the way you care for them, no matter how badly they test you. You're always looking out for others and making sure they're happy, even the ghosts. But what about you? Are you happy?"

"I have nothing to be unhappy about. I have almost everything I need."

"But you need Brodie back to be genuinely happy?" Sol kept a tight grip on my hand, smoothing his thumb repeatedly over the palm.

My heart thundered in my chest. "I do. He's the only man for me."

"I can't accept that."

"You have to. It's my decision, and I've made it." It didn't matter that Sol was handsome, smart, and reliable. He wasn't the man for me.

A series of rapid expressions crossed Sol's face. "Odessa, I'm in love with you. You have my heart."

I stared at him, tightness wrapping around my throat and making it hard to breathe. "I never asked for that. You barely know me."

"I've been by your side every day for months. I choose to be there because I love you."

"Stop saying that. You can't love me."

"I can, and I do." Sol stepped closer. "And now you know. I've been giving you time and space, not pushing anything, but I'm done waiting."

"What have you been waiting for?"

"For you to realize you deserve another chance at happiness. You could be right, and Brodie could have been everything you wished for, and no other man will get close to how incredible he was. But it's easy to distort a memory. And like you said, no one is perfect."

I gritted my teeth. Storm had said the same thing, although she'd been much blunter. "I was happy with Brodie. My memories aren't lying."

"But why don't you deserve to be happy again? You loved Brodie, and he loved you, but that's over. You've been on your own for over three years. Why don't you deserve a second chance?"

"Because I don't need it. And I don't want one. Brodie's—" I stopped myself. No one knew what I was planning once I'd found Brodie's ghost. People wouldn't understand. They'd think it mawkish and unnatural.

Sol stepped closer, wrapped his free hand around the back of my neck, and pulled me in for a kiss. His warm lips covered mine, and I forgot how to breathe. It had been a long time since anyone had touched me like this. The kiss wasn't urgent or demanding, but it fired a spark in me that had lain dormant.

It took several long seconds before I realized what was happening and stopped responding. I jerked away. "I'm married!"

Sol instantly put distance between us. "You're entangled in a memory. You were never married to Brodie. Did he even ask you to be his wife?"

"Stop! I was happy with him. You need to leave this alone. And you have to stop talking about love. You're the one living in a fantasy. We can never be together."

Sol shook his head. "From what I've learned about Brodie, he could be a jerk. You need to look over those memories for clarity and ask other people's opinion of what your perfect life with that guy was like. You won't enjoy the truth."

I scowled at him. We were almost back at the farm, so I stuck my fingers in my mouth and whistled.

"What are you doing?" Sol said.

"I'm done with you. You won't listen to me, so you need to leave."

We turned as the ground shook beneath our feet, and twenty seconds later, Shamrock and Marmaduke appeared.

"Odessa, don't do this," Sol said.

Anger boiled inside me like molten lava. "You insulted Brodie, and you lied to me about going for another job. And… and you said you loved me. I've got every right to get rid of you."

His gaze cut from the scarecrows and back to me. Most men would run in the face of such intimidation, but Sol didn't move. "You're an incredible woman, and you deserve to be happy. Maybe I told you harsh truths about Brodie, but someone had to. Otherwise, you'd spend your life in a daze, imagining things that never happened and forgetting the bad times."

"Shamrock, Marmaduke, get him." I stabbed my finger in the air. "Sol is no longer welcome."

Shamrock and Marmaduke exchanged a glance, their eyes glowing red. Neither of them moved toward Sol.

"You heard me. Follow my order. He's intruding." I was yelling, sweaty, and fuming.

Sol looked at the scarecrows, his expression calm. "They won't attack because they know this doesn't make sense."

I stuffed my hand in my pocket and pulled out a handful of powdered pumpkin encrusted treats. My magic needed a boost so I could get my scarecrows to do what I wanted. I stuffed the treats into my mouth and chewed.

"Why don't I take a couple of days off?" Sol said. "We can think about what we want from our futures. I love working at the farm, but I love you much more."

I choked down the treats. "I don't have to do anything other than get rid of a problem. This is a mistake of my making. I should never have thought an assistant could help me. I'm better on my own if I can't have Brodie."

Sol's expression darkened in a rare show of displeasure. "Maybe you were better off when Brodie wasn't around."

I swallowed the last of the powdered pumpkin treats, and a surge of magical energy shot through me. I pushed it out and slammed it into Shamrock and Marmaduke. "Remove Sol. I don't want to see him at the farm ever again."

The scarecrows surged forward and surrounded Sol.

He raised his hands, his palms out. "Steady, guys. I don't want trouble."

They hovered around him as if uncertain what to do.

"Odessa, don't walk away from this," Sol said.

"Get him out of my sight," I yelled. "And if you won't follow my orders, I'll take you to the stables, and Hettie will feed you to her biggest, meanest stallion."

Sol backed away. "I'm going." He gave me a long, hard look. "Think about what I said."

"I don't need to."

He nodded then turned and walked away.

"And in case you hadn't figured it out, you're fired," I yelled at his back.

Sol didn't even raise a hand in acknowledgement.

Shamrock and Marmaduke followed him for a few minutes before ambling back to me. From the expressions on their faces, they were confused but not as confused as me. And I was still angry. Why did Sol have to complicate things? Everything had been good between us. All the pieces were falling into place with work and Brodie, and then Sol had to slam down his giant man hand full of love bombs and disrupt everything.

"Err... Is it safe to talk to you? Or will you yell at me, too?"

I turned at the sound of Eldridge's voice. He was hovering a few feet behind me. "Of course, it's safe."

"We heard you shouting."

Tuffin sat beside Eldridge. "You scared away Sol?"

"Yes. And he won't be coming back. He doesn't work here anymore."

Eldridge's face morphed into a pale, elongated ghoul with a bulbous forehead and a long, narrow jaw. "But you need time to solve my murder. You can't do that if you have to run the farm on your own."

"I'll still have time to help you. I could handle this place before Sol strode in and took over."

Tuffin snorted and groomed herself with a front paw.

I glared at Eldridge, still full of rage and needing to direct it somewhere. "Have you made progress in finding Brodie? I feel like I've been doing all the work in this bargain."

His features slipped back to human. "I've asked half the ghosts in the village, but no one knows anything about him."

"Keep asking. Someone will know. He's here somewhere."

"I will. But Odessa, I'm running out of time." His form shimmered back to ghoul. "Every time I materialize it feels harder to keep my human form. If you don't solve my murder soon, you'll have to put me down. I... I'm not ready to go."

I massaged my forehead with my fingertips. I needed to get my head in the game and not be distracted by Sol and his unwanted declarations. But how could I focus when my world was falling apart?

Chapter 13

"Thanks for inviting me over." I stepped through Indigo's open front door. "I love the new color on the door."

"Me, too. But the house hates it." She led me along the hallway toward the kitchen. "I figured we could do with a catch up. Just watch the mess, though. The house is sulking about the renovations and keeps moving things. I found six paintbrushes stuck in the toilet bowl this morning."

I stepped over a pile of plastic sheeting. "I thought she'd be happy to have a spruce up."

"So did I, but this house likes things just the way they are. Some things refuse to change, even if it's for their benefit."

Several doors slammed as the house responded to that comment.

I followed Indigo into her kitchen and smiled when I saw Olympus in there, along with Indigo's three familiars, Nugget, Russell, and Hilda. "Hey, I didn't know you'd be here."

"We live here." Nugget swished his tail. "Olympus is a guest."

"I thought I'd make up the numbers," Olympus said. "And don't mind Nugget. He's angry because Monty ripped his favorite toy to pieces the last time we visited. I left him behind today."

"That creature is a menace." Nugget hopped off the counter and strutted out the back door.

"You don't mind me being here, do you?" Olympus said. "I don't want to intrude on a girls' night in."

"You're welcome to be an honorary girl." I tickled Russell's soft, feathered head. "And I'm glad to get away from the farm. I needed a break."

"Trouble with the scarecrows?" Indigo mixed me my favorite rum cocktail and passed it to me.

I took a long drink. "Thanks. Something like that. Actually, I'm glad you're here, Olympus. I could do with your advice."

There was a knock on the front door before I could say anything else.

"Be back in a minute." Indigo hurried out of the kitchen.

"Who else is coming to dinner?" I said.

Olympus simply grinned at me.

A second later, Indigo led Storm into the kitchen. Storm scowled when she saw me. "What are you doing here?"

"You're both here to have dinner and talk things out. I heard you argued, but it's time to make up." Indigo shooed Storm to the table.

I drank more cocktail, keeping my gaze lowered. I wouldn't have come if I'd known this was a setup, but I did feel bad about being mean to Storm.

"Are you even going to speak to each other?" Indigo said.

"I can always take the food to go." Storm continued to linger by the door.

She would as well. Storm was as stubborn as the day was long, and she held a grudge like no one else. But I needed to be the bigger woman here, and I wanted to apologize for what I'd said. "Stay. I've been meaning to come and see you. I've just been busy."

Storm crossed her arms over her chest and tilted her head.

She wasn't making this easy on me. Fair enough. I'd been a jerk. "I didn't mean what I said."

"Which bit?" Storm said.

"About you and your relationships."

She snorted. "That's hardly an apology."

"If I hurt your feelings, I'm sorry. I was having a terrible day. You caught me at a low point."

"That's a start," Indigo said. "Storm, is there anything you'd like to say to Odessa?"

"I stand by what I said about Brodie." Storm uncrossed her arms. "And I do think you should find another guy. What's the point of being that hot and being on your own all the time?"

"You could probably answer that question just as well as me," I said.

"My situation is different. I have other commitments."

"Let's not go over old ground again." Indigo passed Storm a bottle of beer from the fridge. "A small argument won't derail years of friendship. Let's have dinner and catch up on the local gossip."

Storm glanced at me. "I could have worded things differently. I didn't mean to say anything that upset you. But I hate to think of you alone in that farmhouse."

It was rare Storm lobbed an olive branch, so I grabbed it. "I appreciate that. But I'm never alone."

"You are when it comes to human company." Storm strode over, pulled out a chair, and sat next to me. "Unless you're planning on getting up close and personal with a scarecrow."

I gulped more drink. Storm was too close to the truth. But when Brodie was back in the vessel I was making for him, he wouldn't be an animated straw scarecrow. He'd look almost human. It would be Brodie with some... enhancements.

She nudged me. "That was a joke. Ease up."

"I'm fine. It's been a stressful day."

"Dinner's ready," Indigo said. "I'll serve."

"Odessa, you said there was something you wanted advice about," Olympus said. "No trouble at the farm, is there?"

"Yes. Potentially big trouble from the Magic Council. Do you know Selma Black?"

His eyebrows shot up. "I do. What's she up to?"

"Selma wants to put me out of business. She's been investigating what I do with the scarecrows after getting some complaints from villagers. She doesn't think the scarecrows are safe."

Storm lifted one shoulder. "You have to admit, they seem out of control lately. I had to deal with two just the other week. They were trying to smash through the cemetery gates."

"I didn't know about that." I leaned forward in my seat. I thought I had tabs on all my scarecrows. "Who was it?"

"I didn't recognize them," Storm said. "But they were powerful. I could feel your magic coursing through them, but it was stronger than usual. You must have been hitting the powdered pumpkin hard the day you made them."

"I only use the powder to give my magic a boost. And it helps me concentrate." I patted my pocket, where a bag of powdered pumpkin was nestled. "I'll talk to my scarecrows. Make sure they know not to damage the cemetery."

"If they'd gotten through, Silvaria would have destroyed them," Indigo said. "You know how protective she is of that place." She set three large pizzas on the table, along with a bowl of mixed salad and garlic bread.

"Smells delicious. Did you make this yourself?" I said.

Olympus chuckled and shook his head.

Indigo swiped at him with the salad tongs. "I invited you for dinner. I didn't say I was cooking." She settled in a seat next to Olympus. "This is the finest takeout the village has to offer. Enjoy."

We all grabbed slices of pizza and got stuck in.

"How far has Selma gotten with her threats to shut you down?" Olympus said. "She's known for her intimidation tactics. She gets people worried in the hope they'll slip up and make a mistake to give her a real reason for shutting them down."

"Selma said she wanted to search the farm for anything illegal. But she didn't have a warrant, so I refused. She's gone away to get one. I expect her to be back any day."

Olympus winced as he chewed on his pizza. "Be careful around Selma. She doesn't play nice. Get on the wrong side of her, and she'll chew you up and spit out the pieces before grinding them under her heel."

"I can handle an uptight official from the Magic Council," I said. "No offence, Olympus."

Storm snorted a laugh. "He isn't as bad as he used to be. Even I don't mind Olympus now."

"Thanks." He glowered at Storm before his attention returned to me. "Don't take it personally, but Selma is ambitious, and she's been given big targets to achieve when it comes to rural business regulation. I can do some discrete digging to see what she's got on you if it would help."

"That would be good, but she won't find any dirt on my business. Everything is aboveboard." I picked peppers off my pizza. I did need to get my sideline of enhanced humanlike scarecrows under control, though. I could use a concealment spell on the barn, although it would take a lot of power to conceal something that big for so long. It was too risky to move the earlier prototypes. They were delicate and often malfunctioned if I moved them.

"I'll let you know if I hear anything useful," Olympus said. "The easiest thing to do when dealing with Selma is to cooperate. She loves to think she's in charge. Let her in so she can poke around, write her report, and then she'll leave you alone."

"That's if you genuinely have nothing to hide," Storm said.

"I don't. Everyone knows that." I shifted in my seat and grabbed another slice of pizza. Just as I was tucking in, my mobile buzzed, and I pulled it out of my purse. It was a message from John Smith. He had more information on the Chalice family and wanted to meet right away.

"Something important?" Indigo said.

"It could be. Has Storm told you about the ghost I'm helping?"

Storm nodded. "They're up to speed."

"Eldridge isn't doing so well. He's struggling to stay in human form. The sooner I get this problem resolved, the better." I looked at Storm. "John's got more information for me."

"I knew he'd come through. He's not being a problem, is he?"

"No, he's been fine. Would anyone object if I eat and run?" I said.

"Don't mind us. We're just your oldest, dearest friends," Indigo said.

Storm chuckled. "If you don't take too long, we'll save you a couple of slices."

"And I've got profiteroles for dessert," Indigo said. "Come back for a coffee and dessert if you can."

"Thanks. I'll try. But Eldridge really needs my help."

"Don't let John mess you around," Storm said. "He'll always try to squeeze more out of every client. Let me know if he plays up, and I'll have a word."

"I will. Thanks. And thanks for paying John to help me." I squeezed her shoulder as I stood. "And I really am sorry. I hate arguing with you."

She bit into her garlic bread, then blew me a garlicky kiss.

"You really think Eldridge was murdered?" Indigo walked me to the door after I said a speedy goodbye to Olympus and Indigo's familiars.

"He thinks so. And the more digging I do, the more it seems there were reasons for wanting him dead."

"If you have any problems, let me know." Indigo hugged me. "And don't worry about Storm. She regrets arguing with you, but you know she's terrible about apologizing."

I waved a hand in the air. "It's okay. I was a jerk to her, too. We'll be fine."

"You bet you will. And we need more girls' nights in soon."

"Definitely. We can have one at my farmhouse." I hurried away and into the village to meet with John at the inn. As I walked through the door, he was sitting in the same seat at the same table with the exact same drinks order in front of him. Talk about déjà vu.

I slid into the seat opposite him. "Hey. What have you got for me?"

He grinned. "What's that on your chin? It looks like melted cheese."

I rubbed my face and pulled off the dried cheese. "I was eating dinner with Storm and some friends when I got your message. I came as soon as I could."

"Sorry to drag you from your feast, but I thought you'd like to see this. Things just got interesting." He slid a file over to me.

"You've already got more details on the family?"

"Oh, yeah. And it wasn't hard to find. That should make everything clearer for you." John leaned back in his seat. "Do you want a summary?"

I was already reading through the pages in front of me. "Go for it."

"The second husband, Alastair, has a struggling business. He's got a large loan and is only making the minimum repayments. The bank is getting twitchy, and he's panicking. He's been contacting several loan sharks because he has plans to expand."

"That's interesting. I wonder if Alastair spoke to Eldridge about getting a loan from him. He said they never did business together. Could that be because Eldridge refused to help him? That would give Alastair a solid motive."

"You need to ask your ghost about that. There's more. The wife met with a lawyer about divorcing Eldridge a few months before he died."

"Whoa! That means Raina's been lying to me. She said they had a happy marriage."

"You should look into that. And as for the drunken brother, he gave a proposal to Eldridge asking him to invest millions into a luxury resort."

"Eldridge said nothing about that."

"I'm guessing he told Lars no, because it never happened. The guy wanted unicorns and snow in some freaky vacation resort." John shook his head. "It sounded grim."

I kept reading while John sipped his ale. This information showed me suspects had been hiding things. Maybe I'd been too trusting, believing everything they'd told me. I'd believed Raina when she'd said she loved Eldridge, when all this time, she'd been planning a divorce.

"It's better than a soap opera, isn't it?" John grinned at me. "I love my work."

I sat back in my seat and closed the file. "While this is great, it doesn't rule anyone out. They all still have motives for killing Eldridge."

"It's a fun game, this investigation business."

"It doesn't seem fun to me. Why is murder never simple?"

He laughed. "It is. You just don't know the right people."

"I'm glad I don't know those people."

"You're missing out." John leaned closer. "I might find more if I keep digging."

"And I'm guessing that'll cost me."

He shrugged. "I've been paid enough. But I've got a job that would benefit from the addition of a scarecrow to the crew. Can you spare me one?"

"What kind of job are we talking about?"

"It's best you don't know the details."

"Is it illegal?"

"It has elements of illegality. That won't be a problem, though. I know your scarecrows get shipped to people who need private security. They know how to crack heads."

"They're used as security agents, not hired thugs."

John lifted a hand and waved it from side to side. "Thugs or security. It's a gray line."

"My scarecrows won't do anything that breaks the law."

"How do you know that for sure? I doubt you keep tabs on them once you've set them free."

"No, but I vet each client. If I get a hint they'll use my scarecrows for the wrong purpose, I cancel the order."

"I don't want to buy one. I just need extra muscle. A month at the most. You'll get it back as good as new." John waggled his eyebrows. "What do you say? I dig in deep on this family, and you do me a little favor."

I shook my head. "I only use my scarecrows for good."

"A small loan. Call it a thank you for me being so fast at getting you the information."

"Which you were paid for."

John lifted one shoulder. "Whatever you say. Have fun with that information." He stood and left.

I remained where I was as I sipped my drink. Had I been truthful? I'd used my scarecrows to chase away Sol. I'd gotten angry and used my ability to get rid of a problem. And Sol wasn't a problem. He was a good man who radiated kindness. I'd lost sight of that.

And I shouldn't have yelled at him that he was fired when he was being honest about his feelings. It was my issue to deal with how uncomfortable that made me. I didn't want him to leave the farm and work for Alastair.

I needed to make it up to Sol and show him I valued him as an employee. And as a friend.

I tapped my fingers on the table as I smiled. Potentially, I could solve two problems at once. I could go back to Alastair and convince him not to give Sol the job. And, while I did that, I'd talk to him some more about the trouble he was having with his business.

After downing my drink, I gave a satisfied nod. I was getting Sol to stay at the farm, and I had a perfect reason to speak to Alastair again. And with all this new information on the family, things were looking up.

Chapter 14

I was up early the next morning, having given Alastair a call to make sure he was available to meet with me.

I had a good feeling about today. I'd convince Alastair that Sol wasn't right for the estate manager job and figure out a way to chat about his in-trouble broomstick business.

If Alastair had gone to Eldridge for a loan and he'd said no, it was possible that Alastair decided to get not only the money, but the girl as well. All it took was a simple shove on Eldridge's back, and for Alastair to forget he had a conscience.

There was a spring in my step as I reached the Chalice house, and I spotted Alastair coming out the front door.

He gave me a wave. "You're early. We've only just finished breakfast. Come around the back, and I'll open up the office so we can talk in private."

"Thanks. I wanted to get here before you got too busy." I followed him around the side of the house.

"It's no problem. You mentioned you had information about Sol that I should hear."

"Yes. I'll cut to the chase. Sol is a great fit on my farm, but he's not right for this estate. It's a different setup, you see. Sol's experience is in agricultural practices. He knows his way around all my fields and has an affinity with the scarecrows, but he knows nothing about looking after an old family estate like this. I don't want him to be out of his depth and let you down." Yep, I was being sneaky, but I wasn't letting go of Sol.

Alastair pulled back the doors to his office and locked them in place. "It's not so different. Sol wouldn't be dealing with straw and pumpkins, but we have formal gardens, and he'd need to look after the supplies and maintenance. And he seems good with people. Any problems in that area?"

I would not lie about Sol's abilities. "We work fine together, and he's even brought the scarecrows around. They're not keen on anyone other than me, but they follow his orders."

"That's good. Although Sol will only be working with one other person on a daily basis, so that's not an issue." Alastair turned to me. "I like Sol. He had a positive attitude when I interviewed him. He was polite, excelled in the written tests, and has great transferable skills. I can't find a thing wrong with his application."

I walked behind Alastair as he entered the office and turned on the equipment. "I'm not saying he wouldn't be good at the job, but he'll need training. And he hasn't been working with me for long. Maybe he has flaws I've yet to find."

Alastair nodded. "I wondered about the length of time he'd worked for you. Is there a reason Sol decided to leave the farm so soon?"

"Maybe. What did he tell you during his interview?"

"That was the only answer I thought was vague. Sol said he was looking to gain different experience, and while he enjoyed working at the farm, he wasn't learning anything new."

I tried hard to keep my expression neutral. Sol learned plenty on the farm, and we'd talked about giving him extra responsibilities. "He has a point, but the farm changes with the seasons. Every day is different when you work with enchanted scarecrows."

"I don't doubt that, but after interviewing the other candidates, I want to hire Sol. His references are excellent, he's courteous, educated, and when he met the rest of the team in the house, they all had positive things to say about him. Even Piper, and she's usually shy around new people."

I couldn't let Alastair see how desperate I was to keep Sol. "He's personable. I'm not disputing that. But are you sure one of the other candidates isn't more suitable? Maybe they have better experience with a private estate. Sol likes to get his hands dirty."

"He can do that here. I'm considering setting up several large vegetable patches and expanding the home composting. I'm sure there'll be other things. My mind is made up. I'm offering Sol the job." Alastair shrugged. "I'm sorry, Odessa. I don't feel great taking a staff member from you, but we have to keep this estate running smoothly. My time is taken up with this business, and I'd prefer it if Raina slowed down. With Sol in post, I'm certain we can make that happen."

"Sol has spoken to me about traveling. Maybe he'll only stay a year and then leave. After all, he's leaving me after less than six months. Perhaps he's not reliable." I was a horrible person for planting doubt in Alastair's mind, but my anxiety had kicked in.

"No, I don't see that happening. Sol said he wanted to put down roots and find a permanent home." Alastair waved at Piper as she walked around the side of the house. He stepped closer. "And between the two of us, I'm hoping his friendship with Piper will blossom. Then he'll never want to leave."

I jerked back like someone had punched me. "Friendship? What do you mean? They don't know each other. At least, Sol's not spoken about Piper to me. And she's older than him. I mean, not that it matters, but..."

"They've met in the village a few times. And like I said, Piper took to Sol. She kept getting flustered every time he spoke to her." Alastair chuckled. "I wouldn't be surprised if those two don't start dating once he gets his feet under the table here."

"And you wouldn't mind? It must make things complicated when staff date each other. What if they fall out?" My stomach churned and I swayed. Sol would take this job, fall in love with Piper, and I'd never see him again.

"With those two? They're so easygoing, it won't happen. And it would be ideal to have a couple working here. They have their own skills to complement the running of the estate, and couples always stay longer when they work in the same place. I could even set them up with some accommodation on the estate if things get serious."

I bit my bottom lip. I liked Piper, but I hated the thought of her being in a relationship with Sol. "Is there nothing I can do to persuade you he's the wrong candidate?"

"No. And I've given it some thought overnight." Alastair patted my arm. "If it's any help, I can put out feelers. I'm sure someone will take on the role at the farm."

"Thanks. I'm really hoping it won't come to that, though."

"No hard feelings if it does?"

"Sure. And it's Sol's decision, ultimately. If he wants more than I can offer him, then he'll take the job with you."

"That's the spirit. Now, how about you have another go on a broomstick? I'll even offer you a discount since I'm about to poach a member of your staff."

I tore my attention away from the fact I was about to lose Sol and shook my head. "I'm not ready for another ride."

"That's a pity. A few more tries, and I bet you'll get the hang of it."

"No. I'll pass. And you must be busy with other orders." It was time to get my head in the game. I wasn't just here to try to keep Sol. "How's the broomstick business going?"

"It has its ups and downs." Alastair chuckled as he rifled through a pile of post he'd brought with him. "I can't complain, though."

"Since you were so close to Eldridge, I'm surprised he didn't get involved in the business."

He glanced at me and looked away. "I talked to him about it a few times, but broomsticks weren't his passion. I even suggested Eldridge become a silent partner. I'm always looking to expand."

"He didn't like that idea?"

"I assume not, since nothing came of it. It's a shame. The money would have come in handy."

"Did that bother you? After all, you were old friends. You'd hope your friends would help you if ever you needed a cash investment."

Alastair set down the post and crossed his arms over his chest. "We debated it a few times. Why the interest in our business relationship or lack of?"

"It might be the reason Eldridge is still around. He feels bad because he didn't help you when you needed it."

His forehead wrinkled. "I doubt it. And I never said I needed help. I just floated some ideas past him. My business is confined to this country, but I see potential in foreign markets. To do that, you need a huge cash injection."

"Perhaps Eldridge is feeling guilty because he didn't give you what you asked for, and he's too full of regret to pass on."

"I'm not sure. It's possible. Do you really think Eldridge is concerned about that? What has he said to you?"

"When we've communicated, he's made it clear he has an unresolved issue preventing him from moving on. Although he isn't certain what it could be."

"Did Eldridge say it was to do with me?"

"No. He's confused about why he's here." It was time to pull out my trump card and get this murder solved. "Do you think a séance would be a good idea? We could gather in the house and draw Eldridge to us. Having you all together will give him clarity, so he can remember what's keeping him stuck here."

"I'm not sure we should stir things up," Alastair said. "Eldridge's ghost has been quiet. There were a few noises last night, but the number of disturbances have halved. What if inviting him into the house makes more trouble?"

"As I mentioned to Raina, ghosts go quiet to preserve energy. They do it when they're planning something dramatic."

Alastair's face paled. "Dramatic? No, we can't have that. A séance would be perfect. Eldridge needs to leave."

"I agree. And you all need to move on." And a séance meant all the suspects would be together, we'd find the killer so Eldridge could leave, and then I could deal with the problems at the farm.

"We're all free this evening," Alastair said. "Could you do tonight?"

"Of course. I'll be here. I'll bring everything we need for the séance. How does seven o'clock sound?"

"Perfect. I'll let the others know. Now I think about it, we should have done this sooner. Raina worries so much about Eldridge. I don't like her dwelling on the past, not when we have our future together to look forward to."

"Then I'll see you later." I headed to the door and then turned. "Are you sure there's nothing I can say to stop you from offering Sol this job?"

Alastair's look was regretful as he shook his head. "There isn't. I'd be an idiot if I let him go. People like Sol don't come around often. I'm grabbing him before someone else does."

"I understand. I figured I'd ask. I'll see you this evening."

"Wait! I feel bad about this. I want to give you something to make up for it." Alastair opened a cabinet and pulled out a bulging sack.

"What have you got there?"

"I've seen you struggling through the village with piles of clothing for your scarecrows. These are my castoffs. I was planning on donating them to a local charity, but you might find them useful. They're all in great condition. They might do for some of your smaller scarecrows."

"Oh! Well, thanks." It wasn't much of a consolation, but a peek inside showed everything was designer. "The guys will love these. They'll fight over them."

"Your scarecrows pick their own outfits?"

"Always. They have different tastes." I chuckled at the surprised look on his face. "I'll put these to good use."

We said our goodbyes, and I headed away from the house with the heavy sack. I'd just passed a large oak tree on the driveway when a movement caught my eye.

Sol appeared. "Do you really want me to stay at the farm?"

Chapter 15

Heat flashed up from my toes and spread to my cheeks in a matter of seconds. "Were you listening to my conversation with Alastair?"

"I didn't mean to. I came to talk to Alastair about the new job this morning, but then I saw you going into his office. I hung back, but..." Sol shrugged.

"You couldn't resist hearing what we had to say." The flash of embarrassment still burned on my cheeks, so I crossed my arms, trying to look fierce and not like I'd been caught begging to keep Sol.

"I only got interested when I heard you say my name."

I dug the tip of my boot into the dirt. "Maybe I was too hasty yesterday."

"Was the hasty part when you yelled at me I was fired or when you set Shamrock and Marmaduke on me?"

I grimaced. "Both. I shouldn't have yelled, and I definitely shouldn't have used my scarecrows to scare you off. Not that they wanted to. I've never seen them behave like that around another person. They never hesitate when I give a direct order."

"They like me."

"They do. And why wouldn't they? You're a likeable guy."

Sol gestured to the path that led away from the house. "Are you going my way?"

"I need to get back to the farm." I looked over my shoulder at Alastair's office. "I thought you were here to talk to Alastair about your amazing new job."

Sol set off along the path, and I caught up with him. "That can wait. What we need to talk about is more important. Do you want me to carry that?" He gestured at the sack.

"Sure. Thanks." I handed it over as panic threatened to close my throat, but I couldn't keep lying to Sol. I valued him and didn't want to lose him. "I owe you a huge apology. This is becoming a habit, saying sorry to you when I behave like a fool."

"You were angry and hurting yesterday. Don't think I'm not sympathetic to your past. It sounds like you were blissfully happy. You're finding it hard to accept you could have that again with someone else."

I shook my head. "That's just it. I won't. You get one shot at love. Not the teenage crushes we all go through, but serious, full on love. The kind that knocks you off your feet, and you smile for no reason because the guy you're in love with pops into your thoughts." I glanced at Sol, expecting to see pity in his eyes, but there was none. "It shattered my heart when Brodie died. I can't let him go."

"Maybe you don't have to."

I shot him a look of surprise. "That's my plan. I'm going to keep Brodie around forever."

"I'm not sure that's possible."

I shrugged. "Anything's possible when you want something badly enough."

"You can keep him in your memories for as long as you want. When I've been in the farmhouse, I see you have pictures of him around. Maybe you could have a special place on the farm, so when you're thinking about Brodie or want to lose yourself in some of those happy memories, you can go there and be on your own."

I didn't hate that idea. "I'll think about it."

"And there's no set amount of time a person will grieve for when they lose someone they love. Some people recover quickly and move on, while others..."

"Like me, don't want to move on."

"I was going to say, simply aren't ready. But the time will come when you want to step into the world again." Sol had set a slow pace as we walked back to the farm, but my breathing still felt ragged. Talking about Brodie was painful. How was a person supposed to move on when there was so much pain etched across their heart?

"I like the idea of a permanent memorial to Brodie, but it's unnecessary," I said. "I have other plans."

"How are you thinking of commemorating him?" Sol said. "Alastair showed me the memorial bed at the house. That's a nice idea."

"I don't know." I hadn't told anyone about my experiments with the scarecrows. Until I was successful, there was no point.

Sol gave my elbow a gentle squeeze. "Odessa, I care very much for you, and I want nothing more than to see you happy."

I let his hand linger a second too long before moving away. "I'm never unhappy."

"There's always a glimmer of sadness in your eyes. I want to take that away, if you let me."

"You can't. I'm the only one who can do that. I'm responsible for my happiness. Bringing in a substitute for Brodie won't change that."

Sol inhaled sharply. "I have no plans to be a dead man's substitute. Don't expect me to turn into Brodie. That wouldn't make either of us happy."

"No, no, I didn't mean that. Of course, you wouldn't be a substitute. Our relationship would be completely different. I mean, if we had one. Sorry, that was a careless thing to say."

Sol huffed out a breath, but said nothing.

I touched his arm. "I'm figuring this out. It's more complicated than I thought it would be. But I really want you to stay at the farm."

He glanced at me. "You're saying you need me?"

"No, I can handle everything on my own. I don't need a man."

His grin had an edge of wickedness to it, which made my pulse race faster than it should. "But you want me to stay?"

"You're not making this easy on me, are you?"

"You did fire me and almost have me killed by your scarecrows yesterday. I'm allowed payback."

I gritted my teeth. The words didn't want to come out. If I admitted I wanted Sol, it felt like a betrayal to Brodie. I'd been on my own for over three years, and I'd managed, but it hadn't been easy. I'd quickly come to rely on Sol, and that was terrifying. I'd do okay alone, but having a reliable, sweet guy by my side helping to deal with the fires life threw my way made things easier and enjoyable.

"It's okay if you don't want to say anything. This is difficult for you. It's not easy for me, either. Loving a woman who's so deeply besotted with a memory is an ego stamper." Sol's voice was a soft rumble in his chest.

"I wish you wouldn't keep saying that," I said. "I can't tell you I love you."

"I'm not expecting you to. But I need to know there's a flicker of hope. We could be great together. And I might be the only man in the world your scarecrows tolerate. That has to be a tick in the box for me."

I laughed, some of the tension easing from my shoulders. "It's a bonus. And they never liked Brodie. If you leave the farm, they'll miss you. They might even hunt you out in your new job and cause problems so you get fired."

"Is that so? Would they do that, or would you order them to find me and bring me home?"

His tone was light and playful, but a trickle of panic ran through me. Sol already thought of the farm as his home. And why not? He spent so much time there with me. "I might. It would be funny to watch them drag you back."

"My new boss wouldn't think it funny when the scarecrows rampaged all over the pristine lawns and neat flower beds."

We reached the farmhouse, and I stopped and turned to Sol. "You're not a pristine lawn kind of guy. You'll be bored in this new job."

"True, but technically, I don't have my old job. I'm still fired, remember?"

I threw up my hands. "Fine, you're un-fired. I take back everything I said yesterday. I won't set the scarecrows on you ever again, and you can have your old job back. And we'll sort out a pay raise and your new responsibilities as soon as possible." I swallowed, then pressed on. "I want you around. I don't like it when you're not here."

Sol gave a single nod. "That's all I needed to hear."

That hadn't been as hard to say as I thought it would. I did need Sol around. I shouldn't be embarrassed about that.

He took a step closer. "So, now we've confessed how we feel—"

"I've said sorry. Baby steps."

Sol grinned. "I was wondering about going on a casual date. No obligations."

"I can do one better. Come take a look at the suspect board with me. I need a fresh pair of eyes on Eldridge's murder mystery. And I've got new information about the suspects."

"A murder board is better than a date?" He didn't sound impressed.

"Maybe not better, but it's neutral ground. That I can deal with."

Sol huffed out a breath. "I guess that'll do. And I could handle a mug of coffee and a muffin before I start work."

"Working here? You're definitely turning down Alastair and staying with me?" A delicious dash of joy flooded through me.

"Yep. And I'll speak to him later about the job. You were right. It wasn't for me." Sol strode up the porch steps and opened the door for me.

I stepped inside and got busy making breakfast, while Sol set down the sack of clothing and studied the suspect board. Although I was glad we'd made progress and repaired our friendship, I couldn't get tangled up in my complicated emotions. Having this murder to distract me was perfect.

"What are your thoughts on the suspects?" Sol said as he accepted a mug of coffee from me.

"I can't shake the belief that Raina and Alastair are involved. Although I've spoken to them both, and they're not nervous when I ask questions about Eldridge and what happened the night of his death. Raina welcomed me continuing my investigation, and Alastair agreed to hold a séance at the house tonight so the family can speak to Eldridge."

"You don't think he'd do that if he was involved in the murder?"

"I don't know. Maybe they're both playing an excellent game of Lie to Odessa. I've learned Raina was bored in her marriage and consulted a lawyer about getting a divorce from Eldridge. Alastair has been having troubles with his business, but he was open about it when he talked about financing issues."

"Eldridge loaned him money?" Sol unwrapped the muffin I handed him and took a bite.

"No, but Alastair didn't seem to hold a grudge about that. But again, maybe Raina and Alastair have worked hard to get their stories straight. They've had a year to create their alibis and dismiss any motives for why they'd want Eldridge dead."

"And you're holding this séance tonight in the hopes of what?"

"I hope Eldridge can get clarity. He thinks someone pushed him, but maybe this is all a mistake. He'd been drinking that night. He could have simply tripped over his familiar."

"Where is your ghost?" Sol looked around the kitchen.

"I haven't seen him. He's doing his own investigations, but he should be with the family making sure they're terrified, so they keep me involved."

"What about Glory and Lars?" Sol tapped their photos in turn. "Any dirt on them?"

"I haven't spoken much to either of them, so I'll do that tonight. And I need to read over the rest of the information I got on them. Lars had been trying to get investment for a business idea, and Eldridge wasn't keen on lending him money. But I'm not sure about Glory. Eldridge is adamant she had nothing to do with his death."

"It sounds like everything could be resolved tonight," Sol said. "If you want me to, I can come and help."

I was tempted to get Sol more involved, but I could do with some space after everything we'd discussed. "Thanks, but I'll do this on my own. And once you turn down Alastair's job offer, you might not be his favorite person."

"True enough. I'll say you gave me an enormous pay raise and made me partner in the farm to convince him I couldn't take the job."

"Those things could be arranged, if you really want them."

Surprise flickered across his face. "You'd want me to be a partner, not just an employee?"

I flapped my hands against my cheeks, suddenly feeling warm. I had no clue where that sprang from, but I liked the idea more than I should. "It's something to consider."

Sol caught hold of my hand and gently squeezed. "Odessa, you've been alone long enough. I'm here for you. I want to help you with the business and be your partner in every aspect."

His gaze landed on my mouth, but I stepped away. "Thanks. I mean, that's awesome. Brilliant."

Sol let go of my hand, and a playful grin flickered on his lips. "I'll leave you to it. Have fun at the séance tonight." He finished his coffee, placed his mug in the sink, and left the kitchen.

I stared at the closed door for several minutes, not moving. Had that just happened? I'd told Sol I needed him, and it hadn't felt like a massive betrayal to Brodie. I had no idea what I was doing, but I did like Sol. When I got Brodie back, would he think less of me because of my mild flirtation with Sol?

The rest of the morning, I kept myself busy on the farm. The scarecrows were behaving, the pumpkins were being harvested, and everything was working like clockwork. I knew it was partly because Sol was back and we were both happy, even though I kept feeling shivers of guilt about betraying Brodie.

The scarecrows were always sensitive to my emotions, and if I was unsettled or unhappy, it affected them. Since my mood had improved, so had their behavior, and everyone was behaving like angels.

I slid into my experiment barn, my arms full of supplies. I'd happened across an ancient spell of rejuvenation when I'd been browsing a rare spell book from the library. I'd not tried this spell before, and it could be what I needed to stabilize Brodie's vessel.

My feet slowed. I set down the supplies and did a slow turn. The place looked like a whirlwind had whipped through it. There was straw scattered everywhere, and the neat piles of clothing had been shredded. My heart skipped several huge beats. One of my experiments was missing. There was a space where previously there'd been a scarecrow. And not just any scarecrow. It was the vessel I'd planned to use for Brodie's ghost.

I grabbed a handful of powdered pumpkin treats from my pocket and shoved them in my mouth, chewing furiously as I looked around the barn. Maybe he'd gone outside, or he could be hiding somewhere. The powdered pumpkin gave me the boost I needed as I swiftly hunted around the barn. My initial hope faded when the scarecrow didn't show up.

"Odessa, are you in there?" Sol's voice sounded outside. He knew not to come in this barn and always waited for me to come out.

I dashed out and slammed the door behind me. "Sure. What's up?"

"We could have trouble. I just followed a path leading away from the farm. One of the guys has gone rogue."

I glanced over my shoulder as my panic grew. "I know who it is."

"It's not a regular. I did a headcount in the fields, and they're all there." Brodie jerked a thumb over his shoulder. "But all evidence suggests a scarecrow caused this mess."

"It was. I've been... running a few experiments to fine tune my scarecrows. They're in this barn."

Sol's gaze lifted to the barn behind me. "One of them has gotten loose?"

"Yes. Show me the path he made. He's not safe to be out in public."

"This way." Sol turned and marched away. "How did he get out of the barn?"

"I don't know. I lock the place when I'm done. Although I've been distracted by Eldridge. Maybe I forgot to lock it the last time I was in there." Sol was walking so fast, I had to jog to keep up with him.

"He must be a big scarecrow," Sol said.

"A little bigger than the normal ones. I didn't deliberately build him that way, but—" I bit my tongue. I'd almost said Brodie had been a big guy, so he would need a big vessel to be comfortable.

"He went this way." Sol pointed at the path of squashed hay leading away from the farm. "He must have been going at a heck of a pace to make this much mess. Some of the hay bales even got shredded further along the field."

"I wonder what set him off." We dashed through the field, following the clear trail of scarecrow induced devastation. Trees were damaged, hay bales kicked over, and pumpkins shredded. This didn't bode well for his mood when we found him. But I could salvage this. And I had to. This was the closest I'd come to making a perfect vessel for Brodie.

The trail of devastation headed west, taking us past all the houses and businesses. I was relieved my escapee hadn't done any damage in the village. Maybe he'd simply gone walkabout and needed to burn off excess energy.

"The magic trail this scarecrow is leaving feels different from the others you manufacture," Sol said. "Did you use a new type of spell on this one?"

"Something like that. It's more of an experiment. I'm not ready to release this model on my customers."

"It's an intense magic. I don't have powerful abilities, but it's making my skin tingle."

"It's a work in progress. Let's just find him." This was the last thing I needed. With Selma Black breathing down my neck and about to produce a search warrant, I couldn't have any of my scarecrows drawing attention. Especially not this one.

"If we keep going in this direction, we'll arrive at the stables," Sol said.

"You're right. But what's he doing coming out this way?"

A flash of magic up ahead had me speeding up.

"Hettie must be dealing with our scarecrow." Sol broke into a jog alongside me.

"She can't destroy him. I've worked too hard on this model."

"Maybe she should. This guy caused a lot of damage. He could be an unstable model if you're testing new spells."

"No. I've got everything under control." I raced ahead, charging through the large gate that led into Hettie's stables. She looked after a dozen horses and two hybrid unicorns people stabled with her, along with her own small herd.

There was another flash of magic, and I raced toward it. "Hettie! Where are you?"

"Odessa?"

"Yes! I can't see you." I kept running, desperate to find my scarecrow.

"I figured you'd arrive soon enough. Get your butt over here."

She didn't sound far away, and I headed toward her voice. I was speeding along, magic primed on my fingertips. I could contain this scarecrow.

As I zoomed around the first set of stables, I discovered Hettie in a stand-off with my scarecrow. Her body was alive with magic as it sparkled around her in a silver bubble, while my scarecrow swung his huge limbs at her and growled.

"Odessa, what is that?" Sol was still by my side, although he'd slowed, his gaze fixed on the scarecrow. "It looks almost human."

"I've already told you, it's an experiment."

"He's trying to kill Hettie." Sol tapped the silver ring on his right hand. It flared to life, and magic appeared on his palm.

"Only restrain him. Don't damage him. I need him back in the barn."

"Are you sure? The magic is unstable. He looks about ready to blow."

"Odessa! I could do with some help." Hettie sparked a warning blast at the scarecrow.

"He's confused, that's all. He won't hurt you." I shot a glare at Sol. "If you're not going to help, stay out of my way." I charged toward Hettie. "Pull back your magic. You're scaring him."

Hettie's purple eyes narrowed. "I'm scaring this thing? It ripped the wheels off the horsebox, and it looks like it wants to bite my head off."

"He doesn't. Please, let me deal with him. He knows me." I held out a hand and blasted restraining magic at the scarecrow's chest. It bounced off him.

The scarecrow snarled, and his attention turned to me.

"That's it. Come home with me. Everything will be fine. I'm sorry I left you. You must have been confused and wanted to find me."

As the scarecrow advanced on me, Sol flared a ball of magic on his hand and stood in front of me.

I rested a hand on his back and stepped around him. "I've got this. You'll only make him angry if you confront him."

"He's already angry. I'm trying to make sure he doesn't become psychotic," Sol said.

"Back off, both of you." I threw myself at the scarecrow. My legs wrapped around his waist, and

I clamped my teeth on the side of his neck as I poured my power into him, fighting to gain control.

He roared his protests, then dropped to the ground and rolled several times, taking me with him. But I refused to let go as I was bashed around. If I lost this experiment, it would set me back months.

As I clung to the scarecrow, I kept hearing Sol's warning shouts and saw magic sparking around me as Hettie and Sol tried to free me.

I couldn't tell them to leave us alone because my mouth was full of scarecrow. He tasted of salt, straw, and sweet pumpkin from all the magic I'd poured into him.

The scarecrow stopped moving just as he'd rolled over and trapped me underneath him. Magic pulsed around him as I peeked out over his shoulder. Sol and Hettie had connected their magic and were shooting it into the scarecrow's back. They rushed over, pulled the scarecrow off me, and slung him away.

"Have you lost your mind, girl?" Hettie drew back her magic. She extended a hand to me and yanked me to my feet. "That beast could have killed you."

"He would never do that. And I was calming him down." My hand was trembling as I removed straw from my mouth.

"Odessa, he was out of control." Sol shook out his hands as the magic drew back into his ring.

I hurried over to the scarecrow and inspected him. He was no longer moving. I rested a hand on his chest, relieved to feel it moving up and down. "You'll be okay."

"Thanks for asking, but we're fine." Hettie strode over and rested her hands on her narrow hips as she glared down at me. "What are you playing at, creating something like that?"

"I'm sorry. You weren't supposed to meet him. Not until he was ready."

"Ready for what? The finals of a WWF heavyweight knockout contest? That thing packs a serious punch." Hettie rubbed the top of her arm.

I stood, a wave of guilt running over me. "Sorry. I don't know why he came this way."

"I've got an idea. He was looking around the barn and inspecting the pumpkins you brought over. Maybe he doesn't like that his friends are about to become horse feed."

"He's a dangerous experiment you need to end," Sol said. "We got lucky that he met Hettie. Anyone with less power would be dead."

I couldn't think about that. Besides, it was pointless to worry, because it would never happen again. "I'm sorry about the damage he caused, Hettie. I'll pay for the repairs."

"You will, but you've left me in a mess. I need to go away for a few days on a case, and I was planning on transporting two horses back to their owners. I can't do that without my horsebox. Mr. McPumpkinhead Psycho down there wrenched off the tires for fun."

"I'll get you one. I'll hire one. Whatever you need. You find what you want and charge it to me."

Hettie arched an eyebrow. "Well, I could do that, but it's short notice, and I can't be late for the hearing."

I knelt beside the scarecrow again and pulsed calming magic into him. "What hearing?"

Hettie edged closer to the scarecrow. "The county coroner has been on extended sick leave. I'm technically retired from all that, but they begged me to step in until he's back on his feet. I do a few days here and there when they're desperate."

"That's a big change. Dead bodies to horses," Sol said.

"I love it. I've been retired almost a year. I was happy to take a break from the slicing and dicing and poking around in the murky lives people live." Hettie's gaze went around the farm. "It was time to retire when I no longer cared about the bodies. It became a process. Numbers, statistics, and tests. When you forget there was a person behind that information, it's time for a change. So, I turned to my second passion."

My head jerked up. "Were you still working when Eldridge Talbot died?"

Her eyebrows rose slowly. "I was. He was one of my last cases. He fell down the stairs, didn't he?"

I jumped up, keeping my foot connected to the scarecrow, to feel if he stirred. "Possibly. His death was believed to be an accident. But I'm not so sure."

Hettie tilted her head. "How can you know that?"

"Eldridge's ghost has made contact. He hasn't passed over. He's stuck, and it's because he's convinced he was killed."

Her eyes narrowed. "From what I remember of the case, it wasn't complicated. I'd need to check the records, but there was nothing that alarmed me."

"If you're working as a coroner again, do you have access to all the records or just the cases you're working on?"

"I have to see everything. It's the only way I can do my job. Why?"

I looked at Sol to see if he was thinking the same as me, but he wouldn't meet my gaze. "Maybe you can help me. Or rather, Eldridge. If you did his autopsy, could you let me take a look at it?"

"And risk my reputation and career for a man who's been dead over a year?"

"You'd be helping a ghost. And Eldridge is changing into a ghost ghoul. He doesn't have much longer. If I can't figure out what happened so he can move on, I'll have to put him down."

Hettie shuddered and rubbed her hands up and down her arms. "I had an aunt who went that way. It wasn't pleasant chasing her down in the dead of night and extinguishing what was left. She didn't go quietly." She held out a wrist to reveal silver white teeth mark scars.

"Sorry to hear that." I bit my bottom lip. "So you'll help?"

Hettie grinned. "What do I care about my reputation? So long as I have these horses, nothing else matters. I can access Eldridge's autopsy file, but you won't find anything in there. I know the signs of inflicted trauma. If it had been a murder, I'd have spotted it."

"Any information you can give me would be useful."

"I'll do it. But you need to give me something in return," Hettie said.

"Sure. Whatever you need." I had a new lead, and I wasn't letting it go.

"How about one of your worker scarecrows on loan? I won't need him full-time, but I need someone here in the mornings to muck out the stables, brush down the horses, and get the tack ready."

"It's a deal. One of my boys will be happy to help. You'll really let me see the autopsy file?"

"I will. It sounds like you're helping this ghost, so I'm happy to lend a hand. I'll get the information today and drop it off before I leave."

"Thanks, Hettie. Eldridge will appreciate that."

"And I'd appreciate it if you get this beast of a scarecrow out of here before I feed it to the horses," Hettie said.

"Of course. And, sorry again. This was a one off."

Sol helped me get the scarecrow up, and between us, we heaved him back to the farm. From the grim set of Sol's face, he was unhappy. I wasn't sure how to explain the uniqueness of this scarecrow and why the magic inside him had to be so intense. Sustaining life took power, and keeping it stable took even more. Sol must know I wouldn't be using this scarecrow for farm laboring, though. Had he figured out what I was planning?

He looked at me from around the scarecrow. "This is why you're not able to move on?"

I tightened my grip on the scarecrow. "It's an experiment."

"The locked barn, your obsession with Brodie, and the way you still think you're with him. It makes sense. You're trying to bring him back, aren't you?"

So, the game was up. "Maybe."

Sol's sigh was heavy. "This scarecrow isn't natural."

"He's very natural. I just need to work out the kinks. Once I've figured out the right combination of spells, I'll have exactly what I need."

Sol shook his head. "What does Brodie think about this?"

"I know he'll be happy."

"You haven't discussed it with him?"

"There's no need. Brodie wants to be with me."

Sol stopped walking. "You don't have his ghost, do you? Have you even seen his ghost since he died?"

I squeezed the scarecrow like he was a life buoy keeping me afloat in a stormy sea. "He's here. I'm sure of it. And you know how he died. Violent deaths make confused ghosts. Brodie's lost his way back to me, but I will find him."

Sol grabbed up his side of the scarecrow again and continued walking. "You're clinging to this fantasy of bringing Brodie back, yet you don't even know if his ghost is here. And it's been over three years. You know what happens to ghosts if they linger too long. You've seen it with Eldridge. What state will Brodie be in if you ever find him?"

"Brodie was the strong one in the relationship. He wouldn't give up hope that I'd find him." My chest felt so tight I could barely breathe. Sol was wrong. Brodie would be the same lovable rogue he'd always been when I found him.

"There never was a chance for us, was there?" Sol said. "You're making a Frankenstein freak of a scarecrow to stuff your dead lover's ghost inside.

You really want that more than a living, breathing human?"

My bottom jaw trembled, but I kept things under control. "You can feel the magic. When Brodie's ghost is inside, it'll be almost human. Better than human."

"That'll only work if you constantly use your magic to sustain this vessel. Odessa, it'll exhaust you. You'll be drained trying to keep this thing alive."

I let out a sigh, my heart as heavy as the scarecrow. "Sol, just go. I'll deal with this on my own."

He glowered at me. "I'll get this monstrosity back to the farm, but you're right. I need to leave."

There was so much more I wanted to say, but Sol didn't get it. I had to try everything to create the life I'd dreamed of with Brodie.

We walked the rest of the way in silence. The moment we were back at the barn, and the scarecrow had been secured, Sol turned and walked away without a word.

Eldridge materialized beside me as I was debating whether to call after Sol and see if I could fix the mess I'd made. "Odessa! Where have you been?"

"Scarecrow hunting. How about you?" My attention remained on Sol.

"Ghost hunting." He looked at the chained up scarecrow. "What happened here?"

"Long story. Is there any sign of Brodie?" There had to be a flicker of good news to cling to.

"Sorry, and I'm running out of places to ask. No one has seen him. He's long gone."

I sank down next to the scarecrow and rearranged his tattered shirt. "Keep looking." This was a fight I wasn't losing.

"I will." Eldridge's tone was soft as he swirled around the barn, causing straw to fly up. "Have you found my killer?"

"Not yet. But I'm looking at your autopsy results soon. That could help."

He spun around. "You are? How?"

"Grab a seat, and I'll fill you in." Although the start of my day had been a disaster, I could salvage something good by finding out exactly how Eldridge died. One thing at a time, that's how I'd tackle my tangled affairs. Help Eldridge, find Brodie, fix my misbehaving scarecrow, and see if I had anything to repair with Sol.

Chapter 16

I was about to leave for the séance when there was a knock at the farmhouse door. I hurried over to open it and discovered Hettie outside.

"This makes for interesting reading," Hettie said in way of a greeting as she handed me a USB stick. "Plug it in, and I'll talk you through the results."

"Thanks. Come in." I had ten minutes to spare, but didn't want to miss out on useful information about Eldridge's death. I fired up my laptop and plugged in the USB stick.

Hettie pointed at the file I wanted. "It's all in there. My write-up, photographs, and drawings."

"No one questioned why you needed this?"

She smirked. "You're an idiot if you question the boss. Especially when I'm the boss."

I had no doubt Hettie could take down the fiercest magic user. "I wish Eldridge was here to see this. I sent him to the Chalice house to shake things up before the séance tonight."

"You're having a séance?"

"I'm getting the family together and hoping to pull apart an alibi. Someone has to make a mistake soon if they were involved with what happened to Eldridge."

"Nice plan. Scare the suspects into talking. Anyway, open up the pictures. I hope you don't mind corpses."

"Err... I can't say I love them. How gruesome are these going to be?" I tentatively clicked the first picture.

"You'll survive. Keep going through them. That's the one." Hettie touched the screen. "What you're looking at is bruises on the limbs consistent with a fall down the stairs. People tend to drop and slide, plummet and thud to the bottom, or roll down so the bruising is all over them."

I wrinkled my nose. "Okay, so there's nothing surprising there. It looks like Eldridge rolled."

"He did. Go to the next picture."

I grimaced as the picture of a wound on Eldridge's head appeared. "He got that from the fall down the stairs, too?"

Hettie sank into a chair and pinched the bridge of her nose. "When Eldridge's body was brought in, there almost wasn't an autopsy. His injuries were consistent with a fall, and statements from his family supported the accident theory. He also had no marks on his body to suggest he fought with anyone or resisted being pushed."

"Which doesn't answer my question. This wound on his head is making you doubt your findings?" I looked at the photographs of the staircase. "Eldridge could have hit his head on a banister or the corner of the bottom step."

"Yes, but he would have needed to have hit one side and bounced off for his final resting place to make sense. That staircase is wide, and where his body landed was in the middle of the floor." Hettie leaned forward and rested her elbows on her knees. "I suppose it's possible he didn't die right away and crawled to that position before taking his final breath. But there was no blood smear to suggest movement."

"He was found right after he fell. His family heard the noise. If he'd been alive, they would have helped him." I pursed my lips, keeping my gaze off the corpse pictures.

"The more I looked at the injuries and the placement of his body, it got me thinking. What if that head wound happened before he fell?"

"Someone hit him and then shoved him?"

"Or hit him, and in his confused state, he fell," Hettie said. "And that's not all. Something else came up on the autopsy. It wasn't linked to his death, but I noted it in the report because it was a recent injury."

"What injury?" I said.

"Eldridge had healed burns on his chest."

"Like a carpet burn?"

"Nothing like a carpet burn. It was damage from a spell. Take a look at this." Hettie grabbed the mouse and flicked through scanned images until she got to a document.

I read what came up on the screen. "There was a burn mark by his heart. Someone shot Eldridge with a spell?"

"It looks like it. The burn was about three weeks old and almost healed, but there was still a red mark."

"How was this explained?"

"Glory, the daughter, said he used a spell that misfired. He did it to himself."

"Why would he do that?"

"You'll have to ask your ghost buddy. But his brother agreed with Glory. He said Eldridge was trying a new spell, and it went wrong. It ricocheted off something and slammed into him. It made him ill for a few days. Apparently, he was clumsy. And when I looked over his medical records, there was a history of injuries."

"How bad?"

"A couple of broken bones, and he's had concussion twice. Maybe the guy was just super clumsy."

"Or maybe not. Do you remember anything about your visit to the house after Eldridge fell? Anything that stuck out as strange?"

"I do the cutting up, not the crime scene. I wasn't there to see the body in situ," Hettie said.

"What about any tests run on Eldridge's body during the autopsy?"

Hettie shook her head. "It didn't happen. We only do a detailed analysis if there's a suspicious cause of death. This was a simple trip and slip. Or so I thought."

"Looking over this information now, you think Eldridge didn't just fall?"

Hettie's mouth twisted to the side, and she scrubbed at her forehead. "I hold my hands up.

I was no longer interested in my work. I still did a decent job when a body needed attention. But when Eldridge arrived, the official report said he was a drunk idiot who fell down the stairs. His injuries were consistent with a fall, so I did the minimum needed and closed the case." She shrugged, looking shamefaced. "I was done with cutting up bodies."

"I'm not saying you were at fault," I said. "But is there any way we could run more tests? Did you take samples from Eldridge?"

"Sure. Fluids are taken from every corpse. And I'd have run bloodwork to see how drunk he'd been. We keep samples for twelve months and then dispose of them."

"Eldridge has been dead a year. Will his samples still be available?"

"Let me check." Hettie looked through another scanned document. "We're in luck. When samples are disposed of, there's a note and a signature made on the record. There's nothing on this one. We should still have his fluids."

"Can you run tests on them?"

"I can. But what am I looking for?"

"I don't know. Test for everything. Eldridge said he felt confused when he got out of bed that night. What if it was more than the alcohol that made him confused?"

"You're thinking drugs were involved?"

"Anything could be involved." I checked the time. "I'm really sorry, but I need to leave. I'll be late for the séance if I don't hurry."

Hettie pulled out the USB stick and pocketed it. "I can't let you keep this, but let me know if you need to look over it again."

"Thanks. I think I got everything I needed. And it's looking more and more like Eldridge's death wasn't a simple fall."

"Maybe not. And I feel at fault for not noticing that. I'll do what I can to help you make this right." Hettie gave a swift nod. "Enjoy the séance. Maybe a suspect will crack if the ghost gets scary enough."

"Let's hope so. I need a break in this investigation." I walked out of the farm with her and shut the door behind me.

"How did you get on with that messed up scarecrow? If it's a lost cause, I can take it for my horses," Hettie said.

"No. He's fine. He's rehabilitating in the barn. Did you get the horsebox ordered in time?"

"There are no worries there. And the case I'll be working on has been delayed a week, so I can analyze Eldridge's blood samples right away. I'll do it now."

"I'd appreciate that."

We said our goodbyes, and I hurried to the Chalice house. What had started out as a simple mystery was becoming increasingly twisty. A head wound and burns from powerful spells. Whatever happened on the night of Eldridge's death, his luck had seriously run out.

I got to the house with a minute to spare. When I arrived, Eldridge appeared, and a few seconds later, Tuffin strolled around the side of the house.

I pointed at her. "You need to hide. The family can't see you strutting around like you own the place."

"It would give them a fright if they did. I could pretend I've come back to haunt them, too."

I looked at Eldridge for help.

He nodded at me. "Tuffin, I'm glad you're here, but we must be discreet. Raina and Alastair can't become suspicious that Odessa was involved in setting you free."

"I suppose you're making sense for once," Tuffin said. "I'll stay out of sight, but I want to listen."

"You'd fit in my purse." I patted the oversized purse hanging over my shoulder.

"Is it clean in there?"

I looked in at the assorted tissues, scraps of paper, and empty packets of powdered pumpkin treats. "Kind of."

Her nose wrinkled. "I'll risk it."

I set the purse down, and Tuffin hopped inside. It concealed her perfectly, and I eased the zipper partially shut, giving her an opening for air and so she could listen.

"How are we going to play this?" Eldridge said. "I've been making things spooky, so everyone is on edge."

"I was thinking I'd summon you and then run through each motive. I'll start with Lars's failed business proposal."

"Which one? He came to me with so many. I dismissed them before he gave me the details."

"The luxury resort with unicorns. It sounded fun."

"Oh, that was terrible. Okay, that can be his motive. What about Raina?"

"I'll say you were worried she was unhappy in the marriage. Did you know she'd consulted a lawyer about divorcing you?"

Eldridge flashed in and out of focus a dozen times in the space of two seconds. "You're mistaken."

"No mistake. I got it from an inside source. Raina wasn't happy."

Eldridge's expression dropped, and he wavered in the air like he was going to combust. "I had no idea. But if she wanted a divorce, why not do that, rather than kill me?"

"Let's hope the séance gives us the answer. And then there's Alastair. His business isn't thriving. Do you remember him asking for money to bail him out?"

"He didn't put in a specific request. We kicked around some ideas, but nothing came of it."

"He's in debt and is planning to take on more. Maybe he felt slighted by you."

"It's a motive, but it's not one I'm happy about." Eldridge reached for my hand. "Please don't tell me you're going to accuse my daughter of anything."

"I've not had much to do with Glory, but she needs to be included since she was in the house. You don't remember having any problems with her?"

"She used to grumble when I suggested she get a job, but that's what young people do. They don't take responsibility for their futures."

The front door opened, and Piper looked out. "Hi. Are you ready to come in?" She looked around, as if expecting to see more people.

"Yes. All set," I said.

Piper kept looking around. "I thought I saw you talking to somebody."

"Oh, I was going through warm-up exercises in preparation for the séance. Limbering up the old ghost talking muscles." I glanced at Eldridge. "Shall we get started?"

Piper opened the door wider, and I walked inside.

"I hope you don't mind me asking," she said, "but are you sure doing this séance is right? I've never been comfortable prodding the dead."

"I understand your concerns, and I don't disagree with you, but Eldridge isn't at rest. This séance will give him a chance to air his concerns so he can move on."

She led me along the hallway and into the dining room. "I suppose so. I don't like to think of him as troubled. He was always kind to me."

Raina entered the room with Alastair a few seconds later. We exchanged greetings and then settled at the table. Piper left the room, following Raina's instructions to get refreshments.

"Alastair explained the plan for a séance," Raina said. "I hope this brings things to an end. I'm tired of living here and not feeling safe."

"Has Eldridge been causing more problems?" I asked as innocently as I could, while Eldridge hovered around, and nudged a statue off the windowsill, making everyone jump.

"Mainly at night. Although, as you can see, he's making a nuisance of himself this evening. I just want a full night of sleep. We must find out why he's here."

Alastair caught hold of Raina's hand. "We will. Odessa is helping us, so we'll get this figured out."

I didn't have his confidence, but I was sticking to the plan. I had information on the family, Eldridge close by, and a ticking clock counting down to Eldridge's transformation into a menacing ghoul. I could do this.

Piper returned with a tray of drinks and snacks and set them on the table.

I noticed her hand shaking as she passed me a glass. "There's nothing to worry about. Séances can be peaceful experiences. People who've lost loved ones find comfort in being able to communicate with them clearly. I'll act as a conduit and relay everything Eldridge has to say."

She shot me a slightly less terrified look before hurrying out again.

The door was pushed open, and Glory and Lars came in. Lars didn't even have to get close before I smelt whiskey on him so strong my eyes watered. He also carried a large glass of the amber stuff.

"Let me at the ghosts. I'll see them off." Lars swung a clumsy punch and lost his balance. He'd have fallen on his face if Glory hadn't caught hold of his arm.

"Uncle Lars, show Daddy respect."

"You're right. Sorry everyone." Lars straightened, wiping spilt whiskey off his hand. He raised the glass. "Here's to my dear departed brother."

"Sit at the table, Lars." Raina's voice had an air of exasperation to it.

He made an attempt at a salute before pulling out a chair and slouching into it.

"Are you okay, darling?" Raina looked at Glory. "You don't have to be involved if you find it too stressful. I don't want you upset."

"I want to be here," Glory said. "I loved Daddy, but I don't want him to keep haunting us. It makes me feel like I've done something wrong."

Eldridge hovered close to Glory until she shuddered. My heart went out to him. He clearly adored his daughter.

"None of us has done anything wrong. Your father's only here because he's confused. He has a question that needs answering and, with Odessa's help, we'll get that sorted. Then life can get back to normal," Raina said.

"If this goes on for much longer, I'll need a vacation. Maybe you could buy me that apartment in the city I showed you. I could stay there until Daddy stops haunting us."

"Ghosts can travel," I said. "If your dad wanted to visit you, he'd just come to your apartment."

"Tell her I wouldn't do that. I don't want her frightened," Eldridge hissed in my ear.

Glory's face paled as she stared at me. "I don't want a ghost as my shadow. It'll kill my social life."

Ah, the pure heart and intention of the modern youth on gross display for all to see.

"Shall we get started?" Alastair said.

"Good idea. Has everyone been to a séance before?" I said.

They all nodded.

"This'll be straightforward." I eased a hand into my purse, careful not to touch Tuffin, and pulled out a white candle. I set it in the center of the table and lit it. "I forgot salt. Have you got any I can use?"

"Of course." Raina headed to a cabinet in the corner of the room. She took out a large salt shaker and handed it to me.

I took a minute to pour a protection circle around the table so we were enclosed inside it. "This is a precaution. Occasionally, darker spirits will use a séance to force their way into this world. If they get out, they won't get farther than the salt circle."

"Is that likely to happen?" Glory looked around the room.

"It's unusual, but we're protected. And you all have magic, so you can defend yourselves if anything dark comes through."

"I'll get the evil spirit," Lars slurred.

"You concentrate on the spirit in that glass," Alastair said.

Lars chuckled and necked more whiskey.

I settled back in my seat. Other than the anxiety from Glory, everyone seemed relaxed. "Join hands, and I'll summon Eldridge." I looked at him and raised my eyebrows.

He nodded and moved closer to the table.

"Eldridge, your family is here, and they wish to speak to you. What would you like to tell them?"

"That I feel ridiculous," he muttered. "I don't want any of them to be involved."

I slid him a glare. He couldn't get cold feet now. "Eldridge is here. He's confused."

"And I feel like I want to punch someone," he said. "I'm barely holding things together. Being here is bringing up so many memories."

"Eldridge is remembering. He needs to get his thoughts straight so he can move on," I said.

He heaved out a sigh, his icy breath making me shiver. "Let's start by accusing my wife. Ask her about the divorce lawyer."

I focused on Raina. "Eldridge is worried you were unhappy in your marriage."

"I was never unhappy." Raina's gaze lowered for a second. "Of course, we had trying moments. When you're married to someone for a long time, things get stale. It was never anything serious, though."

"Eldridge wants to know if you ever thought about divorcing him," I said.

Raina cleared her throat softly. "Well, I mean, I expect every wife briefly considers divorcing her husband when he's being an idiot."

"Did you ever do anything about those thoughts?"

She licked her lips and nodded. "We had a rough patch not long before Eldridge died. I was angry with him about something small. I can't even remember what it was now. I had an appointment with the family lawyer to discuss changing some investments. While I was there, I brought up the possibility of a divorce."

"She didn't love me," Eldridge mumbled. "Why didn't I know this?"

I wanted to offer him reassurance. "We can all waver. It doesn't mean the love has gone."

Raina simply nodded.

"Did you ever talk to Eldridge about this meeting?" I said.

"Of course not. Why worry him when there was no reason? Is that what's keeping him here? If so, he can put his mind at rest. Where is he?"

"Eldridge is by my right shoulder," I said.

"Eldridge, I would never have divorced you," Raina said. "You can go. I'll always think fondly of you."

"He appreciates your honesty," I said.

"I don't. She should have talked to me. We could have figured things out. Do you think she shoved me down the stairs because we had an argument?"

I nodded slowly to show him I was listening. "Eldridge has questions for the rest of you. Alastair, he's worried about your business."

Alastair jerked in his seat. "I'm sure he's not. It wasn't as if he had an interest in it when he was alive."

"He wants to make sure you're managing. Are you struggling with anything? He wants to know if he can help."

Alastair adjusted his grip on Raina's hand. "I have plans for my business. I mentioned them to you when you were looking to buy a broomstick. I was hoping Eldridge would invest."

"I didn't know you talked to Eldridge about financing your business," Raina said.

"I didn't, at least nothing formal. And he made it clear he didn't want to know, so I let it drop."

"Liar!" Eldridge grabbed the back of Alastair's chair and shook it.

Alastair yelped and went to stand.

"Don't break the circle!" I said. "If you do, none of us are protected. Alastair, are you sure you're telling the truth?"

"Yes! Eldridge, do what you like with your money. I don't want it."

"He can't anymore, since he's dead," Lars said. "What's Eldridge so worried about? Does he think one of us killed him for his money?"

I pressed my lips together and looked at each of them in turn.

Lars choked out a laugh. "He can't seriously think one of us shoved him down the stairs."

"He doesn't. His death was an accident." Raina's gaze cut to me. She looked scared. "He doesn't think anything bad happened to him, does he?"

There was no point in hiding the truth now Lars had drunkenly divulged it. "He does have concerns. Eldridge is worried one of you might have hurt him."

"Oh, Eldridge. We'd never do that. You were a good husband and father. And you always looked out for Lars, even though he didn't deserve it," Raina said.

"Why didn't I deserve it?"

Raina's gaze went to his whiskey.

Lars smirked and emptied the glass.

"They're lying," Eldridge growled out. His features were changing, and he was looking more ghoul-like, with overly large dark eyes that shone with malice.

"Everyone stay calm. Ghosts can become confused. And Eldridge's death was unexpected. That's created muddled memories that he's sifting through to find sense in his sudden death," I said.

"Daddy fell down the stairs," Glory said. "That's all that happened." Her ghostly white face suggested she was about to faint.

"Maybe we shouldn't be so quick to dismiss this," Alastair said. "None of us saw what happened. We were all in bed when Eldridge fell."

"Don't stir up trouble," Lars said.

Alastair stiffened in his seat. "It's only trouble if you have something to hide."

"If this was murder, any of us could have done it. We were all sleeping alone that night." Lars's gaze shifted to Raina. "Or were we?"

"Don't be crude. I was with Eldridge." Raina's cheeks flushed scarlet.

"It would be helpful if you could all think back to that night," I said. "Even if it's just to put Eldridge's mind at rest. You were all in your rooms, in bed?"

"I was sleeping on the couch in the games room," Lars said. "I didn't know anything about it until the sirens blared as the ambulance arrived."

"Passed out drunk again," Raina muttered.

"I need something to take the edge off of putting up with you."

"Which you frequently remind me about. But you know the stipulations in Eldridge's will. I get to spend the rest of my days in the family home. It was a condition of you getting the money."

"You act like you've got the money most of the time," Lars said.

"And I'll continue to do so until you become more responsible and don't drink whiskey like it's sparkling water."

"You never liked Daddy." Glory's glare was directed at Alastair. "And you moved in quickly once my mother was widowed."

"Glory! That's a terrible thing to say." Raina shook her head at her daughter.

"It's true. The second Daddy was in the ground, Alastair kept showing up and hanging around."

"Because he's a close family friend, and we were all grieving," Raina said.

"Don't be so disrespectful," Alastair said. "I care deeply for your mother. It's why I put up with your tantrums."

"You treat me like a child." Glory's bottom lip was jutting out.

"If you want to point fingers, point one at yourself. You're always asking for a bigger allowance, but I know Eldridge refused to overindulge you. He even cut back your allowance in the hope you'd get a job and grow up," Alastair said.

Lars snorted a laugh as he grinned at me. "What does my brother think of all this? Hardly a happy family, are we?"

"I'm speaking the truth," Alastair said. "Eldridge despaired about how lazy Glory was. She's rarely up before noon, and then all she does is shop or play games on her computer. She's twenty-one, not fifteen. It's time she learned some responsibility."

"I'm responsible. But I haven't long lost my father. I'm hardly going to act like everything is normal now he's gone."

"Alastair didn't mean it, darling," Raina said. "But... perhaps you need a purpose. It's not healthy staying here all the time."

"Then buy me a villa in Tuscany and I'll get out of your way."

Alastair tutted. "That's not what Raina meant." He shifted in his seat and focused on me. "What does Eldridge say about Lars?"

I glanced at Eldridge. He was still looking ghoul-like and angry, so I needed to wrap this up. "He's worried Lars is holding a grudge because he didn't invest in his business."

Lars waved a hand in the air. "I was so used to Eldridge telling me I was an idiot and I should stop wasting my time that I was used to it."

"It couldn't have been nice to be called an idiot by your own brother," I said. "Did he really do that?" The question was directed at Eldridge.

Eldridge swirled around the room. "Once or twice. It was all I could do to stop from laughing in his face."

Lars nodded. "It doesn't matter. That's just how he was with me."

"Now you'll never need to start a business and find out how hard it is," Alastair said. "You got everything once Eldridge died. You have the biggest motive for wanting him dead."

Eldridge kept swirling around the room, making it uncomfortably cold.

Raina shivered. "He's not happy, is he?"

"No. And it's time to finish this séance. I'll close the circle," I said.

"No!" Eldridge rushed to the back of Alastair's chair and shook it again. "It's him. I'm sure of it. Glory's right. He moved in on Raina too quickly. He wanted my money for his stupid business, and when I wouldn't give it to him, he found a way to take it."

Alastair's face was as pale as the cloth on the table. "Why is Eldridge so agitated with me?"

"Because he's seen who you really are," Glory said. "You're deflecting. It was you. Daddy knows it was."

Eldridge howled, his human features gone. He grabbed Alastair around the neck, yanked him from his seat, and shoved him against the wall. "He's guilty. I'm going to kill him."

Chapter 17

After a few seconds of everyone frozen in panic, we all moved at once. I closed the séance to make sure no unwelcome guests crept through, then raced over to Alastair, who was suspended in mid-air as Eldridge choked him.

"Die! Leave me and my family alone." Eldridge slammed Alastair's head against the wall.

"Eldridge, this isn't the way to do it. Let go of Alastair." I primed a disabling spell.

"He's killing him. Someone stop him." Raina gripped Glory with one hand, the other waving at Lars. "Do something to save your brother."

"I don't know how." Lars swayed on his feet as he stared at Alastair.

"Do something!" Raina shrieked at me.

This situation was spiraling out of control. I had to get Eldridge thinking rationally. "Eldridge, get control of yourself. You don't want to hurt your friend."

"He's no friend of mine. He killed me to get my wife and my money. He has everything." Eldridge snarled in Alastair's face.

"Eldridge thinks you murdered him," I said to Alastair. "Maybe if you confess, he'll calm down."

"But I didn't do it," Alastair choked out.

Raina opened a cabinet full of vases and antique objects. She threw one. "Go away, Eldridge. We don't want you here." She grabbed a small silver statue and slung it.

Eldridge didn't react as the objects passed through him as he continued to choke Alastair.

Raina grabbed a square paperweight from the cabinet and lobbed it. It bounced off the wall near Alastair's head and landed by Glory.

She scooped it up and backed away, clutching it close to her chest. "How do we get Daddy to stop?"

I sucked in a deep breath. It was time to bust this ghost. I focused my energy, creating a powerful containment spell between my hands. The atmosphere crackled with silver and orange magic as I flung the spell and covered Eldridge in it.

He roared and fought against my magic, but I kept my hold tight. After a few seconds of struggling, Eldridge's energy faded. I wrapped the spell around him until I had him under full control. It was a similar magic I used with my scarecrows to ensure I could contain them if they got over excited.

Alastair wheezed out a breath as his feet hit the floor. He sank to his knees and passed out.

Raina and Glory rushed over to him.

I focused on Eldridge, keeping my magic pulsing through the containment spell as I dragged him out of the dining room and through the front door.

Tuffin trotted out behind us. "That was entertaining."

"Not now," I said through gritted teeth. "Eldridge, if you don't change back, you know what'll happen to you. Don't lose control when we're so close to the end."

The ghoulish version of Eldridge growled and twisted in my spell. It took several minutes, but he slowly transformed. He still didn't look fully human, but he looked much less terrifying than he had in the dining room.

"Are you good?" I kept my spell on him, despite feeling my magical strength fade.

"I've been better," he rasped out. "It was Alastair. I know it."

"Do you remember him pushing you down the stairs, or is that a guess?"

"I... I don't remember. But it makes sense. Seeing them all together, I just knew."

"It makes as much sense as everyone else's motives," I said. "Will you behave if I let you go? I should go check on the family. Alastair might need medical treatment."

He heaved in a deep breath. "I'll be okay."

"I'll stay with Eldridge," Tuffin said, "and make sure he doesn't go psycho on us again."

"Both of you wait here. I'll go see how bad things are with Alastair." I hurried back into the house. Piper stood by the open dining room door, her hands pressed against her stomach.

"Is Alastair dead?" she whispered when she saw me.

"No, but Eldridge got agitated and hurt him. Can you make some hot drinks to help calm everyone down? Something with a lot of valerian would be perfect."

"Of course." Piper dashed away.

I strode into the room. Alastair was still on the floor, Glory and Raina kneeling beside him. Lars was leaning forward in his seat, looking on with interest.

Alastair groaned. "Am I dead?"

"No, but you've had a scare," Raina said. "Stay where you are. You're hurt."

"Eldridge seemed certain you were involved in his fall," I said to Alastair. "Is there anything you want to tell me or the Magic Council?"

Raina glared at me. "My husband didn't do this."

Alastair groaned again. "I promise I didn't push Eldridge."

"Then why was he so angry with you?" I said.

"Because he made a mistake? You said he was confused." Alastair slowly sat and rested his back against the wall as he rubbed his throat. "I could feel the malevolence radiating off him. That ghost is out of control."

"He'll remain out of control until we figure this out," I said. "Did you ask him for money for your business and he turned you down?"

Alastair rubbed his neck again and winced. "Not in so many words, but I tried several times to get him interested in giving me a loan."

"And how did you feel when he turned you down?"

"I was angry my best friend wouldn't help me. I knew he had the money."

"You should have said something to me," Raina said. "I'd have convinced him. Eldridge was always conservative with his investments. He didn't like taking risks."

"I couldn't have asked you for help. This matter was between two business associates. I made it clear I'd repay the loan with interest, but Eldridge didn't want to know." Alastair looked up at me. "Is he still here?"

"He's contained outside. And he's calmer. You must see how this looks to Eldridge, though. He thinks you wanted revenge."

"Not getting a loan from Eldridge was a blow, but it didn't mean the end of my business. It simply meant I had to find other sources, and my expansion plans would take longer. That's not a motive for shoving a guy down the stairs."

I looked at Raina. That wasn't Alastair's only motive for killing Eldridge. Alastair got the woman, lived in this amazing house, and I was certain Raina would give him money for his business if he asked. Maybe Alastair had been biding his time. He was planning to get Raina to invest in his business, but Eldridge's appearance as a ghost put a spanner in the works.

"Daddy was really killed?" Glory was still clutching the paperweight like it was a comforter.

"I'm sorry to say, I think he was," I said. "At least, he believes he was."

Raina stood and turned to me. "So much for getting a resolution from this séance. You've thrown the family into disarray. Odessa, it's time you left. We have things to talk about, and I'd like the doctor to come look at Alastair's neck."

I didn't want to leave. I wanted one of them to confess to Eldridge's murder so we could move on and I could get my life back to normal. But the stubborn set of Raina's jaw meant the time for arguing was over.

"I'll let you know if I hear more from Eldridge. Tonight might have given him clarity. You never know. Maybe he'll remember something useful."

"Thank you, Odessa. We'll take it from here." Raina inclined her head at the door. "Piper will see you out."

I nodded a goodbye to everyone, but their attention was on Alastair, apart from Lars, who was nodding off in his seat. I headed back to the front door with Piper. This evening had been a disaster. I hadn't expected Eldridge to go all-out ghoul and try to kill a suspect.

Piper touched my arm. "Are you okay?"

"Yes, I'm just frustrated. And I feel so sorry for Eldridge."

"Don't say anything to the family, but I was listening to some of your conversation." Piper shot a nervous look along the hallway. "And although I agree Alastair and Raina got married quickly, Alastair is a nice man. He's always very respectful of me. I can't see him killing his oldest friend."

I gestured at the antiques in the hallway. "He's landed on his feet now Eldridge is dead."

"Has he? After all, he's taken on a moody stepdaughter and a man who pours whiskey on his cornflakes. Alastair has had his fair share of stresses since marrying into this family."

Piper had a point. "Does Alastair get much of a say in how the household is run? He acts like he's the boss."

She ducked her head. "I shouldn't say anything. It's not my place."

"I'm happy to listen to any ideas. I'm stumped about what happened here. And the longer Eldridge's ghost remains, the more chance he'll turn into a ghoul. Then he'll never find peace."

Piper shook her head. "I'm sorry about that. I hope you figure this out. I should go. The family might need me." She let me out of the house, then closed the door behind me.

I headed home, covered in the stench of defeat. Eldridge didn't utter a word as we went back to the farm, and Tuffin was also quiet.

"I'm taking off," Eldridge said. "I have some thinking to do."

"Sure. I understand. Don't feel bad about what happened. Alastair will be fine. He was talking when I left, and Raina was getting the doctor out to see him."

Eldridge nodded, then slowly drifted away.

Tuffin grunted. "I'd better follow him. Make sure he does nothing too dumb." She trotted after the sad ghost.

As I walked up the porch steps, Hettie appeared from the shadows.

"Hi. Back so soon?" I unlocked the farmhouse door and gestured her inside.

"I got your blood test results. And you're going to want to see this."

"That was quick. I figured something like that would take days to process."

"I've got a kit at home. It's a hobby of mine."

"Analyzing bodily fluids is a hobby?"

"Sure. I have no social life, I'm not married, and have few friends. Death is my only hobby."

I looked at her with wide eyes.

Hettie shrugged. "People think I'm weird and morbid because I cut up bodies. They stay out of my way. I'm not bothered. I have the horses, and I like my own company well enough."

I dropped my purse and kicked off my shoes. I felt sorry for Hettie. "Would you like to stay for dinner? We can talk about the test results."

"It depends what you're making. I have a sensitive stomach."

"I've got a pumpkin risotto ready to go. It only needs reheating."

"That doesn't sound so terrible. I forgot to eat earlier. I got so engrossed in the tests."

"Take a seat. It'll take five minutes to heat." I pulled out the tub of pumpkin risotto from the fridge and added it to a saucepan to heat on the stove. "Did you find anything useful?"

"You bet I did. Eldridge was one seriously unlucky guy, or someone was gunning for him."

I grabbed drinks and cutlery and set everything on the table. Once the risotto was warm, I served it and settled in the seat opposite Hettie. "So, what did you discover?" I pushed a pot of powdered pumpkin over to her.

She shook her head. "You should be careful with that stuff. The magic in your pumpkins is intoxicating. It always makes my nose itch."

"A little won't hurt." I added a liberal dash to my risotto.

Hettie shrugged. "After reviewing Eldridge's case evidence and running the tests on his blood sample, I'm convinced he was murdered."

"Someone definitely pushed him down the stairs?"

"I reckon they did."

"What about the head wound and the burn on his chest?"

"I can't say for certain the head wound wasn't caused by the fall. I also can't say for certain it was."

"Someone could have hit Eldridge before he fell?"

"You said he was confused that night. Being whacked over the head would do that to a person."

"Eldridge said nothing about being struck, but his memory is hazy. He could have blocked it out." I ate some risotto. "What about the burn?"

"In the report, Glory and Lars said it was self-inflicted after a spell went wrong. That could have been what happened."

"What if it wasn't? What if Eldridge only believes he did that to himself? His memory is muddled because he's been a ghost for so long." I lowered my fork. "A member of his family tried to kill him with a spell. When that failed, they hit him over the head and then shoved him down the stairs."

Hettie whistled low under her breath. "That's cold. But this gets better. We haven't gotten to the blood test yet." She shoveled risotto into her mouth and chewed. "This isn't bad."

"Thanks. So? What about the blood test results?"

"I screened the blood taken from Eldridge during his autopsy. There were traces of poison. Belladonna."

"Poison! Eldridge was being poisoned, too?"

"Wait for the finale. I checked with a contact at the Magic Council and discovered Eldridge filed a report six weeks before his death. The brakes on his car got cut."

"They were deliberately cut?"

"The report is clear. Someone has been trying to kill Eldridge for a while."

"How many ways can a person be killed?" I leaned back in my seat. Someone must have hated Eldridge to keep targeting him.

"That's for you to find out. But whoever did this, they were determined not to give up until they succeeded."

I picked up my knife and fork. "And I'm determined to find out who that person was and make them pay."

Chapter 18

After a sleepless night, I stood in front of my suspect board in the kitchen. "Which one of you did it? You all have sort of alibis, but you also all have great motives."

I shivered and wrapped my hands tighter around my coffee mug as the air cooled. A few seconds later, Eldridge materialized. His shoulders were slumped, and he wouldn't meet my gaze.

"Are you in a throttling mood today, or a happy let's get this murder solved mood?" I said.

"I'm sorry about yesterday. I tried to control myself." Eldridge growled at me, then clamped his hand over his mouth. "I don't mean to be like this."

He looked so miserable, I wanted to hug him. "I understand. This is difficult for you."

"I took the night to think things through. I want my killer found. And after I calmed down, I'm not so sure it was Alastair."

"That's what I was thinking. All your family have good motives for wanting you dead. Even Glory. She didn't behave well last night."

Eldridge let out a long sigh. "She didn't. Although I didn't appreciate Alastair reprimanding her."

"He's her stepdad now. It's his job."

That comment only made Eldridge growl again. His hands looked claw-like, and his teeth were permanently long and more Wolverine than human.

"While you were pondering your killer, did you get around to talking to more ghosts about Brodie?" I said.

"I saw a couple of guys, but they hadn't seen him." Eldridge drifted around the suspect board. "The problem is, all these ghosts have recently arrived, and Brodie's been dead for how many years?"

"Over three years. But that doesn't mean he's gone."

"Sure, but if they didn't know him when he was alive, they might not know him now he's dead. And if he's changing, like me—"

"He's not changing. Well, he might have changed a bit, but he'll still be the same old Brodie." I didn't like the pity in Eldridge's too big eyes.

"While I'm able to, I'll keep asking. But I don't have much longer. My thoughts are getting dark. You have to solve this." Eldridge slammed his arm against the suspect board and sent it crashing to the floor.

I picked it up and set it back on the counter. I didn't want to admit it, but this case was too hard for an amateur sleuth with little clue how to solve a crime. I didn't want to give up on Eldridge, but as he grew increasingly difficult, I might not have a choice.

"Sorry," he growled out. "I'll do better."

"You're doing the best you can. I need to check on my new scarecrows this morning, but then I'll focus on your murder."

"You're useless. A pitiful witch. They should bring back burning at the stake." Eldridge lunged at me.

I blasted him in the chest with a knockback spell and pointed a finger at the door. "It's time you left."

He covered his mouth with his hand again before zooming out.

I'd wanted to talk to Eldridge about his car accident and the brakes being cut, but with the mood he was in, it was safer for me if I wasn't around him.

After a quick breakfast, I grabbed a muffin, headed to my locked barn, and checked my experiments. The escapee scarecrow was calm, and the magic was holding. At least things were looking up in that respect. Now, I just needed Brodie's ghost.

I walked into the village and headed to Olympus Duke's office. I needed to find out more about what happened to Eldridge's car. And since a report had been filed with the Magic Council, this was a good place to start.

I opened the door and froze. Selma Black stood in front of Olympus's desk, her arms crossed over her chest. She turned and looked at me, and her expression soured.

"Your ears must be burning. I've been talking about you to Olympus."

"You actually just said you were leaving." Olympus pushed back his chair and stood. He glanced at me and rolled his eyes. "Selma, I'll let you have that information by the end of the day."

"Make sure you do. I can't afford any more delays." Selma headed to the door and brushed past me. "The paperwork for the search warrant is almost done. I'll soon be by to find out all your secrets."

I pressed my lips together, tempted to stick my tongue out at her back as she stalked away. But I was a grown woman, and that was childish. Maybe just the tip of my tongue poked out.

"What did Selma want?" I headed into Olympus's office and closed the door behind me.

"She's got a bee in her bonnet about your farm. She's digging for dirt while she waits for the warrant. You're lucky. There's a backlog of paperwork at the Magic Council headquarters, and Selma is spitting mad about it." He gestured to a chair, and I sat in it.

"I don't know why she's got it in for me," I said.

"It's just Selma's way. The Magic Council rewards results. And ever since they brought in new targets to achieve, everyone is scrambling to hit them."

"Did you set that up?"

Olympus shook his head. "I voted against it. But they love their key performance indicators. Anyway, what can I do for? I'm guessing this isn't a social visit."

I fished in my purse. "I brought you a muffin." I set the pumpkin muffin on the desk.

"Which is always welcome." Olympus grinned. "But..."

"I'm dealing with a ghost issue," I said.

"Eldridge Talbot," Olympus said. "Indigo mentioned you were still helping him. No luck?"

"Not yet. But I heard something interesting. Eldridge had his brakes cut about six weeks before he died. Do you have the report on that?"

"Sure. I remember it. Give me a moment to dig out the information." Olympus headed to a filing cabinet, and after rifling around for a minute, he pulled out a file. "Here it is. I remember him not being keen on filling in the paperwork, but he caused damage to a neighbor's fence, so everything needed to be filed for insurance purposes. Raina forced him to come here."

"The brakes on the car were deliberately damaged?" I said.

"Is that what Eldridge told you?"

"Not in so many words. Is that what happened?"

Olympus flicked through the file. "There was a clean cut on the cables. They sometimes get damaged if you drive over a bump or hit a pothole, but it looked like it was done deliberately."

"Did anyone investigate?"

"We would have, but Eldridge didn't want any fuss. He filed the report to deal with the insurance, and that was it. He was clear he didn't want any follow-up."

"If someone cut the brakes on my car, I'd insist on finding out who did it."

"Eldridge said it was an accident. And since the insurance companies were dealing with the repairs, we let it drop." Olympus's gaze went to the pile of files on his desk.

"And you're too busy to deal with something so small?"

The wince he made told me everything. "Sorry. You know how the Magic Council can be."

"We have to investigate this some more. It could be important. And I've seen Eldridge's autopsy report. Plus, I got tests done on a blood sample taken after he died."

"How did you manage that?"

"Through my friends in high places." I grinned at him. "I'd better not disclose my source, but she can be trusted. After studying the autopsy report and getting the blood test results back, I'm sure Eldridge was murdered."

Olympus settled back in his seat. "Go on. What do the results show?"

"That someone has been trying to kill Eldridge for a while. Setting aside the fact he died from a fall, he also had a head wound that could have been caused before he fell. He also had a healing burn mark on his chest that was allegedly caused by a backfiring spell. And most damning of all, there were traces of belladonna in his system."

Olympus stared at me, his mouth open. "This guy was unpopular."

"Does this information give you enough evidence to reopen his case?" I said. "Eldridge's death was ruled an accident, but put all this together, and it wasn't. I've been trying to help him, but I'm stuck, and the suspects aren't giving me anything."

"It does. Provide me with the evidence from the blood tests, and that'll be enough to reopen the case. Although I'm not sure how I can justify why the tests were even ordered. Questions will be asked."

"They're legit tests. All done aboveboard by a qualified person."

"Okay. I trust you. But your mystery helper will need to step forward at some point."

I drew in a breath. "It's Hettie Crane."

"You do have friends in high places. Hettie's a firecracker. And smart."

"And she wants to help. Eldridge was one of her last cases."

The door slammed open, and a gust of icy wind blasted in. Eldridge appeared a second later.

"Has your ghost friend arrived?" Olympus said.

"Eldridge is here. You don't see him?"

"I'm not good with ghosts. I sometimes catch a glimpse out of the corner of my eye, but they avoid anyone who works at the Magic Council. They think we'll force them to crossover. Which, under section forty-eight, paragraph nine of the ghost hunting code, we're within our rights to do so."

"He could try to force me to cross," Eldridge growled. "I'd snap his head off if he made a wrong move."

"That's enough," I said to Eldridge. "Olympus has agreed to reopen your case. We're getting the professionals on our side."

He prodded me with an icy finger. "You have to find my killer. This idiot can't even see me."

I shushed him. "That's not nice."

"Your ghost is being tetchy?" Olympus said.

"Eldridge is struggling. I'm almost out of time to help him before he changes for good."

"Then we have a problem. I'm bogged under with current cases and reports. I'll put in a request to get Eldridge's case reopened, but nothing will happen for at least forty-eight hours."

I slumped in my seat. In forty-eight hours, Eldridge would be a ghost ghoul, and I'd have to destroy him. It looked like I was on my own. "Thanks, Olympus."

"Sorry. I wish I could speed things up, but you know what this place is like." His smile was rueful as he led me to the door.

I said goodbye and headed outside, with Eldridge floating beside me.

"How are you going to find my killer? You must hurry." His voice was a low, rumbling growl.

"I know. But I need to find a flaw in one of your suspect's alibis. Something to reveal their guilt." I looked both ways as I crossed the street. "It's time to go back to the beginning. Back to the crime scene."

Chapter 19

I was pleased to see Piper open the door when I arrived back at the Chalice house. "Hey. Is Raina or Alastair in? I wanted to apologize for what happened last night. I didn't expect the séance to get so out of hand."

Piper stepped outside and pulled the door closed behind her. "They're out. I can pass on a message."

"You might be able to help me, actually. Have you got a minute?"

Her hand remained on the door. "Not really. I'm busy."

"Please, it's about Eldridge."

Piper looked around. "Is he back? I barely slept last night thinking about him."

Eldridge had drifted off before I got to the house. "I don't think he'll cause you any trouble, but he is suffering."

Piper chewed on her bottom lip. "I feel bad for Eldridge, but I don't want to get anyone in trouble."

"Someone killed Eldridge. Maybe they deserve trouble."

Her hand remained on the doorknob, as if she was considering fleeing inside and slamming the door in my face. "What can I do to help?"

"I'm interested in finding out more about Eldridge's car accident."

"Oh! I can't help with that. I only deal with the household matters." She inched open the door.

"You didn't hear any conversations the family had about the car? Or any concerns Eldridge had about driving?"

Piper shook her head.

"Did he ever work on that car? Maybe he made a mistake when he was fixing it and damaged the brakes."

"No, Eldridge was terrible at DIY or repairs. He was more a planning and management person. I never saw him tinkering with his cars."

"Did you ever overhear him arguing with anyone before his car accident?"

Piper sucked in a breath. "Odessa, I know I was listening into the séance last night, but I don't make a habit of eavesdropping on private conversations. If I did, I'd lose my job. I like working here. And I respect the family."

"I understand your loyalty is to them. Is that true even if you know something bad about one of them?"

Her forehead wrinkled as she frowned. "They've always been a decent employer. It's why I've stayed so long. And Eldridge was a good man. I'm sorry if something bad happened to him, but I can't put what I have at risk. I don't have the luxury of not working, and I don't want the stress of starting new somewhere else."

"You do know something, though? Who do you think killed Eldridge?"

"I have no opinion on it. He... fell down the stairs."

"But you overheard what happened at the séance. Eldridge is convinced he was killed."

"He must have gotten things wrong. This is a decent household. You should leave things alone." Piper gestured at the driveway. "It's best you leave. Raina wasn't happy with you last night. I don't think she wants you to keep investigating."

"Eldridge isn't going away. And when he turns into a ghost ghoul, he'll come back for this family. They could be in danger if Eldridge's murder isn't resolved."

Her bottom lip trembled, but she pushed back her shoulders. "You need to go. And please return the recipe book I lent you. Raina wants to cook a special meal for Alastair at the weekend. She'll be needing it."

I'd forgotten all about the book she'd loaned me. "I'll drop by with it as soon as I can."

"Piper! Where are you? She's never here when I need her." Glory's voice rang along the hallway.

"I must go." Piper pushed open the door and came face-to-face with Glory and Lars.

"There you are. I hope you're not wasting time gossiping." Glory's gaze cut to me.

Piper bowed her head. "I was seeing what Odessa wanted. She's leaving now."

"Fetch my green coat. And I can't find my umbrella or black patent shoes. Have you moved them?"

"I'll go get everything. I won't be a minute." Piper scurried away.

"I don't know why Mommy keeps her around," Glory said to Lars. "She's so slow."

Lars shrugged and pulled out a hip flask. "I've never had a problem with Piper. She always keeps my whiskey topped up." He nodded at me and took a sip from the flask.

Glory glanced at me. "Was there something you needed? Lars, go get the car."

"Sure thing, Princess." As he got to the side of the house, a blast of magic flashed from his fingers, and a potted plant exploded.

"Lars! Mommy will yell at you again. She hates it when you blow things up."

He laughed and hit another flower pot before vanishing around the side of the house.

Glory rolled her eyes. "He's such an idiot."

"Your uncle blows stuff up for fun?" I hurried over and collected the plants, but they were too frazzled to be saved.

"He does. He's got the perfect aim, even when he's really drunk." Glory arched an eyebrow at me. "Well? Why are you here?"

"Have you got a minute to talk?" I said.

"I shouldn't. Mommy's angry with you. You've messed with everything by stirring up Daddy."

"He was stirred up before I got involved."

She walked past me and stood outside on the gravel driveway. "I barely noticed the haunting. If ever he disturbed me, I'd put on music and pretend it wasn't happening."

"You never tried to talk to your dad's ghost?"

Glory kept her back to me. "I didn't see the point. He was dead. And thanks to you, the haunting has gotten worse. You're interfering and making life difficult for all of us."

"I interfered because your dad asked me to help him. He's really struggling." Glory seemed so cold when she spoke about her dad. She acted like she didn't care about him.

She glanced at me, and her expression softened a fraction, but she shook her head. "Can't you do something about that? You have a creepy affinity with ghosts. Get him to move on, and we'll all be happy. Daddy will be, too."

"He can't move on. He's trapped because something bad happened to him. And it seems he was troubled before he died. I was asking Piper about your dad's car accident."

"What about it?"

"You must have been concerned. Did he get hurt?"

Glory shrugged. "No. He hit the wrong pedal or something and hit a fence. He said it was nothing to worry about."

"Are you sure it was that simple?"

"I know nothing about cars. All I know is his favorite red soft top disappeared after the accident. Not that it matters. And we've got plenty of other cars, so I'll be fine."

It seemed all Glory was interested in was getting a free ride and not learning about what happened to her dad when his brakes were tampered with.

Lars rolled up in a sleek black car and stopped beside us. "Are you ready to go, Princess?"

"Um, should you be driving?" I said.

"Probably not," Lars said.

"He'll be fine. Uncle Lars says he needs to loosen up before he drives." Piper walked around to the passenger door and climbed in. "We have to stop at Lucille's first. And then the Manor Lodge. Then it's Fleurs, Amaretti, and that adorable store with the vintage purses. Also—"

"No. One store."

"Uncle Lars! Don't be so awful."

"You said you wanted to go to one store. That's what I agreed to."

Glory grabbed his flask and threw it out the window.

"Brat." Lars hopped out and grabbed it.

I moved to stand in front of him. "Lars, how much have you had to drink?"

"Just enough to take the edge off and not enough to see double." He flashed out another blast of magic, making me jump as a pot exploded behind me.

Lars roared with laughter. "I'm a great shot. I never miss with my fire magic. It's the only thing I'm good at."

"You're also good at spending money on me, your favorite niece." Glory said. "But only if we hurry."

Lars climbed back in the car, and his gaze cut to me. "What's it to you how much I drink?"

"Odessa is still being Little Miss Nosy," Glory said. "She was asking questions about daddy's accident. Do you remember when he crashed the car?"

"That was his fault," Lars said. "And it served him right for being cheap."

"What do you mean?" I said.

Glory poked him with a finger. "Let's go. And you're taking me to all the stores."

Lars ignored her. "Eldridge let the gardener service the cars. What did he expect would happen? He probably poured oil in the wrong hole."

"Uncle Lars! We need to get to town before it's too late. I've got a dozen shops to get around. And if you don't stop at them all, I'm telling Mommy about the whiskey delivery you're hiding in the cellar."

"Kid, you are a giant pain in my butt." Lars shot me a salute, and they zoomed off.

That was odd. Why would Eldridge ask the gardener to deal with his car? I checked on the other plant pot Lars had blasted, but it was ruined. He really was a good shot, even though his pores leaked whiskey.

Rather than leaving, as everyone wanted me to do, I walked around to the back yard. In the distance, I spotted someone kneeling in front of a flowerbed. As I got closer, I recognized Ben.

He looked up as I approached. "Is there something I can do for you?"

"Hi. It's Ben, isn't it?"

He nodded. "Yep. Most of the family are out. Who are you looking for?"

"It's you I wanted to speak to. I have a question about the work you did on Eldridge's car before his accident. It was you who serviced it, wasn't it?"

He brushed off his hands and stood. "Sure. I always looked over his cars when he wanted them serviced."

"Are you trained to do that?"

Ben tilted his head. "As good as. I do a bit of everything around here. I've been a driver, a locksmith's apprentice, and a waiter. I trained as a mechanic for a couple of years before starting here. I wouldn't mess with an expensive car if I didn't know how to look after it."

"Eldridge was happy for you to do that?"

His eyes narrowed. "Of course. He took pride in his cars. I don't mind doing the gardening, but it's nice to keep my hand in so my mechanic skills don't go rusty."

"Did you notice a problem with the brakes on the car when you were servicing it?" I said.

"They were fine. Everything was fine. I serviced it, put it back in the garage, and two days later, Eldridge crashed."

"Because the brake cable was cut?"

Ben looked at the flowerbed he'd been tending. "I can't tell you about that. I should get back to work."

"Did you see the car after the accident?"

"No, it was taken away and crushed. It probably could have been repaired, but Eldridge said he wanted a new one."

"Do you think the cable could have been cut deliberately? Does everyone have access to the cars?"

Ben's eyes widened for a second. "Sure. Anyone in the family can use them. I even take them out when I have things to pick up for work. The garage is locked, but anyone can get the keys. They're in the kitchen."

"Do you know what's been going on with Eldridge?"

His mouth twisted to the side. "I've heard. Piper told me about the séance. I don't sleep in the main house. I've got a place near the garage, so the haunting has not bothered me. But I've heard conversations about problems in the house. Is Eldridge really in trouble? He can't, you know, move on?"

"Yes, and I think someone here hurt him. Do other members of the family have experience with cars? Could someone have tampered with the one that Eldridge crashed?"

"Not that I know of. But if you're suggesting one of them cut the brake cable, it would be easy to look up online. You just need a sharp tool and five minutes under the car."

"If you had to pick someone out of the family, who most wanted Eldridge out of the way?"

Ben scrubbed the back of his neck for several seconds as his gaze went around the yard. "I don't like to say. And I don't want to get caught talking about something that has nothing to do with me."

"Eldridge is desperate." And so was I. "Any clue could be useful."

He puffed out a breath and rocked back on his heels. "I'd point the finger at Lars. He got it all. The house, all the money, the businesses. And he's enjoying spending it. Mainly on expensive booze. I had to go out last week and pick up a small truckload of Scottish whiskey he'd had imported. It must have cost a fortune. But I guess to a wealthy guy like that, it's nothing. And I know Raina hates him."

"Has she told you that?"

"No, but it's the way she looks at him when she thinks no one else is watching her that gives her away. Her face gets pinched, and her eyes narrow. If she could, she'd kick him out and take everything. But Lars has all the power, so she has to mind what she says around him."

"What's going on out here?" Piper strode over, her cheeks pink as if she'd raced to get to us as quickly as possible. "Odessa, I thought you were leaving."

"Nothing's going on." Ben grabbed his tool belt off the ground.

"What were you talking about?"

He lifted a shoulder. "Just Eldridge and the haunting."

"It's not right to gossip about our former employer. If anyone hears what you've been up to, you'll get another warning." Piper flapped a hand at Ben. "Get on with the gardening. Alastair wants to see this done by the end of the day."

"It will be. I'm ahead of schedule." Ben looked at me. "Sorry, I can't help."

"No, you have been helpful, actually. Thanks."

"Don't listen to what Ben has to say." Piper caught hold of my arm and walked me away a few steps. "He's young, and he has a lot to learn."

A ghoulish looking Eldridge appeared in front of me, and I had to sidestep him awkwardly to avoid walking through him.

Piper looked at me oddly. "What's the matter with you?"

"Nothing. And I didn't mean to stop Ben from working. I was just looking for answers."

"You should leave," Piper said. "I don't want to get in trouble because I let you stay longer than you should."

"You won't. I'll leave right away." I headed off with Eldridge beside me. He kept drifting back and looking at Piper before returning to my side. "She's been with us twenty years. We even kept her on when she was sick. She was off for four months with a liver problem. Ever since then, she's been protective of the family."

"Piper's definitely not keen on me since I've been poking about in your death," I said. "You don't think she could be involved?"

"No. Piper's just worried you'll get someone in trouble. And the staff don't have access to the main house at night. We give them their own rooms, so we all have privacy."

"Neither Piper or Ben were in the house when you died?"

"No, Piper usually finishes by nine o'clock. She waits while we have our evening meal and then retires to her room. Ben is usually done by seven. It depends on what he's working on."

"I suppose that's a good thing. I don't need any new suspects. We have enough people on the board already."

"What were you talking to Ben about?"

"I was asking about the car you crashed. He did the servicing on it just before it happened, and I wanted to know if he saw anything odd."

"Why are you poking about in my car crash? That didn't kill me."

"Because you haven't told me everything. You didn't say someone cut through the brake cables."

"Why is that relevant to me falling down the stairs?"

"Eldridge! The cables were cut! What if that was someone's first attempt at killing you?"

His face flashed several colors in the gray palette. He growled and punched the air several times. "My killer didn't give up until they got me. I just assumed... oh, dear. I've been a fool."

"And that's not all." I looked back to see Piper and Ben talking. "I've got a lot to fill you in on. Do you think you can handle some more bad news, or will it flip you into ghoul mode again?"

"I'm going to have to," Eldridge growled out. He shook himself several times. "I need to know everything."

"Then let's go home. Your death was no accident, and it wasn't the first time someone tried to kill you."

Chapter 20

I'd only been out of bed for ten minutes, and I was enjoying my first mug of coffee, when there was a tap on the farmhouse door. I opened it to discover John Smith standing outside.

"Hey. How did you know I lived here?"

He grinned. "I'm a genius. Got any more of that coffee? I've been up all night."

"Err... Sure. Come in." I poured another mug of coffee and handed it to him.

"Much obliged." His gaze flickered around, taking in everything. I got the impression John missed nothing.

"Did my scarecrows cause you trouble on your way in? They don't like strangers."

"Which is why I came in under a concealment spell. I know all about your scarecrows." His gaze landed on me. "Quite a setup you've got here."

"Thanks. I like it. Is there a reason you came by?" My grouchy level was on medium-high after spending most of the night trying to work out how to find Eldridge's killer and getting nowhere.

John took a long sip of his coffee and snagged a muffin off the counter. "There sure is."

"Are you going to tell me what that is?"

"It depends if you make it worth my while."

I sighed and drained my coffee mug. "I'm not in the mood today. What with suspects coming out of my ears, the Magic Council breathing down my neck, and problems with my scarecrows, I have a full plate."

"What's up with your scarecrows? If you're having trouble with one, I can take him off your hands."

"No. They're not for you." The guy wouldn't give up on getting his sly hands on my scarecrows.

John chuckled. "It was worth another shot. So, I've got new information on the family you're looking into, but it'll cost you."

"How much?"

"Are you sure you don't want to give me a scarecrow?"

"The scarecrows are off the table. But I can pay you."

"I'm not interested in more money."

"What do you want?"

His gaze drifted to my mouth. "How about a kiss?"

"I'd rather give you a scarecrow."

"Then I'll take a scarecrow. I'm open to either. But the kiss would be more fun."

I crossed my arms over my chest. "I don't believe you've got new information."

"If we can't do a deal, then I guess you'll never get to find out."

John was swiftly shooting up the chart to grab the slot of biggest jerk. "I can't understand why Storm works with you. You're not a nice man."

"That's exactly why she works with me. I know which corners to cut to get the information I need and whose arms to twist." His easy smile slipped. "You don't want to get on the wrong side of me."

His threats didn't bother me. I had a scarecrow army and a ghost ghoul on my side. And that particular ghost was creeping up behind John as we were talking.

"I see you're thinking about my offer." John tapped his watch. "You've got five minutes to decide while I eat this muffin. Then the price goes up."

"And you've got thirty seconds to get off my property."

John's hands flexed, and he lowered into a half-crouch. "Is that so?"

"Eldridge, why don't you say hello to John?"

Eldridge's growl made John spin around. His gaze tracked the length of my ghostly buddy. "This is the thing you're trying to save? You're wasting your time. He's too far gone."

"I'm not giving up on him. And if you hand over that information, I might be able to help Eldridge faster or at least stop him from ripping your head off and using it as a basketball."

John inched back, getting closer to me. Eldridge stalked toward him, his black eyes blazing and his newly sharp teeth on display. Magic sparked on John's hands.

I stuck my fingers in my mouth and whistled. It was only seconds before three huge scarecrows blasted through the door, running straight through Eldridge's ghost and simultaneously slamming into

John. He went flying back and hit the kitchen wall, grunting as he slid to the floor.

"Let's try this again," I said. "You've been paid for your services, and I've been nothing but polite to you. But you're trying to take advantage. That ends now. Hand over what you've got if you want to get out of here in one piece."

"Did you just threaten me?" John wisely didn't move off the floor as my scarecrows loomed over him. Eldridge was right behind them, ready to provide backup if needed.

"No, but a few broken bones and a stay in the hospital is the usual outcome if you mess with me. Hand it over."

John's hand whipped inside his jacket, and he pulled out a sheet of paper. "You don't deserve this."

"And you don't deserve me calling off my scarecrows, but that's what I'll do, provided you don't mess me around anymore. What information have you got on the family?"

John's scowl revealed his opinion of me, but he unfolded the paper. "Not the family. I did some digging on everyone else in that household."

"Why do that?"

"Because I always do a good job, and it's easy to leave stones unturned if you're an amateur."

I was going to protest, but he had a point. And I was stuck. "And?"

"And I found something interesting about the housekeeper and gardener."

"You mean Piper and Ben. I know Piper but not Ben. He's newish to the estate. They're not involved in this. They weren't even in the house at the time of Eldridge's death."

"Maybe not. But they know each other really well."

"You're not suggesting they're in a relationship, are you? Piper's at least twenty years older than Ben. I mean, I have no issue with toy boys, but..." There had to be a line drawn somewhere. And younger guys were always too energetic for me.

"Their relationship isn't romantic." John inched forward. "They're mother and son."

I tilted my head as I considered this information. When I'd talked to Piper about Ben's job, she hadn't mentioned their connection. Maybe she was worried people would think the family had shown favoritism to Ben because of his connection to Piper and might not approve.

"When you're done chewing that over in your pumpkin brain, you can let me go. I've got places to be." John attempted to stand, but a scarecrow shoved him to the floor.

"Why were they hiding that information?" I said, more to myself than John.

"That's for you to find out."

"Anything else? What about criminal records?"

"Piper is clean. She's lived a boring life and always worked in the service industry. She's been with that family a long time."

I nodded. "Piper keeps her head down and stays out of the way."

A sly smile crossed John's face. "Not all the time. She got someone's attention when she was younger, since she got pregnant and had Ben. Why is she keeping that secret?"

"Maybe they like to keep things professional when they're working together," I said. "What about Ben?"

"There's not much on him. Average school education, drifted between jobs, never staying in the same place for more than six months. Then he landed this gig. Most likely, his mom pulled a few strings."

"That's what I was wondering. And Piper doesn't want people thinking Ben is underqualified and only got the job because they're related."

"You can puzzle that out on your own time. Now, since I handed over the information, can I have a scarecrow?"

"No, although they'll be happy to show you out. Boys, remove the trash." I pointed at John.

He yelped as the scarecrows grabbed him. Eldridge snarled in John's face before blasting through him and making John groan. "Enough! I'm going."

I made sure the scarecrows marched him off my property, standing in the doorway with my hands on my hips. I never had time for controlling men. They were the worst.

Eldridge drifted back, his features looking slightly more human, but he was still growling. "He won't bother you again."

"Thanks for coming to my rescue." I waved a thanks at the scarecrows as they ambled off, then turned to Eldridge. "Did you know about the relationship between Piper and Ben?"

"What relationship?"

I topped up my mug of coffee and returned to my seat. The recipe book I'd borrowed from Piper was in front of me. "That Piper is Ben's mom."

"She never mentioned a son to me. Where did he come from? How strange?"

"You never heard her once talk about a child?" What kind of mother didn't speak about her kids? Even if it was just to moan about them.

"No. Although I noticed they were close. When I was drifting around the house, I'd often see them talking. I assumed they were discussing work, but they also spent a lot of free time together."

"Now you know why." I stared at some odd annotations next to several recipes as I flicked through the book. "I missed it because they don't look alike. Piper is pale, and Ben... he looks more like you."

"Not really. Although we both have dark hair. Although I was turning salt and pepper before I died."

I ran my finger down some notes in the recipe book. It looked like it had been written in code, so the recipe remained a secret. "Did Raina often bake for you?"

"No. Only on special occasions. Why?"

"I can't figure out her shorthand for these cookie recipes. She's done the same to a brownie recipe."

"Brownies were my favorite. I so miss cake." Eldridge sighed. "I miss being me."

"You're still you."

"Not anymore. We've lost, haven't we?" Eldridge said.

My heart went out to the poor bedraggled part-ghoul. "Don't give up. We still have a little time." But not much. I studied Eldridge again. Ben really did look like him. He wouldn't have—

Shamrock burst through the door, wearing a designer jacket Alastair had donated. He turned around and puffed out his chest, placing his hands on his hips in a model stance.

"Hey! That looks great," I said. "The sleeves are on the short side, but I love the color on you."

Shamrock strutted around, looking like he was on a catwalk.

"Come here a second. There's something on the right cuff."

Shamrock walked over, and I inspected the jacket sleeve. It looked like a grease mark. I sniffed it.

"I should let it happen," Eldridge said. "Why am I holding onto my humanity? I can change into a ghoul and demand answers from my family."

"It doesn't work like that. Once you're a ghoul, you'll only want to destroy. Reason will mean nothing to you." I scrubbed the stain with a damp finger. "Anyone who gets in your way will be hurt."

"But someone is lying to us. Why don't they tell the truth about what they did?"

"I really wish I could answer that, but they all had a lot to gain from your death," I said. "Raina and Alastair were free to marry, Lars got the money, and Glory got her freedom. Plus, your brother is happy to share his money with her by taking her on shopping trips."

Eldridge heaved out a sigh. "As far as they're concerned, I was better off dead. Maybe they all killed me."

I continued to inspect the oil on Shamrock's sleeve. "This could have come from a car. It's not a food stain."

Eldridge shrugged and drifted away.

I looked at the recipe book again. The notes on the page detailed how many drops of a mysterious herb called 'b' was needed to perfect the recipe.

My eyes widened, and I jumped up so quickly I startled Shamrock. "Eldridge, say that again?"

"That I'm better off dead?"

"No! The bit about everyone killing you."

"Why?"

It couldn't be true. But... his car accident, the burn on his chest, poison, the head wound, and the stair fall. "Does belladonna grow on your estate?"

He drifted back to me. "No. We prefer formal gardens. Anything wild gets taken out."

"It doesn't matter. You can get belladonna from the apothecary. And some witches carry it for spells." I tapped the recipe book with a finger. "That's what this means."

"What does it mean? I don't understand." Eldridge stared at the recipe book.

"And then we have the burns. The magic that supposedly backfired and hit you. You never told me about that. Why not?"

"My memory is hazy," Eldridge said. "Everyone said that's what happened, but I don't remember casting a spell. I was a mid-level warlock. I can't think what spell I'd have attempted that caused such damage. But why would my family lie to me?"

"I don't think you cast that spell. But I've seen Lars casting fire magic for fun. He bragged about always hitting his target. What if he did that to you?"

His form shimmered. "Lars tried to kill me? You're not making sense. You said something about oil on that jacket and belladonna. And the recipe book. Now you're talking about my burn. You have a butterfly mind."

"I do. But this butterfly mind has put the pieces together. I need to see if Raina bought any belladonna, I have to talk to Piper about this recipe book, and Ben about the car, but I think I've solved it."

"And then you'll know who killed me?"

"Yes. I know exactly what happened." Although the truth was much worse than I'd imagined.

Chapter 21

"You're certain about this?" I could barely see Eldridge in the gloom as we headed to the Chalice house. "What you suggested will get you in big trouble if you're wrong."

I adjusted the heavy purse on my shoulder that contained Tuffin. "I'm right. The clues pointed me to what happened to you that night. Just stay out of sight when you're listening. You too, Tuffin. No spooky activity to scare the family."

"I'll only reveal myself if someone says something dumb," Tuffin said.

"No. Silence. I have to get this right." My insides were shaking, but I was so sure about this. Even though the truth shocked me. I fixed Eldridge with my hardest glare. "Are you sure you can hold things together for another ten minutes?"

"I'll make sure he does," Tuffin muttered from the purse. "I want this over. I feel icky being a familiar to a ghost ghoul."

"Partial ghost ghoul," I said. "Just help him keep control."

"I'll do my best," Tuffin muttered. "So long as you find the killer."

And that was the tricky part. I wasn't dealing with just one killer. Or two.

"I'm relying on you to drag me away if I become too angry. I don't want to throttle anyone else," Eldridge said.

Tuffin simply snorted inside the purse.

I knocked at the door, and Piper opened it.

Her face was pale as she nodded at me. "I was surprised when Raina said you were coming here this evening. Given everything that happened..."

"That makes two of us. But I won't be long."

"And after our conversation on the phone—"

"Which you didn't mention to anyone else?" I showed her the recipe book I'd brought with me.

"No! Of course not. You said it had to do with Eldridge's murder, so I've kept quiet." Her gaze was on the book. "This is serious, isn't it?"

"Yes. And I hope you and Ben can come along too when I talk to the family. I know you thought highly of Eldridge, so you must want to know what happened to him."

"Of course. Raina said you want us there and were insistent we attend." She cocked her head, a puzzled expression on her face. "Although I don't know how we can help."

"You can. Lead the way." I gave Eldridge a discreet nod as he drifted beside Piper. I followed along behind them and into the dining room.

Raina, Alastair, Glory, and Lars sat around the table. None of them looked happy I was there, although Lars gave me a wonky smile.

"You have news about Eldridge?" Raina said.

Ben entered the room. His gaze flicked around before he hurried over to Piper, who stood with her back against one wall as if waiting for the firing squad.

"Get a move on, Odessa," Lars said. "Some of us have things to do."

"More booze to sink?" Alastair muttered.

"Always." Lars raised his glass. "Cheers to you being the killer."

Before the family could start bickering, I stepped up to the table and set down my purse. "I've finally figured out what happened to Eldridge. But his murder wasn't simple."

"What do you mean by that?" Alastair said. "And how do you know he was even murdered?"

"Because of the evidence I found and the clues left following his autopsy. Someone in this house killed Eldridge."

Raina's trembling hand covered her mouth for a second. "Go on. What happened?"

"Let's start with dessert. Piper kindly lent me one of your recipe books after I mentioned how delicious the cakes at the memorial event were," I said.

Raina glanced at Piper. "I wasn't aware of that. You should have asked my permission before loaning out my things."

"This isn't Piper's fault. And it's thanks to her I found an important clue. And after speaking to Piper before coming here, she confirmed my suspicions about you."

"You can't think Mommy is the killer," Glory said. "That's ridiculous. She loved Daddy."

"Piper confirmed you baked weekly for two months before Eldridge died. Is that right?" I said to Raina.

She sat straight in her seat. "I liked to cook for my husband. Piper took care of most of the meals, but I enjoyed making him something special."

Alastair glanced at her. "You never do that for me. Where are my treats?"

"Piper also confirmed that, after Eldridge died, you stopped baking. You never asked for the recipe book or time alone in the kitchen. It's like you no longer needed to bake. Why would that be?" I said.

"Perhaps it was because my husband had just died following a tragic fall, and I wasn't in the mood for overindulging on sweet things. I was grieving."

"Eldridge confirmed he had a sweet tooth," I said.

"Daddy was always pigging out on the treats," Glory said. "He even used to steal my candy."

"That's enough," Raina said. "I don't see how this is relevant to what happened to Eldridge."

"You didn't erase your poison calculations from the recipe book," I said. "There were three recipes you annotated. And you added a special ingredient. You laced the cakes with belladonna. You poisoned Eldridge."

Glory gasped. "Mommy, you didn't do that, did you?"

"No. Of course I didn't." Raina glared at me. "What I write in my recipe books is my business. They shouldn't have been shared with you."

"It was fortunate this particular book was shared," I said. "Otherwise, I'd never have known about the poison. And the tests recently completed on

Eldridge's autopsy samples wouldn't have been done, so the belladonna wouldn't have been found. You'd have gotten away with it."

"But Daddy didn't die from being poisoned," Glory said. "He fell. That's what killed him."

"We'll get to the fall in a moment." I looked at Alastair. "Thank you again for the donation of clothes for my scarecrows. They love them."

He startled and shrugged. "You're welcome. They'd have only gone to the charity bank. I always collect a pile before making the donation. I've been meaning to get rid of those things for ages."

"At least a year, I imagine."

Alastair pursed his lips. "Maybe. Is that important?"

"One of my scarecrows put on a jacket and showed me. There was a mark on a cuff. An oil stain."

Alastair's face drained of color. "That must have been why I decided to get rid of it. I forget about half the things I give away."

"I expect you wish you hadn't forgotten about this jacket, because just over a year ago, you wore it when you cut the brakes on Eldridge's car. The cuff was stained with motor oil, and you couldn't get it out, so you hid it. It must have slipped your mind it was in the pile of clothing you gave me. I expect you thought it would go to a charity, they'd clean it, and sell it. The evidence of your crime would have been lost forever."

"You caused Eldridge to crash?" Raina said. "Why?"

"I... I didn't. That's not what happened." Alastair stood, his fierce gaze on me. "You should leave. I don't appreciate you throwing these accusations at my family."

"I'm not a part of your family," Glory said, "and I want to hear everything Odessa has to say. You can't be trusted. I always had my suspicions about you."

"Sit down, Alastair." Raina sounded weary. "I want to hear, too. Even if only to prove I didn't poison my first husband."

Alastair was clearly a sensible guy because, after some muttering under his breath, he sat down. "Even if that mark is motor oil, it proves nothing."

"When I ask our friendly local coroner to run tests on that jacket, we should match the oil used in that car to the stain," I said. "And after speaking to Ben this afternoon, I know Eldridge used a specific brand of oil. Nothing cheap for his beloved vehicles. Isn't that right, Ben?"

Ben glanced at me and ducked his head. "That's right. It costs an arm and a leg to get that stuff. It has to be imported."

"I also know how handy you are with DIY," I said to Alastair. "You wouldn't have found it difficult to use one of your many tools from the toolbox you proudly showed me to mess with Eldridge's car."

He crossed his arms over his chest. "I'm not saying anything else until I've spoken to a lawyer."

"You wouldn't need a lawyer if you were innocent." Glory sounded too smug for her own good.

"Glory, what about you?" I said.

She jerked in her seat. "What about me? I loved Daddy. He'd still be here if it wasn't for Alastair."

"I think you did love your dad, but you didn't like it when he said no to you. You'd been arguing just before he died about a change in your allowance and the fact he wanted you to get a job."

"That wasn't anything serious. He was just being mean. I'd have changed his mind."

"Is that why you confronted him that night? You knew he'd had a few drinks and would be mellow. You hoped you'd convince him to increase your allowance to finance your shopping habits."

"I didn't do that. I was asleep."

"Except you weren't. And you confronted Eldridge. When he turned you down, or told you to talk to him about it in the morning, you weren't happy. I don't think you planned to hurt him, but no one likes being told no. Especially not you."

Glory pouted. "I didn't push him down the stairs. Mommy, tell her I didn't do it."

"That's right. You didn't. But you did hurt him." I put my fingers in my mouth and whistled.

A few seconds later, Shamrock blasted through the door. He was holding a muddy square paperweight in his hand.

"Good work, Shamrock." My scarecrows were awesome at hunting things out, thanks to their enhanced sense of smell. "Why was this buried in the yard?"

"How should I know? I've never seen it before. Mommy make her stop," Glory said.

"That paperweight belonged to your grandfather. He gave it to you as a gift," Raina said. "I didn't think about it at the time, but it was in the back of the cabinet when I was throwing things at Eldridge."

"It was. And the second Glory saw that paperweight, she grabbed it. Why do that, Glory? Did you think you'd hidden it well enough, but then your mom shocked you by pulling it out of the cabinet?"

"This is nonsense." Glory gulped.

"Eldridge sustained a head wound before his fall down the stairs," I said. "If we have his body exhumed, this paperweight will match the indentation on his skull. An indentation you made when you hit him because he told you no."

Raina blinked slowly at Glory. "You didn't hit your father, did you? We talked about this. There's no place for violence in this household."

"This isn't the first time Glory's hit her dad?" I said.

Raina's eyes flooded with tears. "She has a quick temper. But Glory never hurt him. She just gets carried away."

"It's more than that." Alastair revealed a large bruise on his forearm. "I've told you she needs help."

"Mommy, shut up," Glory said. "You're as guilty as me. You poisoned Daddy. I always wondered why you never let him share the cakes you baked him."

Raina's eyes narrowed. "Did you hit him on the head and then push him down the stairs?"

"No! Stop accusing me. You did it. You killed him. You didn't love him anymore and wanted to be with that idiot." Glory jabbed a finger at Alastair. "You're in on this together. Alastair cut the brakes, and when that didn't work, you fed him poison. I hate you both."

"Maybe they were in on it together," I said, "but there was another attempt on Eldridge's life before he finally died. That was made by you, wasn't it, Lars?"

Lars choked on the whiskey he'd just downed. "Is there anyone in this room you're not going to accuse?"

"Only one person," I said. "I've seen your fire magic. You said you were a great shot and never miss."

"I don't. But Eldridge didn't die in a fire, so it couldn't have been me."

"Fire magic can be targeted. You can direct a small jet of flames into an object. And it can be mixed with other spells to make it even more potent. And in your case, you wanted to be deadly and accurate when you shot a lethal spell at your brother's heart."

"I didn't do that." Lars suddenly sounded sober.

"You'd had enough of being belittled and made fun of as the misfit younger brother of a successful businessman. Did you want to prove yourself or just want the assets so you could fritter them away on imported Scottish whiskey?"

"Now, hold on. Eldridge didn't die from my fire magic."

"Did you get cold feet at the last second?" I said. "You never miss a target, so you must have changed your mind. Was it too late to draw back the spell, though?"

Lars's gaze lowered to his glass, and he wrapped his hands around it. "I never wanted any of this."

"Oh! You horrible man. You did do it," Raina said. "Why?"

"Because of what she said." Lars's expression was sullen as he looked at me. "You two always made fun of me. I used to hear you when you were having your so-called private conversations. You thought I was a loser. Even when I went to Eldridge with solid business ideas, he dismissed them. I watched him once after I'd given him a proposal. He flicked to the first page, laughed, and threw it in the fire. He didn't even look at the hard work I'd done."

"You do come up with some ridiculous ideas, Uncle Lars," Glory said. "The unicorn theme park was insane."

"That would have worked," he grumbled. "But neither Eldridge nor Raina gave me a chance."

"You admit you tried to kill Eldridge?" I said.

"He was making fun of me again. I got angry, and my magic came out. We were arguing, and it just exploded. I wasn't even aware of what I was doing. The magic was acting on my primal instinct to protect myself. I was done with being the idiot brother. But I never meant to hurt him."

"Fortunately for Eldridge, your primal magic instinct failed, and he lived through that particular attempt on his life," I said.

"Odessa, you've made it sound like we all wanted Eldridge dead," Raina said, "but you haven't revealed which one of us pushed him down the stairs."

Piper cleared her throat and took a small step forward. "You said only one person in this room wasn't guilty. Do you think I had something to do with what happened to Eldridge?"

I shook my head. "You're the only innocent one here. The person who actually ended Eldridge's life was Ben."

Chapter 22

Everyone turned in their seats and stared at Ben.

He stood ramrod straight, his eyes wide. "Why are you blaming me? I barely knew Eldridge."

"It's true. You didn't know him well. You've not been here long, have you?" I said.

Ben edged toward the door, but Shamrock raced over and slammed a huge hand against it, barring the way.

Ben stopped moving, his gaze flicking from Shamrock to me. "No. Why's that important?"

"Because things haven't been easy for you. Piper mentioned you'd get another warning if you got caught talking to me. How many would that be?"

"I don't remember," Ben said.

"Eldridge gave Ben two warnings," Raina said. "He had a rule. Three strikes and you were out."

"You were worried you might lose this job?" I said to Ben.

"I'd have found another. This job isn't worth killing over."

"The job isn't, but there's another reason you're here. It's a reason that made you desperate to stay. And it's the reason you used your locksmith skills to make an extra set of keys. I expect, when we search your room, we'll find keys to get in this house. Or at least the tools you used to make them."

Ben turned to the door, but a growl from Shamrock kept him in place.

"In fact, the Magic Council is doing that now. I've told them everything about this family and my suspicions about your combined efforts to kill Eldridge." In truth, I'd told Olympus, who said he'd get the wheels turning. I hoped he was doing the search, but there was no guarantee.

"I don't understand," Alastair said. "Why would Ben need a set of keys for this house?"

"So he could sneak in and shove Eldridge down the stairs," I said.

There were several gasps.

Piper shook her head, her eyes full of tears. "Please don't do this. It didn't happen that way. Ben's a good boy."

"I'm sorry, Piper. I don't want to take Ben away from you when you've just gotten him back, but he killed Eldridge."

Ben lowered his head. "I... I didn't mean to. I just wanted to talk to the guy."

"And I believe you. Maybe if Eldridge hadn't been drunk, poisoned by his wife, and just been hit over the head by his angry daughter when you shoved him, he most likely wouldn't have fallen. But Eldridge was in a bad way. He was weak and confused. He didn't stand a chance."

"Which means Ben didn't do it!" Piper said. "Everyone else did. They're all involved."

"I never trusted you." Raina's accusing glare was on Ben. "I should have gotten rid of you before now. And Eldridge never liked you."

"I didn't mind the boy," Eldridge whispered in my ear. "But he was headstrong, so I tried to teach him the right way to do things."

I drew in a deep breath. Eldridge sounded reassuringly calm, so I wasn't worried he'd go full ghoul on me. "Eldridge is here, and he heard everything I said. He knows the truth now."

"Can... can I talk to him?" Ben said.

I nodded. "He can hear you."

Ben licked his lips. "I really am sorry, but I couldn't leave. I was just getting to know Piper."

Piper and Ben exchanged a glance, and she patted his arm.

"I know about your relationship," I said. "Do you mind if I share it with everyone else?"

"I'll do it." Piper's breath came out shaky. "Ben is my son."

Raina's face grew bright red, and she stood slowly from her seat. "I thought that had been dealt with."

Piper drew herself upright and glared at her boss. "I did what you asked. You never said he couldn't contact me when he was grown."

"What's going on?" Glory said.

"Eldridge told me Piper was ill when she was much younger, yet you kept her job open for months," I said. "She was only twenty at the time, so I wondered what made her so ill. But she wasn't ill. She left to have her child in secret."

Piper caught hold of Ben's arm and tugged him closer. "I gave up my baby and returned to work as if nothing had happened."

"Mom told me everything." Ben's expression was fierce. "She told me about the threats made about having everything taken away if she kept me. But Mom always kept in touch. She sent me letters and gifts on my birthday and Christmas and said one day I'd be able to join her. I never felt like I had a home until we met. Then I knew exactly what I wanted. I wanted to be with her."

Piper took hold of Ben's hand. "We missed out on so much. I wish I could have kept you, but I was so young, and given the circumstances..."

"You mean the affair you had with my husband," Raina spat out.

Glory gasped. "Ben's my half-brother?"

Ben turned to his mom, and the horror on his face sent a stab of pain through me. I'd figured Eldridge and Piper had been in a relationship, but here was the proof.

"Eldridge was my dad?" Ben sounded wheezy as he processed the news.

Piper pressed a hand against her chest and nodded. "I was so young and foolish. I fell for an older man, and I thought he cared for me."

"But... Mom. I killed him! I was going to lose you and everything we had." Ben's eyes were wide and his cheeks pink. "I didn't know. Why didn't you tell me?"

Tears trickled down Piper's cheeks. "I was sworn to secrecy. I was assured by Raina I could keep my job, and this would be hushed up. Our family is incredibly traditional, and a young, unmarried mother without a job would have been rejected. Raina said it was best if I give you up for adoption. She gave me money, which I've put away for your future, and made me swear never to tell anyone. Especially not Eldridge."

"I don't care about any money. I just want you." Ben clutched his mom's hand.

"I did the best I could. You were found a nice family and didn't want for anything."

"You! I wanted you." Ben raked his hand through his hair. "I hated Eldridge. He was so strict. When I tried to talk to him the night he died, he laughed at me and told me to grow up. He said I had to take responsibility for my actions. He even said it was my fault he crashed the car. I got angry with him, but he wouldn't listen, and the thought of leaving this place and not seeing you every day... I couldn't handle it. So I grabbed him and shook him. Then he was falling. I don't even remember pushing him."

"You know what you did," Raina sneered. "There's your killer, Odessa."

"It happened so fast. Eldridge was trying to get away from me when I saw blood on his head. It made me pull back, but it was too late, and he was already falling." Ben groaned. "I killed my dad."

The sadness in Ben's voice broke my heart. This troubled young man had already had a difficult start in life, and it would only get worse. "With the help of everyone else, except your mom, yes, you did. You're all guilty." I looked at Shamrock. "Make sure no one leaves this room. I'll get the Magic Council in here. They can make the arrests."

Chapter 23

I headed out of the room, closed the door, and leaned my back against the wall. The icy swirl of wind around me told me Eldridge was with me.

"Are you happy now? You know what happened." I opened my eyes and looked at him.

"I wouldn't say I'm happy." Eldridge hovered so close our noses almost touched. "Ben is my son? Are you sure?"

"Yes. Raina never told you what was going on?"

He shook his head. "She always dealt with the staff. I was never good at that. I... I remember some of it now. The lead up to my fall. Glory was there, and we'd been arguing. I had a pain in my head, but I didn't know why. Then Glory was gone, and Ben appeared. I didn't recognize him at first because he was dressed in black and had a hat pulled low over his face. I don't remember what we talked about. Then I was falling."

"If it's any consolation, I don't think he meant to do it. Unlike your other family members, who've been trying to get rid of you for some time."

Eldridge drifted away, his face a mask of ghoulish shock. "I can't believe I never knew about this. Piper kept Ben from me for all these years."

"Don't blame Piper. Raina forced her to give up her baby."

His forehead wrinkled. "I guess my marriage wasn't so perfect, after all."

"Cheating is definitely not the thing to do if you want an ideal marriage."

Eldridge looked shame-faced. "How could Raina do that to another woman? She must have realized what it would feel like to give up a child."

I stopped my snort of sarcasm. Eldridge was hardly Mr. Perfect in this situation. "Maybe Raina did it because she loved you and didn't want to give up on the marriage. She believed she was doing the right thing."

"All these years, I've had another child. And then he kills me." Eldridge drifted away, then zoomed back. "What will happen to them? They all tried to kill me. Ben isn't to blame. I don't want my son to get in trouble. My son! I should have known." He shook his head.

"I'm no expert, but the circumstances around your death are complicated. Raina, Alastair, Glory, and Lars might be charged with attempted murder."

"And Ben?"

"He's not innocent. He made a set of keys so he could sneak in and confront you. That's not the behavior of someone who plans to do good."

Eldridge was quiet for several seconds. "I've lost my entire family. Was I such a terrible person when I was alive?"

"No. Although I can't agree with you having an affair with Piper. And perhaps you could have been kinder to Lars, but you didn't deserve to die."

"They all thought I didn't deserve to live. They'd rather I was dead so they could get their grasping hands on my money. I'm ashamed of my family."

"And your affair with Piper?"

He hung his head. "That, too. It shouldn't have happened."

Eldridge had suffered enough. He hadn't been the best husband or brother, but he'd been stuck as a ghost for too long. "Now you know the truth, can you move on?"

Eldridge's gaze went to the closed door. "I know you'll make sure justice is done. But before I go, I have one more favor to ask."

"What's that?"

"Piper. I was arrogant and too sure of myself when I was a young man. She was a beauty, and I had my head turned. But it wasn't a relationship. And we were only intimate once."

"That's all you need to make a baby."

He cleared his throat. "True. Piper was pretty and obliging, and I took advantage of that. That was wrong, and I deeply regret it."

"Do you want to make amends to her?"

"Yes. I have private assets Raina doesn't know about. Call it an emergency fund, if you like."

I arched an eyebrow at him. "Okay, what do you want done with this secret emergency fund of not at all dubious money?"

"I want Piper to have it. She deserves so much more, but it's all I can give her. She won't want to stay here after everything that happened. Not that there'll be a here if everyone is arrested for my murder. Piper needs the chance to move on. Perhaps she can use some of the money to help Ben once he's served his sentence. She can do whatever she likes with it, but it goes to her."

"That would help Piper. But it might take her a while to accept it."

"She can take as long as she needs. I'll give you the details of the account and how to access it. It's the least I can do."

Although Eldridge was flawed, there was still goodness in him. And I'd help make sure that goodness shone. "It's a deal. I'll make sure Piper is set up for life."

"The gift should be anonymous, in case she doesn't want it when she knows it's from me."

"No, she needs to know. This has to be the end of your secrets. Keeping secrets always ends badly."

"What if Piper doesn't want the money?"

"That's her decision to make. You don't get to decide if she wants your money. She's a free woman and needs to make her way in the world and figure out how she's going to help Ben."

Eldridge let out a long sigh. "You're right. She gets to decide." He turned his head. "Oh! I see a light. It's so warm. I... I want to go to it. Should I?"

"You see it because it's your time to move on. Are you ready?"

He drew in a deep breath and wrapped his arms around me. Icy cold flooded through me, but I endured the hug.

"Yes, I'm ready. Thank you, Odessa. I'll never forget what you did for me."

"I'm glad I could help."

"I'm sorry I couldn't find Brodie. I think he's gone, too."

I wanted to argue against that point, but I knew the truth about Brodie.

"I have to go now. The account information is in the top drawer of my desk in the study. Grab the little brown book before you leave. And take care of Tuffin for me," Eldridge said.

"Wait! What? That wasn't a part of the deal." But Eldridge was gone.

Something hard head-butted my calf, and I looked down to see Tuffin staring at me with a morose look in her eyes.

"Hmmm... What are we going to do with you?" I said.

She slumped onto her belly and heaved out a sigh. "Am I dying now? It happens. I've heard about it. When a familiar's companion dies, it can be too much as the connection severs. And I do feel weak. This is the end for me."

"Um... maybe not. Do you feel unwell?" I pulled out my phone and messaged Olympus about Ben's confession.

"Terrible. I have no purpose anymore. What am I supposed to do?" She rolled onto her side, exposing a fluffy belly I'd have loved to blow a raspberry on. "It's best I find a way to end things. I could jeer at one of your scarecrows until it destroys me."

"Don't do that." I checked the message had been read and then crouched beside Tuffin. "You look pretty good to me. I don't think this is the end for you."

"Only pretty good? Then it's terminal. I always look fabulous."

I repressed a laugh. "Your fur is glossy, and your eyes are bright. I reckon you'll be okay."

She gave another dramatic sigh. "I only stuck around to help that idiot."

I risked a tentative stroke of her head, and she didn't scratch me. "Despite every mean thing you've said about Eldridge, you always loved him."

"Maybe. That doesn't matter now. He's gone. So, what should I do?"

I hummed under my breath. "We can try a familiar bond, but you'll have to share me with my scarecrows."

Her nose did that cute, wrinkly thing. "Must I? They're so dramatic."

"Then you should fit right in."

"You have to order them to stop chasing me. And I can't be disturbed when I'm having one of my half a dozen naps a day. There must be fresh fish for my meals, and—"

"And we're both going to compromise to make this work. You can't have it all your own way."

"I always did with Eldridge."

"And look how that ended."

She gave a little snort.

My phone vibrated, and I was happy to see Olympus was on his way. "I'm sure we can work something out. I'll fix it so the scarecrows accept you, but you have to work on being nicer to everyone."

"You're asking the impossible." Her whiskers twitched. "But I'll see what I can do. Do I also have to share you with Sol?"

My happiness died, and tiny shards of icy pain dug into my heart. "No. Sol won't be around anymore. I'm certain of it."

"If that's true, why can I smell him?"

"You can smell Sol?"

"He reeks of apple wood smoke and pumpkins. And the stink is getting stronger."

I opened the front door to discover Sol sprinting in our direction. "Tuffin, as my new familiar, will you fetch the small brown book from Eldridge's desk?"

"Fetch as in like a dog?" She didn't move.

"No! Fetch as in awesome witch familiar. It's important." My heart raced as the look on Sol's face told me bad news was headed my way.

"Is this a test?"

"Will you do it if I say yes?" I stepped out of the door.

"If I must. So long as I get a reward."

"I promise, you'll get a huge reward."

She grumbled as she mooched away.

I hurried out the door to meet Sol. "Is something wrong?"

Sol gasped out a breath as he slowed. "There's a team from the Magic Council at the farm. They got a search warrant and are going through everything."

"Tuffin, let's move." I didn't wait to see if she'd follow as I raced away with Sol. "Tell me everything."

"They arrived half an hour ago. I tried to put them off and used the scarecrows to prevent them from getting in, but they used magic to freeze them."

"Did you check the warrant?"

"Everything is official. Selma is there barking orders, and she's got six people with her. They're searching everywhere. And I mean, everywhere."

My throat tightened. "Including my locked barn?"

"Yes. I told them there were scarecrows in there that weren't stable, but they didn't listen. I tried to stop them, but my magic will only hold them off for so long."

I'd been so caught up in helping Eldridge that I hadn't perfected the concealment spell around the barn containing my experiments. One look in there, and the Magic Council would know I was up to no good. Well, I was doing good, but Selma wouldn't see that.

"It'll be okay." Sol was breathing heavily as we jogged along. "You run a legitimate business."

"We both know that's not completely true."

When Sol's gaze met mine, there were so many emotions flickering through his eyes that my heart skipped a beat. "Did you get things sorted with Eldridge?"

"Yes. He's crossed over."

"Who killed him?"

"Long story. Basically, everyone had a go at Eldridge, but Ben, the gardener, pushed him down the stairs."

"Everyone tried to kill him? And... Ben? He wasn't even a suspect."

"I promise, I'll fill you in once the Magic Council is out of our hair. That's if you're staying."

Sol nodded. "I'll stay for now. But after the Magic Council has gone, I'm not sure what I'll do."

Things were still broken between us, but I'd fix that. I had to. "You know, we should—"

"Odessa, there's something I need to tell you." Tuffin was suddenly trotting alongside me, balancing a small brown notebook expertly between her shoulder blades.

"Can't it wait?" I was focused on Sol. I had him back in my life and didn't want to let him go. "Sol, let's fix up—"

"No! It can't wait. This is important." Tuffin nipped my ankle.

"Later. Sol, what about—"

Tuffin jumped onto my shoulder and dug in her claws. I caught the book before it hit the dirt. "If I don't tell you now, I never will. I'm doing this in the spirit of friendship, to help our familiar bond."

I unpicked her claws from my skin and caught hold of her so she was in my arms, where she could do minimal damage. "What is it?"

She scrambled up until her nose was by my ear. "I also killed Eldridge."

The shock made me stumble. I held Tuffin away from me and looked at her carefully to see if she was joking.

She leaned against me again, her hot breath in my ear. "I told you I was with him the night he died. That he got up to investigate a noise."

"Sure. What's that got to do with his death?"

Tuffin hissed in my ear. "Shush. This is our familiar witch secret. We're bonding over murder."

"Tuffin, what did you do?"

"I may have weaved around Eldridge's ankles and knocked him off balance just as Ben pushed him."

I sucked in a huge breath. "Why would you do that?"

"I'm a cat. We weave. Ankles are a mini obstacle course for us."

"Didn't you see he'd been hurt?"

"Eldridge got out of bed before me. When I came onto the landing, I saw he was holding his head, but he said it was nothing. I must have just missed Glory hitting him."

This cat was unbelievable. "What about Ben? You must have seen him push Eldridge down the stairs."

"It was dark, and Ben had a hat pulled down low. I had no clue it was him, but when you accused Ben of murder, I recognized the stench of fear drifting off him. It was only then that I knew for certain Ben was the killer. Well, the shover."

"You should have told me this when I first started investigating Eldridge's murder. It would have made things so much easier."

"I didn't trust you. I had to test you to see if you were worthy."

"A test! You made me go through all this and risked Eldridge turning into a ghost ghoul to see if I was worthy of your attention?"

"I won't join with just anyone. They have to be worthy of me."

I groaned. "We'll talk about this another time, when there's no risk of me losing my home and business."

She clung to my shoulder. "You won't send me to jail, will you?"

"I should report this. You were involved in killing Eldridge."

"Accidentally. And I didn't mean to do it. I didn't know Ben would loom out of the shadows and shove Eldridge. I was being sweet."

"You wouldn't have weaved around Eldridge's ankles if you'd known he was in danger?"

"I'd have done my best not to." Tuffin licked the side of my face. "You can't report this to the Magic Council. I've already served my time inside that hideous display case. It was torture, watching that smug, self-satisfied family go about their business and not be able to give them any instruction."

"You were in that display case for a year. You'd get much longer for assisting in a murder." I shook my head as I placed her on the ground. "You're a terrible familiar. I'm just glad Eldridge never found out about what you did to him."

Tuffin kept up the pace as we reached the road leading to the farm. "He'd have loved me, anyway. He was that kind of guy. Sort of gullible."

What was I thinking, taking on a familiar like this?

She flicked her tail and gave me a wide-eyed stare. "I'll try to be better."

"Odessa, we've got a problem." Sol caught hold of my arm and slowed us down.

Standing outside my farmhouse were two members of the Magic Council. I didn't need to get much closer before I saw a barrier spell around the building. "They're stopping me getting into my own home." I raced toward a woman dressed head-to-toe in black. "What's going on?"

She stiffened a fraction, but held her position. "By orders of the Magic Council, this place is under investigation for the illicit use of dangerous magic."

"I own this place. You can't prevent me from going inside." I pressed a hand against the barrier spell. It was hot to the touch and gave a warning spark, suggesting if I got closer, there'd be trouble. "Let me in. You've got no right to do this."

"The paperwork is in place. The search is legal. Please stand back, ma'am."

My gaze shifted at the sound of wood splintering. "You'd better not be doing any damage."

The two women averted their gazes from me and stared straight ahead.

I slammed my fists against the magic barrier. "Let me in."

"You'd better get Selma," the woman I'd spoken to muttered to her colleague.

"Yes. Bring Selma out here so she can explain herself." Fury bubbled inside me. This was my home and my livelihood. And my scarecrows were trapped inside. It was unacceptable.

I grabbed Sol's arm as a van rumbled around the side of the farmhouse. A moment later, six of my scarecrows were loaded into the back. A sharp pain tore through me as I saw my guys being roughly handled.

"Hey! Let them go. They've done nothing wrong." I ran at the barrier and blasted magic at it. It wavered, but held.

"I'll arrest you if you keep doing that," the remaining member of the Magic Council said.

I advanced on her, my hands clenched into fists. "You'll be arresting me for a lot more than that if you don't let me in." Horror gripped my heart as the back doors of the van were slammed shut. "Stop! They'll hate being in there. Scarecrows need freedom."

"To cause more problems." Selma marched out of the farmhouse, a gleam of pleasure in her cold eyes.

"You can't do this."

"I told you what would happen if you didn't compromise."

"You're messing with my scarecrows."

"They're a big part of the problem. They're not safe."

"You know nothing about them."

"I will soon enough. I have plans for those scarecrows."

An icy chill slid down my spine. "What are you going to do to them?"

"Run experiments to see what they're made of. If I find so much as a single spell wrong with them, they'll be dismantled and burned."

"They're living creatures. They have personalities and desires. They... feel."

"You'll be telling me next they want nothing more than to set up a home of their own and have baby scarecrows running around." Selma's sneer made me want to whack her. "These things are unnatural, and they're out of control."

Only Sol's restraining hand on my arm stopped me from throwing more magic. I was so hot with rage that sweat trickled down the side of my face. "If you lay one finger on those scarecrows—"

"You'll what? You're the one in the wrong. This is only difficult because you made it difficult. You have yourself to blame."

I thrust my hand in my pocket, grabbed a handful of powdered pumpkin covered treats and chewed. My magic swirled inside me, and without thinking, I threw it toward Selma. It smashed through the barrier and skimmed over her head.

"That wasn't such a good idea," Sol whispered in my ear.

Tuffin backed away. "You've done it now."

I tossed Tuffin the brown notebook so my hands were free to cast more spells. I was angry and wanted Selma to pay.

Fear flickered in Selma's eyes as she scuttled away. "Arrest them. Don't let them inside the farmhouse. They'll destroy evidence."

"I'll destroy you," I said through gritted teeth. I only made it a few steps before three blasts of painful magic slammed into me, and I was taken to the ground.

Selma loomed over me, fury on her face. "Your freaky scarecrow making days are over, witch."

I struggled under the continued blaze of magic that had me pinned. I turned my head to see Tuffin racing away, a flicker of magic chasing her down, but she was too fast. Sol was also being pinned by two more members of the Magic Council, and magic encircled his wrists and ankles.

"Let him go. He's not involved in this. Sol works for me. That's all."

"Involved in what, exactly?" Selma said. "I know what you're doing here is wrong. We haven't searched everywhere, but we'll find out what you're up to. And when I'm done with you, there'll be no more scarecrows, no more magic, and no more pumpkins for you. Your days are numbered."

As I was dragged to my feet and tugged to the van containing my scarecrows, I had a horrible feeling Selma was right.

About Author

K.E. O'Connor (Karen) is a mystery author living in the beautiful British countryside. She loves all things mystery, animals, and cake.

If you want to be part of the Witch Haven crew, practice spells, solve a few murders, spend time with amazing witches and their talking familiars, and get a **free** book, join her weekly newsletter.

Sign up today.

Newsletter:
https://BookHip.com/QKGDWJW
Website:
www.keoconnor.com/writing
Facebook:
www.facebook.com/keoconnorauthor

Also By

Spells and Spooks
Hexes and Haunts
Curses and Corpses
Muffins and Moonlight
Cupcakes and Cauldrons
Pancakes and Potions
Hauntings and High Jinx
Hauntings and Havoc
Hauntings and Hoaxes
The Case of the Screaming Skull
The Case of the Poisoned Pumpkin
The Case of the Cursed Candy
Fire Fang
Silvaria

If you enjoyed

Hauntings and High Jinx

turn the page to read an extract from the next Witch
Haven mystery.

HAUNTINGS AND HAVOC

ISBN: 978-1-915378-35-4

Chapter 1

This was one of the worst days of my life. And although I'd had a few stinkers, lying in a locked cell under Magic Council scrutiny had to be tying for first place. My business had been shut down, my scarecrows taken, and I was waiting to be charged with who knows what, alongside Sol, my hardworking employee and friend. Well, friend with complications attached.

And to top it all, I had unpleasant magic attached to me, making me want to scratch myself raw. It got slapped on me before I went into the cell so my power was dampened. Maybe I shouldn't have attacked Selma Black when I discovered what she was doing at my farm, but that was my safe place, and it shouldn't have been invaded.

Why was the Magic Council picking on me? There were genuine criminals out there who needed bringing to justice. Instead, they went for an easy target. And now everything lay in tatters, and I couldn't see a way out.

My cell door opened, and Selma Black's sharp face looked in at me. "Are you ready to confess?"

I swung my feet over the edge of the hard cot I'd been resting on. "Nope. I have nothing to confess. And I shall ask for a written apology from you when this is over. It should include glitter and hearts. Maybe even a lipstick kiss."

Selma's cold gaze hardened. "Follow me."

"Where's Sol? Are you still holding him?" I hurried out of the cell, looking for a friendly face, but there was none as we walked along the chilly white painted corridor. I'd been brought to the main holding cells at the Magic Council headquarters, where everything was done by the book and filed in triplicate.

"He's safe."

"But where is he?"

"Somewhere you can't influence him."

We walked through several doors that needed unlocking with magic before we got to an interview room. Selma led me in and gestured to a chair set against a table. She spent a minute getting her paperwork laid out in a neat row in front of her before sitting opposite me.

"Your name is Odessa Matilda Grimsbane?"

"You know it is."

"And you're the owner of the Grimsbane farm on Pokey Lane?"

"Of course. But I won't answer any more questions until you tell me about Sol."

Selma's lips pursed a fraction. "Your partner in crime is being questioned. His answers are illuminating."

I gripped the edge of my seat. "Unless you have an interest in scarecrows, you won't find anything exciting at the farm."

"It's not so much the scarecrows, but it's what you do to make them so powerful. And Sol has provided me with plenty of information we can use against you."

I shook my head. Sol wouldn't say anything against me. I'd always treated him well and considered him a friend. My breath stuttered. Maybe he'd had enough of me. After all, I'd rejected him when he said he loved me. Or he could be angry about Brodie and my plan to bring him back to life. Would Sol turn against me?

He'd be hurting because I couldn't love him. Not that he wasn't easy to love. Sol Vossen was a great guy; he just wasn't my guy.

"What's on your mind?" Selma said. "Feeling guilty about something?"

"The last time I checked, I had nothing to feel guilty about."

She ran a finger down a piece of paper in front of her. "Tell me about the magic you use to animate your scarecrows."

"I use nothing illegal. I form a kind of magical umbilical cord with my scarecrows and channel reanimation magic into them. It makes it easier to keep track of them and get to them quickly if they ever struggle."

"What do you mean by struggle?"

"Not struggle. I'm not describing how it works all that well." I shuffled on the hard seat and released my grip on the chair's edge. "My magic has life-giving properties. It connects us."

"I want to know about their struggles."

"Forget I said that word."

"I can't. Explain."

I huffed a breath through my nose. Selma wasn't letting my tiny slip of the tongue go. "Just like all magic beings, my scarecrows have their ups and downs. I expect you have bad days, don't you?"

"No. You make yourself sound like a god with your magic. That's dangerous."

I raised my hands as I shook my head. "It's not that. I know I'm no goddess. My magic restores. It nurtures."

Selma clicked her tongue against the roof of her mouth. "It does a lot more than that. Are you able to raise the dead, just like your scarecrows?"

"No!"

"Are you certain? We've had incidents of the undead lurking about in the nearby village of Silver Steeple."

"That has nothing to do with me."

"But you could do it?"

I twitched my nose. "I mean, I've never tried, but raising the dead isn't my specialty. My magic isn't dark."

"You must get a thrill from having so much power," Selma said. "You have an army of dangerous creatures at your command."

I hid my hands under the table as I clenched my fists and took a few seconds to deep breathe away my annoyance. "It's always rewarding to see a scarecrow come to life. And they're great protectors. That's their job. They're here to look after the vulnerable, not cause problems."

"Yet they are. These reports show your scarecrows aren't under control. Maybe they never have been. Or maybe you're using a new kind of magic. Something dark and unstable." Selma cocked her head like a bird, her neck sinews bulging.

"I'll give you a list of the spells and potions I use. It's nothing dark, just a powerful combination mixed in with my magic."

"I'll take that information." Selma arched an eyebrow. "And I want to know about the locked barn."

The cold plastic of the chair dug into the back of my legs. "Which one? I make sure all my barns are locked."

"The only one we couldn't get in. I found a gap in the wood. There are scarecrows in there. They look strange, and several were dismembered."

I snorted out a laugh. "You make me sound like a scarecrow serial killer. I create life. I don't destroy it."

"You can destroy your scarecrows, though. If they become unstable, you take the magic back. Isn't that a kind of murder, if you consider them alive?"

"I... no! And I only do that as a last resort." Although I'd been doing it more frequently. I'd been distracted by my continued plight to bring back Brodie, my dead love.

"Someone as powerful as you needs monitoring. Much more monitoring than you currently have."

"I fill in my quarterly appraisals as requested by the Magic Council. You can't expect me to do more."

"You will if you want your business open again. Which is looking unlikely." Selma flicked through a file. "Once I've completed the tests on the scarecrows we collected, I'll know exactly what I'm dealing with."

"You can't do that."

"Because you claim they have feelings?" Selma tapped her fingers on the table. "Is that all scarecrows, or just the ones you're hiding in that locked barn?"

"Um... I consider them family." I'd meant to conceal that barn but had run out of time thanks to a ghost in distress. And although I was eternally grateful they hadn't been able to look inside, I couldn't figure out why the doors wouldn't open. It was a simple spell and a padlock keeping people out.

"What are you doing with those hidden scarecrows?" Selma leaned closer, her nostrils flaring.

Sweat prickled on the back of my neck. "I'm... testing a theory."

"What would that be?"

"I haven't patented it yet, so I can't risk the idea being stolen by talking about it." Selma wouldn't understand I was creating a vessel for Brodie's ghost. What I was attempting broke magical law and would give Selma her reason to lock me up.

"You're running a dangerous operation you have no control over. Your scarecrows are too powerful.

If that power is coming through you via a... what did you call it?"

"A magical umbilical cord."

"Exactly. Since you're the source of that power, there's the possibility you'll lose control, just like your scarecrows. Is your power becoming unstable?"

"Do I look out of control to you?"

"You look like a witch who's panicking. This investigation would have gone more smoothly if you'd told the truth. The Magic Council appreciates honesty. When it comes to your sentencing, it's looked on favorably."

I didn't believe that. All Selma wanted to do was shut down my business and send me to jail. She had me in her sights and wasn't planning on losing focus.

She pushed a piece of paper and a pen over to me. "Write down the list of spells and potions you use on your scarecrows. I'll check it tallies during my tests."

"Don't experiment on my scarecrows. It'll destabilize their magic. It could kill them."

"You make it sound like they're alive."

I gripped the pen. "They are to me. And they're valued by people who take them into their homes."

"We're auditing all sales you've made in the last two years. We want to see how valuable people consider these scarecrows and the troubles they've had with them."

"Then you'll be disappointed. My customers are happy. You only have to check my website to see the glowing reviews."

"Maybe there are some customers who didn't survive after taking in one of your scarecrows. If a rampaging giant straw-filled monster had murdered them, they couldn't leave a review."

Selma was goading me, but I wouldn't let her make me angry. I knew my scarecrows. And sure, they were capable of killing. It was how I made them. They were powerful, bold, fearless, and protective of their masters. They had to be. Being in the magic community wasn't without its dangers, and people needed protecting. That's what my scarecrows did. But they were made to protect, not destroy.

I spent a few minutes writing down my spells and potions, making sure I missed nothing so Selma wouldn't trip me up. I passed it back to her, and she tucked it into a file and stood.

"That's it?" I said.

"For now."

"Can I leave?"

"Not yet. I'm going back to see Sol. From the way he's talking, I won't need anything else from you, other than your signed confession."

"Sol won't betray me." Despite the confidence I pushed into my tone, I was wavering. I'd known Sol less than six months, and after rejecting him, he might be done with me. And I wouldn't blame him.

"We'll see. After this mess, he won't want to stick around."

I scowled at Selma's back as she led me to the cell and locked me in. She was right about Sol. He had no reason to stay. I'd pushed him away repeatedly, and my business was locked up tight thanks to the

Magic Council and their ridiculous bureaucracy. If I could get out of this, I may not even have any work to offer Sol. The guy had said he'd work with me for nothing, but I didn't want to test that theory.

A small black spider scuttled out from under the single cot and waggled a front leg at me. It looked like it was beckoning me closer.

I ducked down until we were almost eye level. "Hilda! How did you get in here?"

She scuttled over, and I held out my palm so she could climb onto it. "Indigo sent me. She's worried about you."

I smiled. Trust one of my closest friends to be looking out for me. "She's not the only one. Selma Black has just grilled me. She's got it in for me. She's also questioning Sol. The Magic Council is trying to find something wrong with my business."

Hilda's black legs quivered. "Indigo and Olympus are working on getting you out."

"They're here?"

"They are, but Selma's got them tangled in paperwork. It could be another few hours before you get free."

"But they can get me free? The Magic Council will realize their mistake and let me go?"

Hilda waggled her two front legs. "Hopefully. They're doing their best, but you know what the Magic Council is like. There are so many rules to comply with."

I sighed and headed to the cot. I sat on it and leaned back against the wall.

Hilda jumped onto my knee. "Indigo wanted to know if there's anything that needs fixing."

I tilted my head. "Fixing?"

"At the farm. Olympus only found out at the last minute about Selma's plans to shut the place down. He was too late to stop her from sending in her team."

"I doubt he could have done anything, but I appreciate the thought. Selma is on a mission to destroy me."

"So, is there anything? Indigo's sure she can creep in and deal with things if you need stuff kept under wraps. Anything, you know, that might not be strictly legal."

Indigo was an amazing friend, but there'd be questions to answer if I revealed what I was up to. "No, it's best she stays out of this."

"There's nothing to hide? You're sure?"

"There are... things that'll need explaining. But I'm working on a plan." Which currently involved refusing to talk to Selma, turning invisible, or faking memory loss.

There was a muffled thump against the side of the cell wall. It was followed by a fizzing noise.

I gathered Hilda up and slid off the cot. "You hear that?"

"I do. It sounds like—"

A flash of white light dazzled me, and I raised my hand, shielding Hilda as chunks of rock blasted around us. A few seconds later, the fluffy black head of Tuffin, a cat familiar I'd adopted from a ghost recently, appeared through a hole in the wall.

"Huh! That dumb scarecrow got it right. He said he could sense you behind this wall," Tuffin said.

I stared at her, my mouth open.

"What have they done, silenced you with magic?" She stepped nimbly over chunks of rock. "We need to move. In case you hadn't figured it out, this is a jail break."

"I... What?"

Shamrock, my ever faithful scarecrow companion, poked his head through the hole. He waved at me, then slammed his fist against the wall twice, making the hole bigger.

"Let's go," Tuffin said. "The guards will be all over this place in a couple of minutes. We disabled two of them, but there'll be more."

"Err... Is this a good idea?" I said to Hilda.

"Don't ask the creepy spider. I spent ages coming up with this plan. Well, a few minutes." Tuffin turned and flicked her fluffy black tail. "Although if you want to stay here and rot..."

"It won't look good if I break out of jail. I can still turn this around."

"Doubtful. This could be your only chance to get free," Tuffin said. "Of course, if you want to plead your case in front of a bunch of poker-faced Magic Council members, who I'm sure will have no problems with the freaky scarecrows you've been creating, then stay. Explain away."

"You're right. Let's move," I said. "But we need to get Sol."

"I knew you'd say that. That's being dealt with. He's next door. Marmaduke is blasting a hole through the wall as we speak."

I looked at Hilda, who was staring at Tuffin, looking undecided if she was friend or foe. "Tell Indigo and Olympus I'm okay, but I need to find a place to hide out for a while until I figure things out. I can't go back to the farm."

"Sure, and we'll figure out a story to explain this hole. We could say trolls attacked the Magic Council headquarters, and your cell just got in the way. I've heard a rumor that trolls sometimes abduct witches for fun."

"Thanks, Hilda. Anything you can do to cause a diversion would be amazing." I set her on the floor, and she dashed through the hole.

Shamrock grabbed my arms and heaved me through the hole before wrapping me in a punishing embrace, the scent of warm straw and pumpkins covering me as he huffed hot breath into my hair.

"It's good to see you too, buddy. I don't want you getting in trouble over this, though. You should have stayed away."

"We were already in trouble," Tuffin said. "The Magic Council is hunting us. I barely got away when we found them poking about at the farm."

"Thanks for coming back for me."

Her nose crinkled. "As if I had anywhere else to go. And Eldridge left me in your care. Besides, we're testing this whole witch familiar thing. Isn't this what I'm supposed to do? Get my witch out of trouble?"

"It is. Nice work." I tried to wriggle out of Shamrock's grip, but he wasn't done squeezing me.

"There's an alert out for any scarecrows you've created," Tuffin said. "I'm included in that alert since we've been spotted hanging out together. I'm a wanted cat."

"Sorry to hear that. Shamrock, you can let me go," I wheezed out. My scarecrows were enormous and sometimes forgot their own strength.

Shamrock lowered me to the ground but kept a tight grip on my arm as we hurried along the wall. There was a second smoking hole through which Sol's head was poking. Another of my scarecrows, Marmaduke, stood beside the hole. I also got a bone cracking hug from him.

"Odessa! Did you arrange for this to happen?" Sol said.

"Nope. But I'm glad it did. We need to get out of here."

He shook his head. "Selma has more questions for me. She'll be back soon."

"Let's leave Mr. Goody Two Shoes behind," Tuffin said. "He'll only slow us down."

"No. We go together. Sol, we have to get out of here before we get charged."

"With what? When I was interviewed, Selma said there was nothing to worry about."

"Don't believe anything Selma Black has to tell you. She wants my farm shut down and the scarecrows destroyed." There was no time for being subtle. "Marmaduke, grab Sol."

"What? Wait!" Sol yelped as all seven feet of hulking scarecrow loomed over him and dragged him through the hole.

Marmaduke slung Sol over his shoulder and took off running.

I wasn't sure this was a great idea, but people were shouting and footsteps were drawing near, so we were out of time. I grabbed Tuffin, jumped on

Shamrock's back, and clung on. "Let's get out of here. Make it fast."

Shamrock took off like a rocket, and my head flipped back so hard I worried I'd get whiplash. Within minutes, we were out of sight of the imposing Magic Council building. The Magic Council headquarters moved around whenever the workers inside felt under threat, which happened on a weekly basis since no one liked them, so it took me a minute to get my bearings, but I soon recognized the surroundings. We weren't far from my home village of Witch Haven.

"Head for the forest. We can hide out there and figure out our next move," I said.

Marmaduke and Shamrock changed direction and sped along.

Tuffin scrambled up, settling her butt against my collarbone and hanging her front paws over Shamrock's shoulder as the wind flicked her whiskers back. "We should get out of here while we can. You can start again somewhere else. I've always wanted to visit a tropical island."

"I'm not abandoning my home or the scarecrows," I said. "I'll take on the whole Magic Council if I have to, but I'm clearing my name."

"It's just a building. And you can make scarecrows anywhere. They'll follow you."

"Nope. My friends are here."

"Odessa, I can't get Marmaduke to put me down." Sol was clinging to Marmaduke, his arms wrapped around the scarecrow's middle. "He's not listening to me."

"It's quicker this way. Just hold on and you'll be fine."

The look Sol shot me suggested he was unhappy with this plan, but we had to get away.

"Go to the distillery," I said to Shamrock. "It's been closed for renovations for at least a week. No one will be there."

"Good thinking," Tuffin said. "We use it as a base. You gather your assets, assuming Selma hasn't frozen everything, and then we leave for our island sun paradise."

"No leaving. But I do need time to think. Once Selma understands how my business runs, she'll back off." Although I was wondering if I'd see Hell freeze over before that happened.

"There's no chance of that. Selma Black wants your head on a pole."

My nose wrinkled. "That's a disturbing image. Although she does hate me. Maybe I wronged her in a former life."

"Most likely. You can be annoyingly cheerful. I reckon Selma plans on tearing apart the farm and the scarecrows until she finds enough evidence to ruin you."

"Selma needs a fun hobby," I said, "one that doesn't involve persecuting innocent witches."

"Or a boyfriend. After all, you get distracted when there's a good-looking guy around." Her gaze landed on Sol.

"That's not true." I'd always been loyal to Brodie. He was my one and only, even though we'd been parted by his death over three years ago. I hadn't given up hope we'd get our happily ever after.

My gaze cut to Sol, and my cheeks flushed. I had experienced a moment or two of weakness with him. I'd even considered becoming more than his employer, but it was wrong to betray Brodie. And once Brodie was back, I'd be focused. No one else would tempt me. Not even a good man like Sol.

Marmaduke made short work of smashing the lock on the closed distillery entrance door. The place was quiet and dark as we entered, and I decided to keep it that way, so I pointed to the lights and shook my head.

This wasn't an alcohol distillery, but a magic distillery run by the Frost family. It wasn't a popular business, but it had made the family rich, and they had sites around the world. The Frost family offered payment for magic. People's powers were distilled out of them and sold to the highest bidder. It was an enterprise you only used when you were desperate and had no other option.

"Marmaduke, you can put me down," Sol said. "There's no threat here."

Marmaduke grunted and looked at me for his orders.

"Let me down, Shamrock. Marmaduke, let Sol go, too. Both of you go look around." I patted Shamrock's arm. "Make sure we're alone. Then come back."

Shamrock set me on my feet, while I kept hold of Tuffin so she didn't fall, and he dashed away with Marmaduke.

Sol raked a hand through his hair. Despite looking disheveled, he was still a handsome man. Big, broad, kind of hairy in a manly way, with several days' dark stubble on his chin. "Listen, Odessa. We should go back to the Magic Council. I was making things right with Selma and explaining what you do."

"What were you telling her?" I jammed my hands on my hips. "When she interviewed me, she said you were singing like a canary. You could have gotten me in trouble."

His expression hardened. "I wouldn't do that. You know how I feel about you."

I huffed out a breath. "I also know I rejected you. You told me you..." I couldn't bring myself to say the L word.

"Yeah. I love you. And that hasn't changed, no matter the crazy mess we've found ourselves in."

"It should. If you weren't involved with me, you wouldn't have been arrested."

Sol's walk was confident as he approached. "I'm prepared for everything they throw at me. But I'm not happy you suggested I'd tell the Magic Council something bad about you to save my neck."

I bit my bottom lip. "I'm panicking. And I never said that exactly."

"But you meant it. You don't trust me?"

Guilt gnawed at my insides. I had doubted Sol. "I trust you. But it feels like everyone has turned against me."

"Not everyone." He cupped my face in one of his big, tanned hands. "Sure, this is a mess. But we could have stayed and straightened things out with the Magic Council. Running looks bad."

"And given them time to find something to charge me with? Maybe you, too. And then my business would never reopen. What will I do without my farm, scarecrows, or my amazing pumpkins? It's all I've ever known. I'm not letting that go."

"But was running the best thing? Doesn't that suggest we're guilty?"

"We'll cover that up," Tuffin said. "That spider said something about trolls. Or we could blame the scarecrows."

"Spider?"

"Indigo's familiar came to see me," I said. "Olympus and Indigo were trying to get us out, but it didn't sound like it was going well."

"You can thank Wonder Cat for your rescue," Tuffin said. "Is there any fish in this place?" She leaped out of my arms.

"I doubt it," I said.

Tuffin's nose crinkled again. "I'll go look for fish. You two focus on figuring out a good cover story to clear your names."

"We don't need a cover story," Sol said.

I rested my cheek against his warm hand, reassured by his presence.

Sol smiled down at me. "We'll figure a way out of this together."

Tuffin hissed, and her fur puffed up. "Something is in here."

I looked around the dense blackness of the distillery. "I don't sense anything."

She hissed again, then yowled as she was dragged back by her tail and slung out the door. A few seconds later, Shamrock and Marmaduke suffered the same fate, growling and snarling as they were taken outside, and the door slammed behind them.

Sol grabbed me as I sparked up a spell. "You see anything?"

"Not a thing," I whispered. "But something doesn't like us being here."

He yelped as an inky black shadow grabbed him and pulled him away from me into the gloom, leaving me alone.

Hauntings and Havoc is available in e-book and paperback

ISBN: 978-1-915378-35-4

www.ingramcontent.com/pod-product-compliance
Lightning Source LLC
Chambersburg PA
CBHW050751190726
48285CB00005B/1619